Last Heartbeat

T. R. LYKINS

Last Heartbeat

©Copyright 2014 T.R. Lykins

Editor: Mickey Reed http://www.mickeyreedediting.com

Re-edits by Karen Mills-Tribble

Cover Design by: Juliana Cabrera @ Jersey Girl Graphics

http://jerseygirlgraphics.wordpress.com/

Paperback layout and design by Marcy Rachel of Backstrip Publishing

http://www.backstrippublishing.com

Promotions by: Ena Burnette - Enticing Journey Book Promotions

This book is also available in digital format at most online retailers.

Dedication

My husband, who shows me how love is supposed to be and loves me the way I am supposed to be loved.

To my two sons for bringing out the motherly love I have for them and showing me that I can love unconditionally.

Loraine
Just hang on
a little longer
Enjoy
JK Rifkins

Prologue

*A*s I lie on my hospital bed, I can barely breathe, even with the oxygen tube turned on high; my heart is on its last beats. I never thought that, as a fifteen-year-old kid, I would be dying. It's only been eight months since I heard the diagnosis of viral cardiomyopathy heart disorder. My heart was damaged so badly that, on the day of the diagnosis, they only gave me a short time to live and put me on a heart donor list. We all know that receiving a heart from the heart donor list can take a long time, but time isn't what I have right now. Both of my parents are with me and won't leave me because the doctor told them I might not make it through the night. So we are all just waiting for me to die.

The doctor just came back to check on me, but he seems to be happy about something. I'm glad he can still be happy even though I'm barely breathing and my heart has almost stopped beating. *Breathe* I keep telling myself. He is telling my parents something and they are smiling and looking at me. I'm glad they are smiling; I haven't seen them smile in a while. Maybe he told them a funny joke or something. *Just breathe, Alexia,* I tell myself, *and hang on.* You can do it. The pain is so bad that it is hard to hang on. I really don't want to die at age fifteen without knowing what the world has to offer. I only just started this life, and now I'm going to die.

As I look up, a group of nurses and more doctors come in. This must mean I'm going to really die in an only a few minutes for sure, since everyone is doing so much to my body. My doctor, Dr. Wright, comes over and listens to my heart, before he looks at me with a big smile. Dr. Wright tells me that I'm going to surgery; I have a donor heart waiting on me! I stare at him and can't believe that what he is saying is true. Normally people have to wait for a donor heart with a perfect match for years, so that means it can't be true. I know I'm in shock. Then they wheel my bed out of the room and into the operating room, is all I can remember.

One

FIVE YEARS LATER

As I'm sitting in the airport, I take a look around. I see all the people and think about the time I wasn't going to be here. Five years ago, I almost died. I was at my last heartbeat, but someone else died in my place that day. These people can't comprehend that life goes on even if you're not here anymore. They wouldn't see a young twenty-year-old girl waiting on her flight to go to college and get to live her life for another day. I was lucky the day of my heart transplant, but five years ago, my heart donor wasn't. I don't know who that person was, whether boy or girl, but I'm going to take this gift and appreciate it every day that I live. I take one more look around before I board my plane and smile because life goes on, even when we least expect it.

As I board the plane, I decide to make the best of everyday because I know I'm on borrowed time. Who knows if my new donor heart may decide to fail or reject me? The plane I board is really nice because my parents decided that I should fly first class to head off to my future. My parents have always shown me love, and when I was sick, they stayed close by my side. So close that I have been sheltered most of my life, and this is the first time I have been away from them.

I didn't have too many friends since I became so ill at an early age. The ones I have graduated while I was sick, so I didn't get to graduate with them. Being in and out of hospitals for so long, I just now finished high school. I know what you're thinking. I should have tried being homeschooled. I just felt so tired and didn't have the strength to do it. My new heart is so much better that I feel like I can do anything. This heart must have been from a strong, healthy person.

I sit in my awesome seat and get ready to take flight. A few minutes later, a guy sits down next to me. I don't say anything to him or look at him at first, but he is being so noisy I look up and see him for the first time. What I see is the most amazing-looking guy I believe I have ever seen. My heart speeds up a little and that sort of worries me a bit. He has dark brown eyes and brown hair that is messy but looks good on his oval-shaped face. He seems tall because his legs are so long. He looks up from what he is doing and smiles so his dimples show. *Wow,* is all I can think and my hands start sweating.

He reaches his hand out and introduces himself. "Hi, my name is Phillip Ryan. Where are you headed off to?"

I shake his hand and hope he doesn't notice how sweaty it is. "Hi, my name is Alexia Morgan. I'm headed off to college," I say in a nervous voice. What just happened to my voice? I am never nervous. *Ugh.*

Phillip smiles at me and says, "Wow, small world, because I'm headed off to college too. Where are you going to college?"

I look up at his dimples. "Coastal Carolina University. Where are you going to school?"

He never takes his eyes off me and exclaims, "No way! You can't be going there too. I have been going there for two years and I've never seen you there before. I would have remembered your face if I had."

"This is my first year there. I hope I am going to like it." Still looking at him, I see a big smile showing off his perfect teeth.

"I see. You're a new college girl and I get to show you around. You don't look like a freshman. Maybe sophomore or junior, are you transferring?" Phillip asks.

This question I knew would be difficult to answer when I got ready to go to college, but I didn't expect to have to answer it so soon. I look at him, and he's still waiting for my answer. "I just took a break from school for a couple of years, so yeah, I'm going to be a freshman." I laugh. "A twenty-year-old freshman. How funny is that?" I turn away, staring out the window, and think that I'm just really lucky to be a twenty-year-old anything.

I shake it off and turn back to Phillip, who still is looking at me, but he seems a little sad behind his eyes. What made him sad? I was just trying to joke, but now I don't know what to do. If my parents hadn't sheltered me and had me out more, maybe I could come up with something witty to make him smile. Ugh! Here goes the best I can come up with.

"So," I say, "does that make me a freak or what?"

There it is. He is smiling again.

He says, "No, because I also took off a year before college, so that makes both of us freaks I guess. No, really.

Sometimes life gets in the way of what we want and we have to take a break before we get to move forward."

There is still sadness behind what he just said, behind his smile. I can still see it, and wonder what that could mean. What is he hiding that could make his perfect smile still show sadness in his eyes? This boy definitely had something bad happen to him in the past or is going through something now.

As I'm thinking about what it can possibly be, he starts talking again. "I should be a senior, but I'm going to be a junior. All my friends left me behind when I decided to take a break. That's okay with me though. They went to off to so many different colleges. When I decided to take a break, I wouldn't have been able to see them much. You're going to like CCU. It is so close to the beach and there is so much you can do around the town. When you're not in classes, you will be busy. Maybe we will get to hang out sometime."

"The beach is why I chose CCU, I love walking and reading on the beach. Hopefully I will find the perfect place to do homework at the beach. Somewhere quiet so I can just relax, watch the waves, and study. Listen to me... I really love the beach, and I can get carried away," I giggle. What is up with me? *A giggle*? I never giggle. Phillip must really think I took a break because I'm a childish and giggling fool. *Ugh.*

He laughs at me. *Just stop being crazy in front of this boy.*

The next thing he says is, "My brother used to love the beach so much. He would ask my parents to take us every year. They did most of the time and Myrtle Beach was his favorite place. Most people say Florida beaches are the best, but not him. That is why I chose to go to CCU... so I can be close to the beach.

I know how you feel about the beach, sand, and waves. You just can't get enough of the place."

"Is your brother going to CCU too?" I ask him.

He looks away for what seems like forever and turns back to me with the saddest eyes. "No. He didn't get to go to college. A drunk driver killed him when he was eighteen. I was with him in the car and I was injured, but I lived and he died. My injuries were really bad too and I had to get my spleen removed. I had to get a transplanted liver, which my brother, who was a donor, gave me. I just felt, like I needed to go to college where he had planned to go. Once I got there, I realized I loved it. Sometimes I just wonder if I got some of that feeling from him, because a part of him is in me? I know that is crazy. Still, I just wonder. I hadn't even known he'd signed the donor card on his license. If he hadn't, I wouldn't be here today to keep living on. He did do wonders that day. He saved a lot of people. Someone even got his heart. I hope they appreciated the gift and are taking care of it." Looking miserable for a minute, he looks over at me and says, "I'm sorry for all that information I never talk about it to anyone. I just met you and out it came. You must think I'm crazy." He laughs off his bleakness.

I look at him and now know that is what the lonesomeness is in his eyes. I tell him, "You're not crazy. I can understand everything you just said. You loved your brother and miss him. What he did when he became a donor was awesome. That many lives he saved although his couldn't be saved is a miracle in itself. It was meant to be, so you could live. The other people, I'm sure are very grateful too." I'm afraid to tell him I have a donor heart; for some reason, I don't. I didn't want to depress him more. I try to change the subject. "What are you majoring in at CCU?"

"Graphic design. One day I want see my art designs on a lot of different places. I'd love to have a building or airplane or something big with an awesome design on it that people will know was made by me. What about you? What are you majoring in?"

Most people freak when I tell them my plans. They think that I must be so smart, but I'm not. I just want to help people. I look up and say, "Exercise and sport science to focus on cardiac rehabilitation." Yes, that is the expression everyone gives me when I say that out loud. I smile at him for that look.

"Wow, you must be smart to become a doctor for cardiac patients." He's looking like he doesn't know what to say to me now.

I laugh out loud. He looks like I insulted him, so I tell him, "I'm not going to be a doctor. More like a physical therapist who helps patients recover from cardiac-related rehab. Sometimes patients need to learn to walk and do exercises that help them with recovery and strengthen every muscle so they can get on with life and feel better."

Phillip looks at me and says, "I know about physical therapy. I had to do it before I could go home when I had surgery. I used to be a football player, but I had to quit. If I got hit in the liver, I would most likely die. I didn't want to take the chance to lose the gift my brother gave me. It would be a waste for sure. I gladly gave football up."

"That is a great thing you did and sacrificed. You truly do appreciate what an awesome gift he gave you. I know I would be appreciative too. You were lucky to receive a donor so quickly. Since he was your brother, he helped you to have a perfect match. Most of the time, people have to wait a long time and even die before they have a donor. I want to help the ones who are lucky enough to get another chance in life. I could have been your therapist and someday, hopefully, I will be someone's." I say this knowing how hard I had to work to get my strength back. Now, I can finally get on with my life. I'm sitting on a plane with the cutest guy ever and ready to live every day, for as long as I can.

The fasten seatbelt light comes on and the pilot says that we are getting ready to land. I didn't even know it took off. How could that have been so fast? I look at my watch and realized that I talked to Phillip so much that time flew by. Yes, *flew by*, get it? I just made a really bad joke. I'm grinning to myself and Phillip looks at me.

He smiles, "What is making you grin so big and beautifully?"

"I thought how fast the trip was and thought, *it has flown by*. I thought it was a funny joke" can't believe I said that out loud. Now he must think I'm crazy.

He turns and laughs, shaking his head, "That is sort of funny. Maybe you should become a comedian." Laughing again, he says, "It really has flown by, and I can't believe I have told you stuff no one else knows about me. You must think I need a psychiatrist. Or maybe it's your sweet, beautiful face that makes me want to tell you everything. If I see you on campus, please don't tell my secrets. People actually think I'm a little bit cool. Okay?"

"I really won't say a word. I probably won't be around you much anyway. I'm sure you will be hanging with all the older cool kids and I'm too much of a nerd to hang with you. I'm cool with it though. I probably will be sitting on the beach doing my reading and that would probably bore you too much. I really have enjoyed talking with you. I hope you have a good school year." I say, getting ready to get off the plane.

Phillip puts his body in front of me and says, "I will never think you're not cool enough to hang out with me, and you can do it any time. Just say the word. I think you are beautiful, and your eyes look at me like they see right through me and know everything about me. They are the bluest eyes I have ever seen and I would like to see them again. You do something to me that makes me want to be better. You know people think I'm a player at this school, but it isn't true. Don't listen to a word of the rumors, okay?" With that confession, Phillip turns and exits the plane before I can even take a breath, which I was holding.

As everyone moves about the plane, I get it together and think about what he just said. Wow! What a confession. I was sitting beside the most awesome boy. Turns out that he is a player. Why would he tell me that? Now that makes me wonder if he just lied about everything he'd said just to talk to me. I am so glad I really didn't tell him much about myself. Time to shake off what just happened and get on with my new life. The life that doesn't include spending time with a boy, because I'm on borrowed time and that wouldn't be fair to any guy.

Two

PHILLIP

ow! What just happened to me? I never talk to girls that way and tell them my deepest, darkest secret. I never even talk to my parents about my brother, so why her? I know that now I have to stay away from her. Now I am afraid everyone will know the truth about me. Not just that I have a deceased brother but that a part of him saved my life. It still makes me sad that I lived and he died. It messes with my mind too much and makes me a bit crazy at times. Maybe that's why everyone calls me a player. Sometimes I hook up with a girl every now and then just to forget. It has not been that many really. Other guys I hang out with go out with a lot more girls than I do. I can even count them on two hands and I still know their names.

As I head out of the airport to get my luggage, I see Alexia coming to the luggage area. I quickly turn around so she doesn't see me. *Hurry* luggage! *Get out so that I can hurry out the door before I run into her again*! The buzzer goes off at the luggage area and I see my baggage first thing. I grab it and make a run for the door so that I won't run into her again.

As I get to my car, which is in the parking garage. I start thinking; I should have asked Alexia if she needed a ride. *No.* If I did that, I might spill more of my secrets to her. I almost decide to drive around and see if Alexia had gotten a taxi. I turn my car around and see her coming to the parking garage and see her get into a parked car.

Why would she have a parked car here? Maybe she is like me, living off campus and already been flying back and forth from her hometown. I didn't even ask where she is from. Now I will never know because I am staying away from her. I can't even think about her.

When I see her look up at me with those big blue eyes it makes my heart skip a beat. No one has ever done that to me ever. Even the girls I have hooked up with have never done that.

Well, I better get back to my condo and get ready for my first class tomorrow. As I turn out of the airport, I head toward the beach. I like driving next to the beach with my windows down so I can smell the salty air and feel the breeze in my hair. It takes longer to get to the condo this way because of the traffic, but I don't care. It's worth this feeling of being free and alive.

My parents had bought my brother a condo on the beach so he wouldn't have to live at the dorms. They also bought it so that we could visit often to beat the cold Ohio weather. In the summer, while I'm gone, they rent it out to tourists. They are choosey about who gets to rent it. Being picky keeps the cost down for damage. The condo is our little piece of heaven on earth and sometimes, it makes me feel closer to my brother.

I sure hope the cleaning crew did better with the cleaning this summer than last year. I think my parents will fire them if it's not clean. Last time, I had to do most of the cleaning myself when I came back for school. I really didn't mind, but my parents said that if they hired someone to do the cleaning, it should be done right. I agree with them, but I'd hate to have someone to lose their job.

I pull into the condo parking lot and already hear the waves lapping up on the beach. The breeze relaxes my body. I hurry and take my luggage into the condo. Walking through the front door, I can see the ocean from the big balcony doors. I run and open them to see what is going on at the beach. Knowing that at this time of the day not too many people will be out, I decide to hurry down to put my feet on the sand and in the water.

Oh, how I have missed this place. I can't wait until this school year starts tomorrow, and knowing that I get to spend every day at the beach makes me smile. Maybe I'll even study more at the beach this year instead of on campus, which is what Alexia said she'd be doing. Maybe that will actually make me study more here at home, than on campus. I just have to see what comes up and see what my friends are doing. My parents would like more studying from me. I do a fair job at school but I could always do better, so maybe this year I will.

I know I could be on borrowed time because my body could reject my brother's gift. I like living every day to the fullest. So far, studying has been the last thing on my mind. I just have to see what each day brings. Maybe that blue-eyed girl could be the best of every day. *No,* I have to leave her alone.

It's time for this guy to relax on the beach and stop thinking about the blue-eyed angel. When my friends find out I'm back, time for relaxing will be over. Partying is what they all will want me to do but they don't think I'll be back until tomorrow. I'm glad I took that earlier flight so no one knows I'm here except Alexia, and no one even knows her yet.

There I go again, thinking about her. I have to stop or there will be no relaxing for me. I can't relax when I keep seeing her and it rouses me up too much. I hope I don't have any classes with her on campus. It would be hard being next to her when I need to stay away. The rumors about me being a player might help keep her away from me. I hope so, because right now, if she were here, I would become more than a player and do something I shouldn't. What is up with this girl I know nothing about? I can't keep her off my mind and now I want to know more about her.

That's it. I'm going to call my friends and go out to clear my mind. Even the beach hasn't relaxed me. Why is that? I pull my phone out and call my best friend Jacob to meet me at Hamburger Joe's our favorite burger hangout. As I get there, Jacob is with Tyler, another of our friends, getting our seats. They wave me over and I go sit down. We order our favorite wings and burgers.

Jacob says, "Phillip! Glad you got back early. Thought you weren't getting back until right before class tomorrow?"

"Decided at the last minute to come back early," I answer. "I planned on relaxing a bit and seeing how the cleaners did with the condo. Didn't want a repeat of last summer."

Tyler laughs "Yeah, that was a disastrous mess. Your parents should not have kept that cleaning crew."

"I didn't mind cleaning it. With how much my parents paid them, they should have done better job though. Glad that when I came home this time the place was spotless. I had time to hang out with you guys before tomorrow," I say but really trying to get that girl out of my head. So far, it isn't working.

Jacob smiles "Boy, we are really glad you called. We are going to have fun partying tonight. There's a party at Megan's private beach house. Now let's get eating. The party is supposed to start soon. I hear it will have a lot of people from CCU. Supposed to be the biggest party of the year."

"This guy is sure ready for fun tonight." I smile. Hopefully, I will forget about Miss Blue Eyes tonight.

Tyler says, "Hope you don't get all the girls. We know how you like so many different girls and they like you. Don't be selfish with them all."

I laugh. "I don't get the girls. That is Jacob's job. Just hope to talk to one or two." I wink at them.

After we finish eating, Jacob jumps up and says, "Let's hit the road. Don't want to miss this one."

We get up so that we can pay and hit the party of the year.

Just what I need after all, I hope.

T. R. LYKINS

Three

ALEXIA

As I enter the airport and head off to the baggage claim area, I spot Phillip's messy head of hair. I stop and think about everything he said. His being a player makes me think that I don't want to talk to him. I just need to get my luggage and leave without acting like I saw him. That is what I am going to do.

As I get closer, I see Phillip run up and grab his luggage quickly. Then he is out of the door before I can even breathe. *Wow!* He must really want to avoid me to get out of the airport so fast. What does that mean? Am I that bad of a person that I need to be avoided? *Wait just a minute.* This is great! Now I won't have to be worried about running into him. Yay for me! But why do I feel like that is not what I really wanted?

So many questions are going on in my head that I almost miss seeing my suitcase. I have got to get my head back in order and that includes no brown-eyed, messy brown-haired boy with awesome dimples to think about. *Okay, Okay*. Now I think I'm going crazy. Stop it!

As I pull my luggage to the parking lot, I am grateful that my parents had my car delivered to the airport. I will have something to get around town in, and I plan on making many trips to the beach. The college is about twenty-five minutes away from the beach, so I need a car to get around. They also sent most of my belongings to my college dorm room and they will be waiting on me when I get there. They spoil me too much, but at least I do not have to lug it all to my car right now.

Great! My car is right where the car should be, and that makes me happy. As I get in my car, I think, *Should I make a detour to the beach or go to campus? Which one, which one?* Darn, I wish I didn't have to go the dorm first to make sure everything is there. I would definitely go to the beach, but I am worried about my things not being there. I head to campus instead of the beach.

Pulling onto the campus, I am astonished by all the beauty. I almost make a wrong turn to my dorm. Once I find the parking lot and retrieve my keys, I head to my room. It's on the second floor, which is lucky for me. Being up on higher floors means a lot of steps and that would make me tired. They do have elevators, but I still like getting some exercise.

I get to my door and wonder if my roommate is here. Should I knock first? It's my room too. I try the doorknob and it's unlocked. *Yay!* She must be here. This makes me both a little nervous and excited. I never had a sister or brother, so hopefully we will get along well.

I enter the room and see her for the first time. I am a little shocked at what I see. Don't know why, but she isn't crazy looking. She is normal like me. We have talked on the phone, so

I thought she would be a punk rocker or Goth. This eases my nerves even more.

She squeals and jumps out of her chair, running to me as fast as she can. "Hi, I'm Kristen! I'm so glad you finally got here!" She gives me a big hug. "I was getting ready to leave to go to the biggest party of the year and now you can go with me. It's going to be at a private beach house and everyone will be there. You need to hurry and get ready. We should leave in about thirty minutes, so we can make it there early. I like watching everyone come in the door and seeing all the hot guys." She smiles wide at me.

I look at her surprised. I don't know what to say. Am I really ready to go to a party since I just got here? I am a little tired from traveling. "I didn't know there was going to be a party this soon and I just got here. Maybe I should sit this one out and unpack."

She looks at me with a big frown on her face and says, "You can't miss this one! It's the biggest and best of the year. Mostly upper classmen go, but we got invited, and no one turns down Megan's invitations. Her parents have a private beach house, and the party is mostly in the backyard, which is the beach. I know you love the beach since we have been talking about it before you got here. *Please* go! We can ride together. You can unpack tomorrow. How many classes do you have on the first day? I only have one."

I really love the beach and I've never been to a beach party. It may be nice to go, just to hear the waves and feel the breeze. My classes start late tomorrow. Can I get enough rest? *Ugh*, I really want to go. Just arriving and turning around to go the beach party might be a bit much though.

I say, "I have two classes tomorrow and the first one is at ten."

She squeals again and says, "Perfect! You would have time to sleep and still go have some fun. Please come! We won't stay out too long. If you want, you can drive, that way you can leave whenever you need. You can leave whenever you need. *Please. Please.*" She begs. How can I turn her down?

"Okay, I'll go, but I'll drive separately. I just want to stay about an hour so I can get back and relax a bit. I hope the party isn't too big though." I've never been to a party, and if it is huge, I might get nervous around so many people.

"It will be big but if you're only staying for about an hour, not everyone shows up that early. You should be good with the crowd. I'm happy we get to go to our first party already! Now get dressed so we can go." She smiles and turns to finish getting ready.

I go to my bags and look for something to wear, still wondering if I should go. I am a little tired and don't want to push myself too hard. But I really do want to see the beach.

I pick out my favorite shorts and a cute top. Add in some flip-flops and I'm almost ready to go. After freshening up my makeup and brushing my hair back into a ponytail, I'm all set for the beach. Just took me fifteen minutes to finish. Kristen is still putting on makeup.

"I'm ready" I inform her.

She looks up and says "Wow, that was fast. Just give me a few more minutes. You're a natural beauty, but it takes me a long time to look halfway decent."

I laugh. "You are a beauty and I am not. I just don't take a long time to get ready. Doesn't really matter how I look. Everyone will have eyes on you. I just want to hit the beach."

"Look, I am finally ready. Do you want to follow me?"

"I will follow you. I don't know where the beach house is and I can leave early."

We head out to the party and I like the drive to the house. The sun is still shining, but it's starting to set. Everything looks amazing with the sun bursting over the water. As we get closer to the ocean, I can see it in between the houses we drive by. This makes me want to hurry and get on the beach. How much farther can it be?

Luckily, I see Kristen put on her turn signal and she pulls into a massive beach house. Even the driveway is huge. There are a ton of cars already here. I see where Kristen parks. She gets out. I pull up beside her and ask where the best place to park would be so I can get leave early. She tells me and I direct my car there.

The front door is massive in size. That makes me a little bit scared to go to this party. I have never seen a house this big up close. These people must be loaded. I get ready to tell Kristen that I've changed my mind, but the door opens and I am curious to see what this house looks like. Entering the front door, I can only concentrate on the view of the ocean, through the floor-to-ceiling windows. The sun setting over the ocean makes me feel alive, and I want to walk out to the beach right then.

Kristen grabs my arm to start introducing me to some of the people she knows. I get introduced to Megan, our party hostess, but she seems to be the typical rich girl type, a little bit stuck up. That's okay with me.

I keep moving to the back doors. Kristen hands me a cup of beer and I take it. She doesn't know I won't drink it. I can't with the medication I'm on for my transplant. So I just hold on to it and pretend to sip from it.

I finally get to the beach and there are people everywhere. I look around to see what everyone is doing. Everyone seems to know each other. Some are so drunk already that they don't know what is going on. There is dancing, a bonfire, and even a table set up with kegs of beer. Megan really did go all out on this party. I wonder what her parents think about this or how can they afford such a nice house.

After seeing the perfect spot down the beach a little ways off from everyone, I start sneaking off before Kristen spots me. It's not that I don't like her, but all these people are a bit too much and too loud for me.

As I get to my spot, the last of the sun finally sets with an orange glow, which makes the waves, sparkle just a little. "Ahhh," I say to myself. "Now this is what I came to this party for." I sit there for a while and listen to the waves, the music and all the partygoers, which surprisingly makes me relax. I lie back on the sand and close my eyes. *Peace at last.*

I barely have a minute to myself when, all of a sudden, sand flies in my face. I jump up quickly and dust of the sand off my skin. As I look up at the reason for my sandy face, I see him... Mister Brown Eyes. *No, no!* Not this quick! I was hoping to never see Phillip again.

Phillip stumbles over to me and says, "I am so sorry. I didn't see you laying there." He's smiling at me with a big grin. "Did you fall down and do you need help getting up?" he asks, while looking at my overturned drink cup.

Oh no. He thinks I'm drunk. I look at him and say, "I am fine. Just go on about your business so I can get on with mine." Where did that rudeness come from? I'm never rude to anyone, but Phillip just brings it out of me. That's not me at all. Then I just wave him off and look away before those eyes suck me in.

He doesn't leave me like I asked him to. Instead, he sits down next to me and speaks, "Truly I'm sorry for kicking sand on you. Please forgive me. I didn't mean to do it. I was just running and didn't see you laying on the sand. Are you here for the party? I came with my best friends Jacob and Tyler. They are already drunk, so I'm staying sober to drive them home. If you're drunk I can take you to campus. I don't really mind because I sort of owe you that for kicking sand in your face."

"Really you don't have to take me anywhere. I'm not drunk, just relaxing, and you don't owe me anything. I came to the party with my roommate. I drove because I'm leaving soon."

"Who is your roommate?"

"Her name is Kristen. I just met her, but we have talked on the phone before I got here. She told me about this party and asked me to come. I only came because I wanted to relax at the beach for a little while." I get up and say, "Well, it's time for me to go back and unpack. You have a great time partying."

He grabs my hand, "You should stay awhile longer. I would like it if you did."

I look at him and try to figure him out. "You don't want me here I might cramp your player status." The tension between us was growing, and I wondered why.

He laughs, "Player status? I told you that wasn't true, and you have to keep my secret. It will be our little secret." He winks at me.

Then I hear a loud noise. I look up and see two guys stumbling over to us. They laugh at Phillip, mumble. "Who is this or which number?"

Phillip says something to himself quietly and tells them to shut up. Then he introduces me to them. "This is Jacob and that is Tyler. Guys, this is Alexia. She is starting CCU this year."

The Jacob guy laughs, "Nice to meet you. I'm letting you know this guy gets around a lot, but I don't, so maybe we can get to know each other."

"Nice to meet you, but I don't need to get to know either of you," I reply.

Tyler laughs. "This girl sure is smart and I like her already. She knows a player when she sees one."

"Guys, be quite for a while. You also need to stop drinking so much. Your liver can't handle much more. I am sorry for these guys acting like drunken losers." Phillip smiles.

I get ready to respond when I hear a girl's voice calling Phillip. *Oh,* that's Megan. I remember her from the introduction from Kristen. Phillip looks up and sort of makes a face like he doesn't like her, but then smiles at her. I wonder if she saw that face before he turned on that beautiful smile in a second heartbeat.

She must not have. She runs up, jumping right into his lap and giggles. "Oh why are you all the way over here when the party is in full swing? I have been looking for you all night. If I didn't know better, I'd think you were just ignoring me tonight," Megan says with pouty lips.

Phillip says, "Not trying to hide from you Megan. No one can do that. Just hanging out here with some friends. You know

Jacob and Tyler, but have you met Alexia yet? I just ran into her sitting on the beach."

Megan looks at me and snarls her nose up and says. "Yeah, she came in with Kristen and we have met." She looks me in the eye. "You're not trying to steal my man Phillip, are you?" She asks with evil eyes.

"No, I don't want Phillip. He is all yours. I just met him, so why would I want him?" I say and get up. "Thanks for having me at your party, but I have to go." I turn and walk away.

Wow! What was that? I thought Phillip said that he wasn't dating anyone. Maybe she is one of the girls he strings along. I know he is incredibly handsome, but I will not be played by anyone. I don't have time on my hands for that, being on borrowed time, so I must make sure I make the best of every day I have. Time for me to head out and get some unpacking before my class tomorrow.

I look for Kristen and find her inside dancing with some guy. I walk over and tell her that I'm leaving. Then I ask her if she will be okay by herself. She says she will be, but not to wait up for her. I laugh and shake my head.

Once I get to the dorm, I'm still thinking about Phillip while I get unpacked and ready for class tomorrow. I can't get him out of my mind and I don't know why. He has one girlfriend too many, by the way. I know it must just be my hormones kicking in. He is too gorgeous, for my hormones to not go into overdrive. I never have felt like this about anyone before. I sigh and lie down on my bed, thinking that I will never get to sleep tonight.

The next thing I know, I wake to my alarm going off. I jump up and look around to get my bearings. I did sleep well last night and I had an amazing dream, which included Phillip.

Blushing, I look over to see if Kristen is still asleep, but her bed is empty. I hope she just went home with someone and didn't crash her car into a tree or something. I hope she is really okay. I really like her and believe we can be good friends in time. I think about that, as I get ready for my first day of college.

Four

PHILLIP

Jacob, Tyler and I get to Megan's party a little later, and it is already going strong. The music is so loud that I wonder if the neighbors will call the cops. As soon as we get to the door, we walk in and see people everywhere. Bodies grinding against each other to the loud music and cans of beer litter the party. The crowd is so thick that you can actually smell the sweat in the air along with the beer. Girls in short shorts and tank tops so small they don't hide much from your eyes are on the dance floor. Maybe I will get lucky and get my mind off Miss Blue Eyes.

The guys head to the kegs to get started with drinking. Jacob hands me a beer and I tell him that I'm driving, so not tonight. He downs the beer in a big gulp and goes for another one. I laugh at him and tell him that I'm going out to the beach. He waves me on.

I get outside and the breeze feels good. It's a breath of fresh air from being inside with all those sweaty bodies. Sort of makes me feel alive. The sun is just setting as I get closer to the edge of the water, and it makes the waves seem to glow. It's so relaxing out here that I almost forget I am at a party.

I turn around to go back into the party and see my blue-eyed girl, just lying in the sand, off to the side so no one will bother her. She looks beautiful and peaceful lying there. I should just leave her alone. Just turn around, go back to party, and leave now. I turn to leave, but my feet take me toward her. I fight my feet and stumble, kicking sand on her. *Oh no. Not so smooth Phillip. Now she will think you are drunk for sure.*

As I look down at her, she sits up in a hurry dusting off the sand I just kicked on her. I can't help myself but smile at her. She is the most beautiful girl I have ever seen. I have been around a lot of girls. Something about Alexia just does something to me that no other girl has done.

She finally gets all the sand off and looks to see who did the nasty sand kicking. She frowns at me. I know she is mad, but I think she is maybe happy to see me again. No, I am wrong. She is more than mad; she is pissed off big time and about to give me an earful. This girl has a lot of spunk for being so little. I think I might actually try to get to know her after all. I tell her that I am sorry, but she is still angry.

What is all that noise? *Ugh!* Why are Tyler and Jacob coming out here? They both look plastered already. How do they do that so quickly? Oh no, Jacob has already spotted Alexia. Now how will I keep him away? Jacob starts flirting as soon as he stumbles over to us. Alexia is angry, so I know she won't put up with it; at least I hope she won't. *Ah, there's my girl.* She is already telling him off and me too. How did I get into their conversation?

Then I hear a voice and I know who is coming, Megan. I have been trying to stay out of her sight for a long time. She never gives up. Megan runs right up and jumps onto my lap. I look up and see Alexia. The face Alexia just made. What was that? That makes me think she doesn't like Megan. I'm glad, because I don't either.

I introduce them, but they have already met earlier. Alexia gets up and says her goodbyes, but I really wish she'd stay. These three bozos just ran her off, and I want her with me, not this bunch.

After Alexia leaves, I pick up Megan and sit her on the sand. "Why did you jump into my lap? You haven't ever done that before."

Megan frowns "Why not? You know I want to go out with you. Give me a chance like all your other girls. Maybe you will like what I have to offer." She smiles up at me and bats her eyes.

"Whatever you think you know about me is something you know nothing about. I am picky with who I am with. You haven't been so nice, so I am not going to give you a chance." I get up and then go walking down the beach to clear my head a bit.

I love walking on the beach anytime of the day, but the night is so relaxing and peaceful. I think about Alexia and now I know she must believe I really am a player. I wish I hadn't been with the few girls I had been with and just saved myself for the most special girl. I know most guys would have just laughed at me for thinking that. Being with someone just for the physical need and not for love isn't good for anyone.

What has me even thinking like this? As I try to come up with some reason, I see Alexia in my mind. No, I can't think about her. The three amigos just ran her off. Time to get my best guys home before they start puking. I don't want that in the car for sure.

Five

ALEXIA

hy did I wake up so early? I'm not even a morning person. I need to go find coffee and in a hurry, so I will make it through my first class. I walk across campus to the food court and get my coffee, deciding to get a bagel too. Walking back across campus to my first class, I am so lost in thought about how lucky I am to even be able to go to college that I almost run into Kristen.

"Good morning sunshine," I say, smiling.

Kristen frowns. "It is too early to be good. I stayed at my friend's room last night, and he has an early class so I had to leave. Now I am going back to bed. I made sure all my classes were late. I'm not a good morning person. How about you? Did you find a guy to hook up with last night?"

If she knew I was a virgin she would probably be shocked. I just smile, "No one caught my eye, so I just came back to the room and unpacked."

"Sorry about not getting lucky. Well, I'm going to the dorm and crash for a few more hours. See you later." She turns and goes on her way.

I think to myself, *I'm not disappointed about not getting lucky.* I want to wait on that perfect guy. I wonder why everyone is in a hurry to have sex. Maybe it is because I'm still a virgin and think I might be missing out. I guess I am too old fashioned in thinking that I should wait on the guy who I am in love with. I made my mind up to stay a virgin until I am in love, and I know I can do it.

I head to my first class thinking that maybe I should have slept in a little later and not gotten up so early. As I get to the building's doors, I see Phillip ahead of me. I hope he doesn't see me. I head to the correct room and enter my first college class - Biology.

I find a seat near the back because I don't like being in the front. I put my backpack on the back of the seat and get my things out for class. I wonder how many students are in my class. Looks like the room is half full so far, so maybe I'm not the only crazy person to have biology as a first class. I start doodling on my paper, waiting until class starts. Then hear someone sit down in the chair next to me.

I look to see who it is to greet them. To my surprise, it is Phillip. *Oh no. This can't be happening.* Why do I keep running into him? He must be stalking me. So I say, "Hey, are you stalking me or something?"

He laughs "I can't really be stalking you if I have to take this class to graduate. I did get lucky to wait until you came to CCU. Now I will have you to take all the notes so I can sleep in class. Sounds like a plan to me."

"*Really*? You think I'm writing all the notes so you can sleep? I don't think so, mister. How are you even up so early after partying so late and being drunk? By the way, your girlfriend is pretty." That sounded mean and I sound jealous.

He looks at me and frowns. "Megan isn't my girlfriend. Just so you know, I don't have one. She just likes hitting on me. I don't even like how she acts or looks. I wasn't drunk last night either because I had to get my drunken friends home safely. I don't mind being here early. I like the early morning time. I waited to take this class later in college because I really don't like biology. I am so glad I did wait to have a pretty girl to cheat off of." He smiles and then says, "This day can't get any better."

I think he is really crazy. He thinks I'm going to let him cheat off me? I don't like cheaters of any kind.

The room is getting full, so now I can't find another seat. I wish I could. This guy is going to drive me crazy for sure, and now I have to sit by him for a whole hour. Hopefully tomorrow I can change seats.

Just before the professor comes in, I say to Phillip, "I don't like cheaters, and that means you can't cheat off me. I believe you're wrong about how I look. You need glasses, because I'm not pretty."

The professor comes in and introduces himself, telling everyone what is on the syllabus and what is expected of our work in class. Then the professor does something I thought only happens in grade school. He says to take a look at our seats and who is beside us, because from this day forward, that is where we will be sitting the rest of the year. *What*? *Who does this, nowadays*? Now I have to sit beside Phillip every day! I am wide awake now, that is for sure.

I can't even concentrate on what the professor says next. This is going to be one long day. I stew over what the professor just said for a long time. I look up to see what is going on and notice everyone leaving. I look over and see Phillip putting away his things.

"Where is everyone going?" I ask Phillip. I must look confused to him.

He turns and says, "Class is over. Time to go. By the way, I'm glad the professor assigned us to work on the project together. We will have to get together soon to get started on it. When will be good for you?"

What did he just say? I'm confused. What project is he talking about? Oh no! I must have missed something while I was being angry about the assigned seats. *No. No. No.* Now I have to ask Phillip what I missed. He will think I have lost my mind for sure. "

Um... What project do we have to do together? I must have missed what the professor said." I frown at him.

"I almost missed it too, because he was talking so fast. Who assigns seats in college anyway? He must think we are still in grade school. But we have to do our first syllabus assignment with the person sitting beside us, which happens to be you and me. No one was sitting on either side of us. Now you're stuck with me the rest of the year." He smiles at me like he is going to enjoy this much more than I am.

It really can't get any worse, this day, can it? How can I be stuck with this one guy? I should be staying away from him. I look up at him to see him still smiling at me. "Well I guess you have to work hard to be my study partner," I tell him. "I have to get good grades in this class. I have another class soon. I guess we need to get together soon to study." Reluctantly, I write down

my phone number and hand it to him. "Text me when you can."
I turn to leave, but he grabs my hand and turns me around.

He looks into my eyes. "I will text you soon. I can't wait to
study with you. I believe we will be a good team together. You
know, I'm not a cheater. I was just joking, okay? Believe me
when I tell you, you're pretty. Wait, no. You're not pretty."

"I told you I wasn't"

He smiles. "You're not pretty, but you're the most
beautiful girl I have ever seen. You shouldn't interrupt me when
I'm not finished talking. Well, I have to go. Don't forget, I'll be
texting you soon. Never think you're not beautiful." He turns
and walks out.

Wow! What a way to start the first day and my first class!
I am so confused about this guy that I can't think straight. *Why
him*? Why does he think I'm beautiful? I know what I look like,
and I'm just a plain average-looking girl. There's nothing special
with how I look. I think I need more coffee before my next class.
I need to forget everything that just happened. First day of
school and there's so much drama already going on. How could
one girl be so lucky?

I leave the building and walk back to get my coffee. I have
plenty of time before my next class, so I decide to find a nice
quiet place to read my new book. I get coffee and even found a
muffin to go with it. Now to find my quiet place, I look around
and find a nice shady spot under a big tree. Sitting down, I pull
my books out to get my biology book and skim over my syllabus.

I'm looking at it and see that this class shouldn't be too
hard, but I'll be learning a lot too. What is the project I have to
do with Phillip? I am so confused about Phillip and the way he
makes me feel. I have been extremely sick before, and my

hormones have not been active like this for other boys. I know I will get over this soon.

Six

PHILLIP

*T*his has to be my lucky day to walk into biology class and see her sitting in the back by herself. I know I shouldn't do what I am about to do, but I can't help myself. As always, my feet are already headed in her direction, so I move toward her and then sit down right beside her. I hope she doesn't look up just yet so I can look at her for a bit. But no, she notices me first thing and then her smile turns down. Her smile is so gorgeous, and I can't think straight.

Then she asks me if I am stalking her. I laugh and tell her that I'm not. Who knew that waiting to take biology the third year would make me lucky, that I'd have class with this beautiful girl? She has this wittiness about her that draws me in. I have never met anyone like her.

I try to play it cool and tell her that I have someone I can cheat off and do my homework with now, but she seems to get mad at me for trying to be funny. *Okay*... That didn't go so well. Maybe I should take that back. Does she really think I cheat? I hope not, because I have worked hard to do as well as I have since I came to school. Not like most of my friends, who like to party too much and barely get by. This class is going to be my favorite - having her in it is the reason.

She tells me that my girlfriend is pretty. *What girlfriend?* She looks a little bit jealous too, and that puts a smile on my face. I let her know that I don't have a girlfriend really fast. That is why she left the beach so quickly last night. How could she think Megan was my girlfriend? Maybe because of the way Megan jumped in my lap. That won't happen again I'll make sure of that. The professor calls everyone to his attention as soon as he gets in the door.

What! Did the professor do what I think he did? Yes he did! I laugh to myself, because the look on Alexia's face says, *Yes*. She seems surprised by getting assigned the seat right next to me for the rest of the year. Yes! This will be the best class ever.

The professor is going over the syllabus and I believe Alexia has spaced out over something. I try to listen so that I can tell her what he is saying. It is hard to keep paying attention when I can even smell her perfume. It smells so good like flowers and vanilla. Makes me want to get closer to her and take a deep smell of her skin.

Okay, now I know I'm in over my head and don't know what to do. Who does that? Who wants to smell someone's skin because they smell good? Especially since they first met the day before.

I have never in my life wanted to smell any girl I have been with before. Maybe I will not be lucky after all. Having to sit here day after day with this torment? It is already killing me to not just reach over, put my arms around her, and pull her close to me.

Then the professor starts to talk about an assignment we have to do with the person right beside us. I listen closer to what he is saying. I glance then to both sides of me to see who will be my partner, but the only person next to me is Alexia. *Yes*! Maybe not though, being around her more could be too much to handle. I think that maybe if I get to know her I will get over this infatuation. That is what this has to be - yes, infatuation. This assignment will fix that for sure, and maybe we will be just friends.

I write down the assignment and put my books away. I noticed Alexia looking a little bit confused. Why, I wonder, is this girl looking this way? Then she asks where everyone is going and I tell her that the class is over. She really must have been spacing out over something important. I let her know about us being partners on the assignment and she makes a face. This girl and her faces are going to be the death of me.

I laugh and tell her that we have to get together soon for studying. I also make a joke about the assigned seats and being stuck with me the rest of the year. She smiles at me, but it's not a full-on smile. Is that the reason she didn't pay attention in class? Is it really that bad for her to sit next to me? It has to be something else. Maybe I should ask.

Before I can do that, she hands me her phone number and says not to bring her grades down. *Wow*! She must think I'm a loser who doesn't study. I will show her that I am not. I wonder if this is her cell phone number. I'll text her soon to make sure.

I tell her that I will text her soon and that I can't wait to start the assignment. I decide to tell her that I'm not a cheater and let her know that I was just joking. I even do something as stupid as telling her that she is pretty, but then I take it back. She interrupts me to say, "I told you I wasn't." That makes me angry because she is beyond pretty.

I smile at her, "You're not pretty but you're the most beautiful girl I have ever seen. You shouldn't interrupt me when I'm not finished talking. Well, I have to go, but don't forget I'll be texting soon. Never think you're not beautiful." I leave before I say something else to embarrass myself.

I can't believe she doesn't know how beautiful she is. I know she thinks she looks like everyone else, but she doesn't. To me, she is something special.

I really should text her to make sure she gave me her right number. I start texting her number, but then I hear Megan before I get to finish, so I put my phone away. I turn around and go the other direction to avoid her. The more I see her, the more I dislike her. Megan is this spoiled girl who thinks she should be able to get whatever or whomever she wants. I know one guy who isn't into her and that is me. I guess my friends would probably think I'm crazy because she is really nice to look at and would let me do whatever I would want to do to her, but that isn't who I want to be. The best thing I can do is just ignore her.

I walk out the opposite side of the building, which makes my walk longer, but I'm good with it. Who doesn't need extra exercise? I head back to my car so I can go to the condo. I think, *I need to hit the beach for a while, before my next class.* I have three hours before that time, and I need to clear my head. Nothing a little sun, sand and waves can't take care of. Who wouldn't love living in a condo on the beach? I smile, turning my music up and rolling down the windows.

Knowing what waits for me when I get home makes me happy. Pulling into the driveway to the condo, I already feel more relaxed.

Seven

ALEXIA

*T*he rest of my day was uneventful. My next class went by surprisingly well and I even paid attention in it. There were no assigned seats in that class either. I tried not to stress over my biology class the rest of the day and just went with it. No need to stress over something I can't help. Maybe Phillip won't call or text me to study today. I think I'm going to stay in the room and rest. It has been an exciting first day for me. I ate before I came back to the dorm so that I could just chill a bit and read. I don't have much homework. A nap might be what this girl needs. Kristen isn't here because she has late classes and now would be a good time for a nap.

I lie down on my small bed and shut my eyes; yes, this is what I have been waiting on all day. I am almost asleep when I hear the door open. Kristen comes in being really hyped up and loud. She must be on a caffeine high. I guess my nap is over for now. Maybe I should head out for a drive and find a nice place at the beach to relax. I need to go find a chair that I can keep in my car so I can always have a seat at the beach.

Kristen walks in with a grin on her face. She must have had a good day. "You look happy. How was your first day of classes?"

"It was amazing. And I found out that the guy I hooked up with was in my class. I didn't even know his name, but I found out what it was today. His name is Chris, and he has an amazing body and blue eyes that can drown you. He asked me out again and I can't wait to go." Still smiling, she sits down on her bed.

How nice it must be to be able to do what you want and when you want. I am afraid to let myself go around boys because it is best if they don't get attached to me. I might die too soon, and that wouldn't be fair to him. I know I should live every day to the fullest, but I still feel guilty getting close to people. I don't want them to feel bad when I die and leave them. I have had this fear, ever since I first got sick. Watching how sad my parents were when I could barely breathe did something to me. It would break my heart to leave all of the people I get attached to. My parents say that life must go on and that I should not fear this. They say that I'm easy to love and get attached to. I don't believe them though because I really don't have too many people in my life. I did that on purpose.

Kristen looks over and says, "Why so sad? It is good he asked me out. Most of the time guys will hook up with me and move on, but this time, maybe it can grow into something good."

"I am glad for you and hope for the best with Chris. I will have to meet him if it will last a while. When is the big date going to happen?" I smile at her so I can get myself out of my depressing thoughts.

"He is taking me out tonight. Can you believe that? It surprised me too. I need to get ready now. He will pick me up outside the building in an hour. What should I wear?

"Depends on where you're going. Do you know where?

"He said to eat and play putt-putt golf."

"Maybe you should go with some cute shorts and top to match. Sandals too."

"You are right. That sounds perfect. I know the best outfit for my date." She goes to her little closet and pulls out these really cute red shorts and a black and red top to match. She looks up for my approval and I give her two thumbs up. She laughs and says that she has to run to take a shower.

I wonder if maybe I should take that nap now, but I decide to go over my lessons from today. Right when I am almost done, Kristen runs back in to get dressed and fix her hair.

She gets done and asks, "How do I look?"

"You look beautiful and that outfit looks good on you." I smile. "I hope you have fun tonight. It still is warm and sunny out, so kick his butt at putt-putt."

"I plan on it, but so you know, if I don't come back early, everything went well and don't wait up. Oh, I have to go. Hope you do something fun tonight." Wow! She is so full of energy; I wish I could be like her.

As I put my books away, I get a text. It's just my parents checking on my first day and me. I let them know that I had a great day and I am fine too. We get done and I put my phone down beside my bed. I lie back on the bed, but now I am not tired at all. Maybe I need to go out for a drive and take a walk by the beach. That would relax me a bit.

I just wish I weren't so scared to let someone in. It would be nice to go out like most people. Sometimes I get lonely. I don't have siblings, just my parents. I don't have many friends because I don't let people around me to get to know who I am. The little bit of interaction with Kristen was the most fun I have had in a while. I really should get a life, not worry so much and not be negative about myself.

I get up and put on some shorts, a t-shirt and flip-flops. I decide to go get a chair, sit and relax at the beach. As I am on my mission, I stop at the beach store for my chair and I get another text. Wondering who could be texting me, I look at it and can't believe who it is from. It is Phillip and he wants to get started with studying, but I have plans. I buy my chair, head out to my car, and reply before I start driving.

Me: Sorry I am just headed to the beach. We will have to plan another time.

Phillip: We can study at the beach if you want to. I live in a condo at the beach. You can come over then we can go down to the beach to study and maybe get pizza.

I really like this plan more than going to the beach by myself. Should I go? I have never been to a guy's home by myself before. I have to do this project with Phillip even if I don't want to. As I am deciding, he texts me back.

Phillip: Are you coming? I will order pizza and it should be here by the time you do. What kind of pizza do you like?

His actually asking me what kind of pizza I like makes me want to go. No guy has ever asked before. Well, I haven't been around many guys either, but I am curious about what his condo on the beach looks like.

Me: Sure I'll come over. Text the address to me. I like about anything on pizza, so surprise me.

He texts back the address and I put it in my GPS. It is really close and I should be there in twenty minutes, so I let him know. I am lucky, that I had my backpack full of books with me. I don't have to go back to the dorm first. I roll down my window and turn up my music for the drive over. I love the salty air and breeze in my hair.

Smiling as I drive toward the beach, I start to relax. The beach always has this effect on me. Maybe it won't be bad to study at Phillip's place. We will be at the beach and that should help us finish faster.

T.R. LYKINS

Fight

PHILLIP

I'm so glad I decided to go to the beach for a while before my next class. After I ate lunch, I came down to the beach for a jog and then swam in the ocean. I even sat under the cabana, which is exclusive to my parents' condo building. Every resident who owns a condo gets a private cabana. That really makes it nice to relax, and sometimes I need to get out of the sun so I don't get sunburned. Yeah, I believe I might have it made.

Now if I can clear my head of Alexia, I might find a cute girl around here to talk to. I watched a lot of girls on the beach through my sunglasses. That way they don't see me looking, but none of them can compare to her. We should hurry and get started on our project so we can finish quickly.

I see some girls coming my way and think that maybe my luck is getting better. Then, as they get closer, I see, that I'm not going to be lucky, because one of them is Megan. She comes up and stands over me blocking the sun.

"I saw you today at school and yelled at you too, but you went the other way. If I thought you were that mean, I would believe you did it on purpose, like you were trying to avoid me," she says with a pout.

Oh no, she knows what I did. "No, I just didn't hear you or see you." I smile up at her and hope that she buys it.

She smiles back. "What are you doing out here today? Are you done with school for the day? We are, so we plan on hanging out at the beach for a while and working on our tans."

"I'm not done with classes today. Just taking a break for a while. Who are your friends?"

She looks a little worried about introducing us, but she does anyway. "Oh this Beth and Jessica. They came in for a few days before their school starts and I'm just showing them around." I look at each girl and notice they are as pretty as Megan, but none of them can compare to Alexia. We need to get the project done so I can move on already.

I say, "Hi Beth and Jessica. I hope you have a good time while staying here. Be careful and don't get sunburns today."

They both giggle at me and smile. They tell me that they're glad to meet me after what Megan has told them about me. They both hope to spend more time with me too.

Then Megan says, "Oh, Phillip, I am having another party tonight so Beth and Jessica can meet everyone. You should bring your friends too."

"I don't know if I can tonight. I already have a biology project. I have to start when I get back from my next class."

"Well tell Jacob and Tyler. Maybe they will come. I know they won't miss a party to do homework," Megan's says sort of angrily.

"Okay I will let them know about your party. Is it at your parents' beach house?"

"Yes it is. You know there isn't a better place than the beach house to party at."

"Nope there isn't"

"So please come then. You can even walk over if you wanted to. My house isn't too far from here."

"I know, but I have to get this biology project done fast."

"I could help you if you want me to. I did get a B in that class."

"No I don't need your help. I have a project partner to help me and we have to start tonight." Megan's helping would be bad and I would never be able to avoid her then.

Megan pouts and says, "Well, you know where I am if you get done in time. And bring your partner. He may like the party too."

"My partner isn't a guy. You met her last night at your party. Her name is Alexia."

"I remember her. She didn't stay too long. She was the girl sitting on the beach with you and your friends. She didn't look like your usual girl you go out with," she says kind of hatefully to me. "So why do you have to do a project with her?"

She looks at me with her hands on her hips and expects me to answer. I start saying, "I don't have a usual girl, but if I did it very well could be Alexia. She has nothing wrong with how she looks and I think she is beautiful. We have the same class and we got picked to do it together. I will tell the guys about the party. I have to go now for my next class." I get up and leave Megan and her friends.

So now my relaxing turned out to be a bust. Megan just got me angry from talking about Alexia like that. How could she? I was trying to get Alexia off my mind and now I can't. I feel like I should go back to Megan and tell her off for Alexia's sake. See what this girl is doing to me? She is turning my world upside down and I don't want her to.

I look down at my watch and notice that it's getting late. I better hurry to my class so I can text Alexia and get this project done quickly. I have to get over her and fast. I head to my room, grab my books, and head out. Once I get to campus, I start walking to class. I turn toward my building and see Alexia going out and across the lake to the dorms. That was close. I want to try my best to avoid her every minute until this project is over, but then I think about how, I don't like avoiding her. I should have just asked her to meet me after class. Now she is already out of my sight. I will text her after class.

I get to class and it goes okay. My mind is still a little upset over how Megan thought Alexia wasn't much to look at. How could anyone think such a horrible thing? Looking at Alexia makes me think of the ocean, because of her beautiful blue eyes. Yeah, this infatuation is really getting bad.

I pay a little bit of attention to my class and now it's over. I get my books together and put them in my backpack to leave. As I walk across the school grounds to my car I see Tyler and Jacob coming over to me.

"Hey guys. How did your classes go? Did you have a bad hangover this morning? I asked them.

Jacob looks like he still has a hangover, but says, "It was bad this morning, but I'm good now. Classes? What classes? Because I think I fell asleep in mine."

"That isn't the best way to start off the school year." I let him know.

"I know and I really have to do well in my classes or I won't graduate in the spring. Maybe I should stay away from the parties this year." He smiles, knowing that he won't.

Tyler laughs at him. "Sure that is going to happen. Better find someone quick to cheat off so you can pass. My class was pretty boring. I hope is gets better."

I check the time and find it is getting late. It's time I should head out. "Hey, Megan is going to have a party again tonight at the beach house and told me to let you guys know."

Jacob grins real big. "Megan huh? I thought you didn't like her much. I don't know why. She is pretty hot."

"I don't like her because she is stuck up and thinks she is better than everyone else. I'm not going anyways. I already have a biology project I have to start on. You guys should go. She had some really cute friends with her that I met today." Maybe they aren't too much like Megan."

Tyler says, "What? You're not going to go to a party? You are missing out on Megan. She is really into you and you probably can get whatever you want out of her, if you know what I mean." He winks.

Jacob winks too. "Yeah, Man. You are missing out. I think I am ready for another party. What about you Tyler?

"Yeah let's go and maybe we will get lucky while Phillip misses out." Tyler laughs.

"I'm not missing out, and Megan gives me the creeps guys, so go for it. Well, I have to get going so I can start this project. Have fun tonight and don't drive drunk. If you drink call me and I'll pick you up," I say and walk to my car. I decide to text Alexia when I get back to the condo.

The traffic isn't bad as I hit the road, so I get home really quickly. As I ride up the elevator to my room, I realize I'm hungry. I think I will get pizza delivered. Then I wonder if Alexia has eaten yet. I text her asking her to come over to work on our project and if she wants pizza, maybe I shouldn't have asked about the pizza. I like a lot of different things on mine. She texts back saying that she is busy going to the beach. *Well that is perfect, I think to myself, because I am at the beach already.* I tell her that and she agrees to come over and will be here soon. I am smiling as I get off the elevator and almost run into my neighbor, Jack.

He asks, "What is with that big grin on your face, boy? Must be a girl. It is always a girl with you boys."

"Well, actually it is, but not what you're thinking. I have to do a school project and she is coming over in a few minutes," I tell him.

"With a smile that big on your face, it must be a really good project you have to work on." He smiles wide and gets on the elevator.

I laugh and turn to my room. I order my favorite pizza, and I bet she won't like it, even though she said to surprise her. I go jump in the shower really fast before she and the pizza gets here.

Nine

ALEXIA

The drive over to Phillip's is quite nice. It is a private area, which I believe is close to Megan's beach house. I turn down the next street and see her house right there. What a coincidence. I pay no attention to that because he told me that his parents rented out the condo during the summer and it has to be in a nice area where people would like it.

A few more turns and my GPS says that I am here. I look up at the condo building and see that it is even nicer than I thought. *Wow*! It must be nice to live here rather than at the dorm. I can't wait to see more of this area. It has to be private too, because there isn't much traffic around this area.

I find a parking place and then text Phillip to let him know I am here. He said that he would have to come down and let me in. I get out, sit on the bench near the doors, and wait. He texts backs and says that he will be right down. As I wait for him, I can feel the nice breeze coming from the ocean. I close my eyes and relax for a minute, knowing that it shouldn't take long. I could really get used to this.

I hear the door open and look up. I see Phillip grinning at me. Seeing him takes my breath away, and that shocks me a little bit. Wow! I really am in trouble.

He comes over and sits down beside me. "It is almost time for the pizza delivery guy to get here, so we can sit here for a minute if you want."

"That is fine with me. I like the feel of the breeze, this evening. It really is nice here."

"Yeah, it does feel good. Oh, here comes the pizza. I am starved. Are you hungry too?"

"I can always eat pizza, and I like about anything on it too. I can't wait to see what kind of surprise pizza you got for me."

Oh my. He just keeps grinning at me, like he is happy to see me. I like that. He makes my tummy do flip-flops.

After he gets up and pays for the pizza, he turns around and says, "Well, let's go see what kind of surprise I have for you then."

We walk into the building and he stops at the security desk to tell the guy sitting there, to put my name down and let me in whenever I come over. He turns and heads to the elevator, and I follow him in. This elevator ride seems to be taking forever, and being so close to him, I get a good smell of him. He smells delicious. It's definitely not the pizza kind of smells either. *Hurry up, elevator,* I say to myself. He smells way too good.

Finally, the door opens. We go to his condo and he opens the door. As you can imagine, I am blown away with the awesome view. I head over to the open balcony doors and look out. I love it here.

I turn to him and smile. "This is an amazing view. You are lucky to live here and not at the dorms. I think I would even sleep on this balcony."

He laughs. "I do sometimes. I love it here too. Do you want to eat the pizza out here?"

"Can we please?" I ask looking up at him with a smile.

"Yes I'll go get some plates and something to drink. I mostly eat out here instead of inside. I'd rather be out here every chance I get."

"Can I help with anything?"

"Nah, I got it. You go sit right over there and enjoy the view. What would you like to drink? I have coke, maybe tea and beer."

"I would love to have tea, but if you don't, I will take a coke. I don't drink beer."

"I will see about the tea. I don't drink beer either, but I keep it here for when I have friends over. You met Tyler and Jacob last night. They can put it away fast." He heads back inside to get the food and drinks.

I am amazed that he doesn't drink, but then I begin to think about what he told me on the plane and that makes sense. He can't drink and be on transplant medicine. This makes me sad for him. I know how it is to have to watch what you drink and eat, because of a transplant. The medicine might stop working or you could have a reaction. No time to think about that. I have to try to get through this project and hurry. The more I am around Phillip, the more I like him.

"Here we go. Pizza and Coke what more do we need? Sorry I was out of tea. Hope you like this pizza. It is one of my favorites." He sits down beside me and opens up the box. I can't believe my eyes! He got my favorite pizza from my favorite pizza place. I look up and see him smiling at me.

"How did you know my favorite pizza is The Moon Doggie? I have loved this pizza for a long time. This is from my favorite pizza place when I am here. I like all of their pizzas, but this one is the best." I beamed at him.

"You have to be kidding me. This is the best pizza ever! My brother and I ate so many of these pizzas when I was growing up. We couldn't get enough. Finding out that someone else loves it too is amazing for sure. Well, let's eat so we can tackle this project and be finished with it. Have you looked at what we have to do?" He places pizza on my plate and hands it to me.

"Yeah, I looked at it a little bit today. I had another class. I really didn't get into it much. Can't believe we have to do the project on properties of DNA. I wasn't into biology in high school. I hope you are you are good with this biology stuff." I take a bite of pizza and make a groaning sound because it is the best pizza.

He laughs at me for making that sound. "Glad I picked the right pizza so you could make that sound. I like it. I will have to surprise you more often to get you to make that sound again." So he takes a bite and groans too. After he gets done chewing, he says, "I believe this project might take a while longer than we planned, because I was hoping you knew more about biology than me. I guess we will have to work on it every day. How about you come over after classes every day this week, and maybe we can finish it fast?"

"Sure I can come over as long as we can work on it on this balcony or at the beach. I could get used to being here. It is so nice here. Maybe tomorrow I will buy the pizza so you're not out too much money. I feel like I at least should help pay for pizza or some food if we will are going to be working so hard."

"That's okay. My parents set me up with a really good food allowance. They know I like to eat more than most people. I think we should get started so I won't keep you too late."

"That sounds like a plan. I will put these dishes in the dishwasher, grab my books, and go to the restroom. Then I will be ready. Where is the restroom by the way?" I get up and grab the plates to take with me.

"It is right down that hall to the left. I will get my books and computer. I will be sitting out here when you get done." We both go our separate ways to do our things so we can get to studying.

I put the dishes in the dishwasher and find the bathroom. I take a few extra minutes to compose myself. Being around him is already getting to me. While we were eating and talking on the balcony, I felt at home here with him. I felt like I was supposed to be here, and this confuses me. I'm not supposed to get attached to anyone. I told myself I wouldn't before I came to school. I won't leave someone behind to be hurting over me when my time is up.

"Quit feeling sorry for yourself," I say to myself. "Enjoy the now. You deserve to be happy even for a little while." But I don't want people to get attached to me. I am making this harder than it should be. *Ugh*! My thinking is driving me crazy, and I am taking too long in here. He probably thinks I have fallen in or something. I wash my hands and decide to just get this project over with. Go with it for now and not worry about everything else.

Here goes. I open the door, retrieve my books, and head to the balcony. When I get to the balcony, I see Phillip leaning against the rails. Oh my goodness, he looks like a model standing there. His hair is blowing in the wind and his muscles are flexing the way you would see in a magazine. *I am so in trouble,* I think to myself, but I step outside anyway.

Ten

PHILLIP

I get the text from Alexia saying that she is here and waiting on me downstairs. She is a little bit early. The pizza should be here soon. I grab my wallet to take it with me. Hopefully, the pizza will arrive when I get downstairs too. I head for the elevator and ride down. I like taking the stairs sometimes, but I don't want to be sweaty by the time I see Alexia.

As I get to the outside door, I look out and see her sitting on the bench. Her eyes are closed, the wind is blowing her amazingly long hair, and she looks like she is enjoying the breeze, so I watch her for a moment. She looks so peaceful. I hate to interrupt her. She is so beautiful that it hurts to look at her, and now sitting here at my condo makes my stomach feel funny. Maybe I am really hungry. I hope that is what this really is that I am feeling in my stomach.

While I stare at her for a moment longer, Jack comes up to me and touches my arm so I don't get startled. He grins at me and turns his head toward Alexia. "That must be the girl who has that smile so big on your face. If I had a chance with her, you would have to work hard to keep her away from me. So are you going to invite her in or are you just going to look at her all day?" He turns and heads off laughing. I just realized that I really have it bad. I need to figure out what to do with it. Should I go with it or ignore it? Maybe I need to let nature take its course and see what happens.

I open the door to head out, and Alexia opens her eyes. I smile at her. That is all I can do because seeing her eyes again takes my breath away. Yeah, I can see I have it bad. I walk over to her and sit down beside her. I get a good smell of her because the breeze blows her scent my way. She has the most amazing scent. I could smell her all day. I wonder if I hugged her close and put my nose close to her skin if she would freak out. I am freaking myself out just thinking about it. She would run off screaming.

I quickly let her know that the pizza is almost here so we should wait on it. I really just want to sit here and let the breeze fill me with her sweet scent. Then I think the pizza guy should hurry before I reach over and grab her to hold her close. I even want to kiss her so badly.

Thank goodness the pizza guy saves me. This project keeps getting harder and harder and we haven't even started on it. I get up and pay him giving him an extra tip, because *hey,* he just saved me.

We go inside with the pizza and I head over to Jake, who is the security officer. I tell him who Alexia is and let him know that she is my study partner. I tell him when she comes over he should let her in, so that she can come on up whenever she likes. He smiles really big at me like he knows something I don't but puts her name on the list. I don't have many people down on the list. I like keeping it that way. Just a few of my friends can come and go.

I turn to Alexia and we head over to the elevator. The ride up seems it takes like forever. Being this close to her sets my skin on fire. I don't know what this is, but I think I like this feeling I am having around her. *Let nature take its course*, I think to myself. Maybe it will be something more, or maybe not.

We get to the condo and I open it up. Then I see her face light up like a Christmas tree, because the view is amazing. She is looking at the view of the ocean, but my view of her is even better. Her eyes just glow, or maybe it's the reflection of the light. No, I believe they are glowing, and it's the best view I have ever seen. She heads straight for the balcony and steps out. I put the pizza down on the table so I can follow her. The wind blowing her hair is so breathtaking that I almost trip on my way out. She looks like she loves it here and says so. I would love to keep her here that is for sure.

She turns and smiles up at me. She says that she would sleep on this balcony. I let her know that I do, but now all I really can think about is her sleeping with me on this balcony would even be better. She is really getting to me. I suggest we eat out here, being that this is where I eat most of the time.

I ask her what she wants to drink. So she doesn't like beer... That's good to know. I let her know that I don't either. She seems surprised by it. Maybe she forgot that I can't have it with the medicine I am on. Even if I weren't on it, I wouldn't drink. That is how I lost my brother. Since that day I vow never to drink and I plan on keeping my vow. I keep this to myself because everyone would think I am crazy but I know how bad drinking effects people. They do crazy things when they drink, just look at my friends.

I go get plates and drinks. I hurry so I don't miss seeing her. I put everything down on the table outside and ask her if is she ready for her surprise pizza. I see her eyes light up just at seeing the box, and I find out that this is her favorite pizza place. I open the box and learn that this is Alexia's favorite pizza too.

Now I know that I have to get to know her more. She is full of surprises. Anyone who likes my favorite pizza is the greatest in my book. I hand her some pizza and her drink. We talk about how wonderful this pizza is and that it was my brother's favorite too. Alexia is easy to talk to and she makes this place feel more relaxing for me, like she should always be here with me. Having her here with me makes the pain of losing my brother easier. She has this calming effect on me

We discuss the project and how we both don't like biology. I ask her to come over every evening, so we can get the work done fast. Looks like it may take longer because we both aren't as good at biology as I hoped. As we talk, it just seems so natural. I have decided for sure to let things happen. I really don't know if I can stop it at this point anyway. I really like being with Alexia, and maybe she will feel the same way, if we see more of each other.

Alexia gets up and takes the dishes to the dishwasher. She looks like she belongs in that kitchen. She goes down the hall, and all I can think about is how much trouble I am in. I get up and lean against the balcony rail to see what is going on at the beach. I can see a bunch of people over at Megan's party. I should feel like I am missing out on the party, but really I don't because this feels right being here with Alexia.

I hope Jacob and Tyler don't get into much trouble. I told them to call me for a ride if they get too drunk. I believe they will, because they are responsible sometimes. I hate that people don't heed the warnings about drinking and driving. People only think about themselves too much and not the cost of someone's stupidity. How, in just a fraction of time, a life can be lost or so many lives can be changed.

I hear Alexia coming. Now it's time to get studying. She waits for a moment before she comes out. I wonder why. I turn around and see her. I smile at her and grab my books. I love the way she just looked at me.

Eleven

ALEXIA

*H*e smiles at me when he sees me coming out the door, and my heart starts beating faster. Yeah, he has that effect on me already. I think I like how he makes me feel alive. I am going to just go with it because he probably doesn't feel anything for me though. Since he is a player, he probably has many beautiful girls. He won't even look that way at me. I better get my books and get this work done. I don't want to burden him. He probably had other things to do tonight.

I walk over to the rail to look at what he may have been looking at and see what looks like a party a little ways over at a beach house. He probably was wishing that I would hurry back so we can finish studying and he can go to the party. Looks like a lot of people are there.

I turn to him and say, "If you had plans this evening, we could do this another night. I see that party over there and I bet you were supposed to go to it. Looks like a lot of things are going on."

He walks over to me. "No, I didn't want to go. Megan asked me to, but I told her no. Jacob and Tyler are over there. I hope they call if they get too drunk to drive. I'd rather stay here and do biology homework than go to another party at Megan's. Let's get this work started so I don't keep you out too late."

We get our books and computers out of our backpacks, to start our first night of studying. It goes by so quickly that I hardly notice that two hours have gone by. We got a lot done. We definitely need several more weeks to get everything that is on the list done. I hope he doesn't stop our study session for a little while longer because I like being here. Every now and then, we can hear the party still going strong, but Phillip doesn't look sad about missing out.

He asks me if I want something to drink and then goes to get it. I get up to stretch and lean against the rail to see the water. The breeze still feels so good. I hear Phillip answer his phone and say, "I will be right over." Then brings me out my water.

He looks at me a little bit sad and says, "That was Tyler. I am sorry. We have to cut the studying short for tonight. Jacob has gotten too drunk. Tyler can't get him to leave the party. I have to help get him out of the party before he gets into trouble. He tends to cause trouble when he is heavily intoxicated."

"Is there anything I can do to help? Maybe I can help you convince him to leave."

"I don't know how you can unless you bat those pretty eyes at him. He may follow you anywhere." He laughs.

"Sure he would. My eyes work that way on every guy." I laugh at my joke.

He stares seriously at me. "I know if you batted your eyes at me, I would follow you anywhere. Just try and see." He winks.

I believe he is flirting and I do as he asked. "Well, let's go save Jacob, sweetie," I bat my eyes at him. I even throw in my biggest smile. Two can play this flirting game.

He reaches over and grabs my hand. "Let's go. See? It worked just like I knew it would. You keep that up and you won't get rid of me." Still holding my hand, he grabs his keys and we head out the door. We make it outside with him still holding my hand. His hand is larger than mine, but it feels so right in my hand. I hope he doesn't stop holding it anytime soon. When we get outside the door, I think we are going to his car, but instead we head to the beach. He sees my confused look.

"It is quicker this way to get to Megan's. I really don't want him to get sick in my car either. I will bring him back to the condo and let him rest it off before taking him back to the dorm."

"I can take him to the dorm so you don't have to. I have to go that way," I offer.

"No. You will not be taking Jacob back, especially when he is drunk. He gets flirty with the girls and fights with the guys. Our mission is to get him to leave and get him back to the condo."

"Okay. I will do my best eye batting to get him to leave. Maybe if I ask him to leave he'll think I am flirting, and I won't even have to bat these eyes." I laugh.

"You think I am joking about your beautiful eyes making me want to do anything? I am serious girl. I don't want Jacob to fall for your cuteness and try to run off with you. He is the real player between us."

"Sure he is. You're just saying that to make me think you're not, but you seem really flirty with the girls. I have seen you around. You even flirt with me and I know that doesn't mean you like me. You just do it out of habit," I say, but I feel a little jealous thinking about him and other girls.

We still are walking to the beach house when I notice that he still has my hand. He pulls me to a stop and turns me to him.

"What makes you think I don't like you? I flirt with you because I do like you and I like being with you. I know this is soon, but I like you more than I have liked anyone. I can't explain it, but you do something to me."

I am stunned.

Before I can say anything back to him, we hear a loud noise. He starts pulling me toward it. It sounds louder the closer we get to it, and I might be a little scared, but I keep going.

"Jacob must have already started something so we have to hurry," he says.

He's still holding my hand when we get to the party. We see everyone standing around two guys who seem to be getting ready to fight. I think, *Oh no*. I have walked in on something I shouldn't have. Phillip pulls me closer, and most of the people glance at us, but he pays them no attention. He has one thing on his mind and that is to get to Jacob.

We get to the guys and he says, "Jacob, buddy, what are you doing? You need to stop whatever it is and come with us to leave." As soon as he says this the other guy laughs at Phillip. Phillip tenses up like he's getting ready to step in front of Jacob. He then lets my hand go.

The guy says to him, "What, you have to fight Jacob's battles now? I knew he was a wimp." The guy laughs.

Phillip does something that surprises me. I thought he might go grab Jacob and make him leave, but he walks over to the guy instead. He gets up into his face, and the guy doesn't seem to be backing down either. I feel like I need to do something, but I don't know what I should do. I'm scared that the guy wants to fight.

Phillip continues his stare down, and the tension that flows off his body makes everyone back up. Even Jacob is now quiet and maybe a little more sober. Tyler comes up beside Phillip and also gets up into the guys face.

Phillip says, "James, whatever Jacob did, you know he has had too much to drink. Back off or you will have to go through me to get to him."

Tyler says the same thing too. By the look on James's face, he doesn't seem to want to back down. Jacob decides to join them and James holds his hands up. "Okay. I will stop if he stops hitting on my girl."

Jacob slurs, "Which girl are you talking about?" He smiles at James to further his provoking.

"Misty the redhead, who you decided to put your hands all over a few minutes ago."

"Oh. Misty. She is hot, but I just tripped and she was there when I needed help standing. I just grabbed her so I wouldn't fall," Jacob grins. I wonder if that is true and by the look on James's face he is thinking the same thing.

I decided, to do what Phillip said, I could do. I walked over and batted my eyes to Jacob before turning to James and smiling. "Oh here you are Jacob. I have been looking for you. I am glad I found you. What are you and these guys doing outside? I am sorry if he is causing trouble, James, but I really can't take him anywhere without him drinking and tripping over his feet. Now come on, Jacob. It is time to leave." I grab him by the arm and pull him away from everyone down at the beach. I hear James say that it is okay but to put a leash on him as we leave.

Jacob slurs, "Thanks baby, but who are you? I think we have met, but I don't remember where. Did we hook up some time ago?"

I get ready to tell him off, but Phillip comes up behind me and pulls me away from Jacob. Phillip gets up into his face saying, "You met Alexia yesterday at Megan's party where you were also drunk. You have to stop all this drinking or I will not come to your rescue again. You need to get serious with school and stop the drinking. Every now and then is fine, but not every night. School has just started and you are already getting into trouble. *No*, you haven't hooked up with Alexia, and you never will hook up with her. Straighten up now! Tyler take him back to the condo. I have to go ahead so I can cool off or he will not be staying tonight."

Before we get moving, I hear someone calling Phillip's name. Phillip tenses up. He seems to know who is coming our way.

I turn around and see Megan running over to us. "Oh Phillip, don't leave the party! You just got here. Come back and hang out with me. We can go find a place that is quiet in the house if you want to," she says suggestively.

I look at her and think that she's really full of herself and totally a slut. I hope he doesn't take her up on it. I sounded jealous with that thought. Before I can think about how this makes me feel, Phillip shakes his head.

"Megan I told you I didn't want to come to your party, and as good as your offer sounds, I have to pass. Please just go back to your party. We have to get Jacob home before something else happens with him." He walked over to me.

Megan adds, "When you get done with him, you can come back over if you want too." She smiles, looking hopeful. I think, *Really*!

"I am sorry, Megan, but that won't happen tonight or any other night. Goodnight Megan." He takes my hand and she looks over at me like she would stab me, if she had a knife. I smile and squeeze his hand. *Yeah look, Megan. Phillip has my hand.*

Megan says one last thing before we get to leave. "You will be sorry, Phillip. You missed out on the best thing you will ever get." She stares us both down with evil eyes.

Phillip looks at her and then to me and says, "No I haven't." He pulls me along the beach and away from her dirty looks. Tyler drags Jacob along behind us. *My*, what was all that about? Phillip looked at me, like I was the best thing, and that makes me feel lucky. After we get up to the condo, the guys come staggering in.

Jacob says, "Phillip you should have taken Megan up on her offer. You know she is crazy about you. I will take care of this little blue-eyed girl you brought along to save me," Jacob half-smiles at me.

Phillip gets up and grabs him. "You will never touch Alexia. I mean it. I don't like Megan and I will never hook up with her. You need to apologize to Alexia now! Never talk bad to her or about her again."

"Okay, man. Back off. I was just joking. What has gotten into you all of a sudden? Alexia, please forgive me for being a jerk. Are you guys hooking up?" Jacob asks and almost falls asleep.

Phillip is about to grab him again, so I reach over and touch his hand. "Please stop Phillip. He is drunk and he doesn't know what he is saying. He will be sorry in the morning" I say to try to calm him.

Phillip's tension goes away while my hand is on him, "He has no right talking to you that way, or anyone for that matter. I want to smack him until he tells you he is sorry the right way." He then smiles and stares at me, "I knew taking you there would be a good thing. All you had to do is bat those eyes and you stopped a fight that would have been probably really bad. You stepped in with your sweet smile and turned those eyes on. They made all the guys stop to look at you. You were so brave when you did that. I almost had to beat them both down because they were looking at you. Now I have to keep all the guys at school from stalking you. You are going to be trouble for me."

I laugh at him. "Trouble? Me? I don't think so I am just plain ol' me. Nothing for anyone to remember, so you won't have to keep anyone away."

Tyler speaks up before Phillip can reply. "Wow, what a night. I know Jacob probably won't know a thing in the morning. He probably won't remember he has an early class and he will have a killer hangover. I didn't drink as much as he did, but I sure feel the buzz too. I don't know if I can make it back to the dorm. Are you going to take us back Phillip?"

Phillip says, "If you want to go, I'll take you back, but you and Jacob can share the guest room."

"Do you still have twin beds in that room?" Tyler asks.

Phillip smiles "Yes. They are still there. What, you don't want to share a bed with Jacob?"

Tyler laughs. "Heck no man. Have you ever slept in the same bed as him? He snores and tosses like crazy in his sleep. I did it once and never again. I guess we should get him to bed, and I am going to hit it too. Thanks, Alexia for your help tonight. Pay Jacob no attention. He won't remember being a jerk to you in the morning." Tyler smiles at me.

"You're welcome Tyler, and thanks. Get some rest and drink water. Don't forget to take aspirin so you won't have a bad hangover in the morning." I smile at him and wave him goodnight. Tyler and Phillip drag Jacob to the bedroom. I wait a minute to see if Phillip comes back to say goodnight to me.

While I do, I pack up my schoolbooks and computer. I look over at the clock and realize it is already two o'clock in the morning. There has been so much excitement; I didn't notice how late it has gotten. I stand up and stretch. Yawning, I turn around and see Phillip standing close by me. He even looks more relaxed than he was a few minutes ago and I like that.

"You look like you might be tired. I didn't notice the time until now and it is late. I'd hate for you to drive back this late. You can stay here if you want and sleep in my bedroom. I will sleep on the couch," Phillip says, reaching my arm to rub it.

"I'd hate for you to sleep on that small couch. You are so much taller than it is long. I don't mind driving back." I reason, yawning again.

He smiles and yawns too. "It is settled. You can't drive this late and you are tired. Come on and stay. We can share the bed if you don't mind. I will sleep on top of the covers. I will loan you a t-shirt because it will be like a gown on you." He grabs my hand and leads me to his room. "Look, the bed is a king-size one and there will be plenty of room for both of us. Please stay the night, and I promise not to bite."

I look around the room and it seems relaxing. The bed is huge and much bigger than the dorm room. I even notice the double doors and see a balcony. I think about it, and I really do feel extra tired. It would be nice to wake up and see the ocean in the morning. "Okay... as long as you keep to your side of the bed. You can sleep under the covers. I believe I can trust you to keep your hands off me. I would like to borrow that shirt. I wish I had a toothbrush though."

He goes to the dresser and gets me a shirt. Then he enters the bathroom and brings out a toothbrush still in the pack. "Toothpaste is in the bathroom. Go change and brush. I'm tired, so let's get to sleep."

"Be right out in a minute." I hurry to the bathroom. I change into the shirt, and it does make me a nice gown, stopping just about at my knees. I wash my face and brush my teeth. Looking in the mirror, I see a woman who is nervous. This will be the first time I will share a bed with a man. I don't plan on doing anything but sleeping. I'm still nervous and don't know why. I shouldn't be because it just is sleeping. I finish and go to the bedroom. I jump in the bed and notice that Phillip is already in it, sitting on top and waiting on me.

He smiles at me. "You look cute in my t-shirt. I may have to keep you here every night."

"I don't think so. You wouldn't have time for all your girlfriends to visit." It makes me sad that I said that to him when he is only trying to be nice to me.

Now he looks unhappy. "I don't have any girlfriends. *Or* a girlfriend for that matter. I really don't. I know it might seem like I do to you, but you're wrong. Unless you are going to be my girlfriend?" He smiles over at me with a twinkle in his eyes.

"Are you for real? Asking me to be your girlfriend? I think you're a big jokester. You don't even know me. I know you are playing me right now." I angrily jump up off the bed to put my clothes back on.

Before I can start, Phillip has his arms around me and has my back pressed to his chest. "I am not joking to you. I know we just met, but this feels right. You and me just feel right. I can't explain it. It does. We can hang out together and take it slow, but believe me, I want you to be with me." He keeps his arms around me, holding me close to him. I feel his heart beating as hard and fast as mine. This does feel right, but I am so scared to get close to him. I said that I would let things happen, but now I don't know if I can. I'm scared of what might happen to me.

I turn around in his arms to face him. He looks down at me like I am the most special thing in the world. His brown eyes have turned darker with passion, and that makes my breathing stop. He bends down and kisses me like a man who knows what he wants. I kiss him right back, like I even know what I want. It lasts forever.

Then I want more of him, which wakes me up, and I realize that this isn't fair to him. I pull back, catching my breath and look at him. How can I do this to him? I turn away from Phillip and wipe a tear, because I have to tell him the truth.

He leans down to me and says, "Just think about it, but not tonight. It is late and we need sleep. I meant every word of what I said. I want you to think about it, and no rushing into anything. I won't even kiss you again until you're ready. So come back to bed and rest." He guides me back to the bed, and I crawl back under the covers.

I smile at him as he gets in the bed. He asks me what time my class is in the morning and I tell him that it's at ten but need to get up at 8:30 so I can go to the dorm and get changed before class. He sets the clock before he reaches over, grabs me and pulls me close to him. I snuggle up to him like I was made for him. It does feel right to be next to him. I didn't think I could sleep, but I fall to sleep rather fast.

Twelve

PHILLIP

I grab my books off the table and watch Alexia lean over the balcony. She sees the party and frowns. I wonder if she'd rather be there than here with me. She asks if I had plans that I am missing out on. I tell her no. So she is concerned about me missing the party. That is funny because I'd rather be with this girl than at any party. I let her know that I'm not interested in Megan's party. I tell her about Jacob and Tyler being there and that they may need a ride if they get drunk. She is okay with me leaving to get them, if I need to.

We start studying and I actually enjoy doing this with her. This is the first time I have ever enjoyed doing any studying. Most of the time, I would rather skip it altogether. If I had Alexia here more often, I might get better grades. She really is helping with this project, and she is making me learn a lot. She said that she wasn't too good in biology, but the way she gets us moving on this project, I think she is wrong.

I look at her when she is reading from her book and my heart flutters as she looks at me. I have never had this reaction around anyone before. I hope this takes a while longer to finish, because I am going to hate it when she leaves. The guys better be good tonight because I really don't want to have to pick them up and leave Alexia.

I notice that we have been studying for two hours. I get up and stretch. I see if Alexia needed something to drink. I'm inside getting us some water, when my phone rings. I look at the phone number and I know that if I answer it, our time together will be over. I have to answer it. I promised the guys I would come. Tyler sounds upset about Jacob, who is about to get into a fight. I let him know that I'll be right over.

I take Alexia her water and tell her that I have to go get Jacob and Tyler. She surprises me and asks if I need her help. I think about this for a minute and decide that she could be great distraction for Jacob. I don't really want her to leave and I know I am being selfish. I tell her that if she bats her beautiful eyes, he would do whatever she wanted. She doesn't believe me when I say this. I let her know that she could and that I would do whatever she wanted me to with her beautiful eyes batting at me. *Yeah*, I know she has this power on me like no other girl possibly can. I really don't care at this point. I keep flirting with her and she thinks I am joking, but I'm not. I let her know quickly that I'm not joking. I grab her hand and we head to get Jacob out of trouble.

We take to the beach. It is faster, and I want to walk on the beach with Alexia, just holding her hand. It feels good to walk hand in hand with Alexia. Her hand feels good in mine and it is so small and fits perfect into mine.

Then she offers to take the guys back to the dorm. That is something I can't let happen. A drunken Jacob would hit on her as soon as he got in the car, thinking she might want him too. It is a nice offer, but I let her know that it isn't going to happen. Over my dead body, would I let that happen. Thinking about this makes me have a strange feeling of jealousy. Jacob will have to stay at my condo and sleep by himself.

As we get close to Megan's, I hear a bunch of guys arguing. I hurry and pull Alexia along with me to get closer. I never let go of her hand. I love the feeling of it in mine, and it is helping me not lose it as I get closer to the argument. I glance over and see James, who looks like he is going to beat the crap out of Jacob. I wonder what Jacob has done now. I have to let go of Alexia's hand so I can help stop the fight.

James isn't the kind of guy who likes to fight just anyone who crosses his path. Jacob must have done something really bad to get into it with James. I step up and get between the guys. I ask James what Jacob did and he explains that Jacob was hitting on his girlfriend. I notice Tyler coming to stand beside me looking right at James like he is going to punch him. Good, I have backup.

This makes James step back. Jacob asks who James's girlfriend is and James tells him, and Jacob says that he knows her and wasn't hitting on her. He claims he tripped and grabbed her by accident. With that smile on Jacob's face, I know he is lying to James, and I can see what will happen next. This fight is going to be ugly. This isn't in my plans for tonight.

As I tense up, reading myself for a fight, Alexia comes over and grabs Jacob. She goes on and on about looking everywhere for him and how she can't take him anywhere. She bats those blue eyes at James, and I can see him melting into them the way I do. Now I really want to beat him down, but she ends up getting us all out of a fight and drags Jacob off. I start to follow and hear James tell her to keep him on a leash. I smile and follow closely behind Alexia and Jacob. Yes! This girl is amazing.

I hear Jacob ask her if they hooked up and if that's how he knows her. This makes me want to explode my fist into Jacob, but I calm myself down. I walk up to Alexia and grab her hand. Then I explain to my friend who is so drunk, that he hasn't nor will he ever hook up with her. I tell him that he is going to have to stop with all his drinking and get focused on his classes. I am calming down from my rage toward Jacob, because Alexia still has her blue eyes on me. She has this effect on me like no one ever has and I'm starting to like it more and more.

We get ready to move toward my condo and then I hear this annoying voice. I don't even have to turn around to know who it is, but I do because I'm not rude. Megan wants me to go back to the party and hook up with her. She just basically asks me this in front of everyone. *Really,* this girl is unbelievably slutty. I quickly let her know that I have no interest in her and her party. She tells me that I'm missing out on the best thing I'll ever have while giving Alexia dirty looks. I let her know that I'm not missing a thing and grab Alexia's hand pulling her close to me.

I have to get us away from Megan and fast but not before hearing her say that I'll be sorry. That girl is unaware of what is going on around her. Can't she see this beautiful girl beside me with her hand in my hand? I will never mess up being with Alexia for anyone. I'm not missing a thing. I smile at Alexia and she smiles right back at me. I think my heart jumped a beat when she did that, and I love having her next to me. I just don't know the reason for that yet.

Jacob says another stupid drunken thing - that I am missing out and that he would take care of Alexia for me, so that I can go to Megan. I tell him that that isn't going to happen ever. These drunken people don't have feelings. If they did, they would see that I am already head over heels for this blue-eyed girl standing beside me.

He is making me so mad that I grab him and tell him that he is to never touch Alexia and needs to apologize to her. He half-drunkenly does this, but I don't believe him. I'm getting madder by the minute at him. Alexia touches me and reminds me that he is too drunk to know what he is doing and won't remember his actions in the morning. Her touch automatically calms me and her smile melts the anger away, so I let go of Jacob.

I turn to her, smiling back, and let her know that, with her batting her eyes, everything would be okay. I tell her that she is going to cause so much trouble with all the guys wanting to be with her and I am going to have to keep them away. She doesn't believe me and says that she is just plain. How can she not see how wonderful and beautiful she is inside and out? Everyone around her lights up when she is around, but she doesn't know this. She is perfect and not full of herself like Megan.

Tyler comes over and says that he is tired, wanting to know if I was taking them home. He says the same thing Alexia does, about Jacob being drunk and he won't remember a thing in the morning. I ask if he wants to stay in the guest room with Jacob. I know that no one can sleep with Jacob because he is like a bear wrestling in his sleep. I tell Alexia that I will help Tyler get Jacob in bed and be right back.

We drag him to the room, and I turn the bed comforter back. We lay him down, and I take his shoes off because I will have to clean the sand off the bed if I don't. With him settled in the bed, I turn around and find Tyler lying on top of the other one. He still has his shoes on, and I take off his too. I'm glad to have these two here and not driving. They both know I don't like them drinking and driving so they always call me to pick them up. Maybe one day I will tell them about my brother and how he died. Alexia is the only person here that I have ever told.

I walk out the door and notice how late it has gotten. How did it get so late so fast? With all the excitement of the evening, time has flown by, and I feel guilty because now Alexia has to drive back to the dorm. That isn't going to happen. She will have to stay and I'll sleep on the couch. I look over at her collecting her books and see the biggest yawn. She is really tired, and I can see it.

I walk up to her and she smiles at me. My heart beats faster every time she does. I ask her to stay, but she is hesitating. She yawns again and I know she will have to stay because she is too tired to drive. I tell her that I'll sleep on the couch and she can have the bed. She says that the couch is too small for me. I agree but don't want to offend her with asking to share my bed. I do ask and offer to sleep on top of the sheets. I'll even let her borrow a t-shirt. Now that will be nice to see her in my t-shirt.

I show her that I have a king-sized bed and tell her that I'll keep to my side. She says okay. I get her a shirt and I go to the bathroom. While I'm in there, I brush my teeth, wash my face and take my medication. I dig out a surprise toothbrush for her. I keep extra around in case I need an extra. I come out with my surprise and she smiles at me. She goes in and takes only a few minutes. Glad she was fast because I am tired.

While she is in there, I change into pajama bottoms and sit on top of the bed. I start thinking more about Alexia and feel nervous about having her here in my room alone. I have to keep myself in check or I'll have my hands all over her sweet little body. She has these curves I want to hold onto. I sigh and let out a breath. *Oh no* I believe I am already falling for this girl. How did this happen so fast? I barely know her, but she feels like home to me.

She comes out of the bathroom and jumps on the bed beside me. *Wow*! I think I better leave. All I want to do is grab her and have my way with her. She looks freaking hot in my t-shirt. I start to think about how she would look with nothing on at all. *Okay now*. Calm yourself down before she runs out of here screaming. I take a deep breath and tell her I like her in my t-shirt, that I might keep her here every night.

That sounded creepy, and I hope she doesn't think so. Then she smiles and says that if she were here every night I couldn't have any girls or girlfriends over. I have never have had a girl over here, but she doesn't know that. I tell her that I don't have any girlfriends unless she wants to be my girlfriend.

I can't believe I said that. Where did that come from? She asks me, if I'm for real about asking her to be my girlfriend and if I'm playing her now. She doesn't know me much. I have never asked anyone to be my girlfriend. She seems mad. Then gets out of the bed and goes to her clothes. No, she isn't leaving here tonight, and I now know what I want for the first time ever. She is here in my room with my t-shirt on. For the first time ever I want to have a relationship and with this girl only.

I get up and move behind her, pulling her back close to me so that she is touching my chest. I let her know that this feels right, and I mean it. Everything I say to her, I mean it. This girl has taken me over completely. I don't want to scare her off. I tell her to think about it and not rush anything. I kiss her and my heart explodes in my chest. I know she can feel it because I feel hers beating as hard as mine. I better stop now, because if I don't, I will have to do more than kiss her.

I tell her that it's late and pull her back to bed. I ask what time she needs to get up and set the clock. I pull her close to me and cuddle her up next to my chest. She doesn't fight me and relaxes into my arms. This feels like home to me, and hopefully I don't mess this up with my girl. That makes me smile. She hasn't said yes yet, but she will.

I hear her breathing change, and I know she is already asleep. I lie there for a while, watching her and she really is the most beautiful thing I have laid my eyes on. I can see her face with what little light is shining through the window, and I know that she really is my angel. I don't know how long I lie there watching her, but when I fall asleep, it is the best sleep I have had since my brother died.

I wake up earlier than she does, because I want to make her breakfast before she leaves. I can't cook much, but I make some eggs and bacon. I put on a pot of coffee. I think she likes it. If not, I will find out what she does and fast. It is time for the clock to wake her, so I put the eggs and bacon in the oven to keep warm. I run back to the room and get back under the covers. I want her to wake up in my arms. I make it just in time. The clock sounds and she turns over and tries to smack at it. I laugh, and she turns back around. She looks at me and laughs because she must have forgotten where she is. I turn the clock off and tell her good morning. I kiss her on her sweet face. She smiles at me. I wonder what my beautiful blue-eyed girl is thinking. I hope she can see how awesome I think it is for me to wake up next to her.

Thirteen

ALEXIA

I hear the alarm clock go off and think, *Ugh,* give me five more minutes. I turn to hit the snooze button on my clock, but I miss it somehow. Then I hear someone laugh and I remember where I am. I slept so well last night. It was the best I've slept in forever. I turned back around and see Phillip smiling at me. My heart rate picks up as soon as I lay eyes on him. He is turning me into one of those girls who you read about in books. You know, the girl whose heart beats fast and breathing becomes difficult. I really get it now that it is happening to me.

He kisses me on my cheek and I smile at him. I like waking up in his bed. Is that bad of me? We didn't do anything but sleep. This feels so natural, like I should be here. Now I believe I am getting ahead of myself, because he can't feel that way about me - *yet.* He did ask me to be his girlfriend last night. I think he did or maybe it was a dream. I was awful tired last night.

Phillip rises up and says, "I made you breakfast and coffee. We better go eat it while it is still hot. I made coffee, but I'm not sure you like coffee. I will learn what you like and soon."

He pulls me out of bed and I notice that he looks down at my legs. I then look down and see that the t-shirt has slid up to my belly button. I quickly pull it down. I am embarrassed and my cheeks are on fire. He puts his hand on my cheek and that calms me down.

"Hey. Don't worry that I saw you like that. You are beautiful and have nothing you should hide because every bit of you is something amazing." He looks into my eyes and moves closer like he is going to kiss me.

Before he does kiss me, I remembered my morning breath. I step back out of his trance and move toward the bathroom. He yells at me to hurry so that we can eat and he leaves the bedroom. I yell back that I will.

I look at myself in the mirror and my face still has a crimson color. I then notice my hair. *Oh no!* Look at my rat's nest. He must think rats have taken up in my hair and are never going to leave. I try to smooth it down. Then I brush my teeth and use the bathroom. I reach over to grab my shorts to put them on, but I keep his t-shirt on. I hurry out of the room and head to the kitchen.

As I reach the kitchen, I see the outside balcony table set with plates of food, coffee, and orange juice. It looks picture perfect and the ocean background is what makes everything so peaceful. I feel as if I am in a dream and when I wake up, something bad will happen.

Phillip looks at me and says, "Come join me." I go sit down beside him and thank him for the breakfast. We start eating, and when we are almost done with our food, we hear noise inside the condo. Phillip frowns. "I forgot about those two staying the night. Hope they don't scare you off with their bad hangovers. They usually would still be sleeping in, but I guess they woke up to go to class. That is a big surprise."

I take a few more bites and look at Phillip. "No they won't scare me off. I have to leave soon too so I can get ready for class. This food is really good. Where did you learn to cook?"

He laughs, "This is all I can cook. I wish I could make other things, because I would cook dinner for you sometime. What time do you want to study tonight?"

"I can cook some things. Maybe if we are studying here, I can fix you something sometime. I only have two classes today and should be done around four. Let me know what time will be good for you."

We get up and take our dishes back inside. I load up the dishwasher. When I turn away from putting the dishes in the dishwasher, I run right into Phillip. He laughs and pulls me in close enough that I can smell his wonderful scent. My tummy does flip-flops.

Jacob comes rushing in the kitchen but stops and looks at Phillip with a big smile on his face. "What do we have here? Are you two an item or just hooking up?

Phillip seems to get angry with Jacob, "We are not hooking up, Jacob. I am really interested in being her boyfriend, if she will have me. Right now we are hanging out and getting to know each other until she accepts me to be her boyfriend. I will wait on her to decide."

Jacob turns to me, smiling wide, "Why are you keeping my boy hanging? I am waiting on an answer, sweetheart."

He makes me angry. Phillip sees it and he tries to get me to calm down, but I say, it is a little bit too soon to answer because we just met. Now that I think about it more, maybe I will be Phillip's girlfriend. Only if I knew he really was interested in me, but I am sure he isn't. I turn to leave, picking up my backpack and purse.

I realize that I am still in Phillip's shirt, but I don't care. I am leaving now. Phillip tries to stop me. I'm out the door and in the elevator before he can get to me.

What was that all about? Why did I get defensive over that question? Maybe I already know the answer. I do feel something for him. As I come to this conclusion, the elevator doors open and there stands Phillip looking hot and very sweaty. Did he just run down all those stairs?

He pulls me into his arms and says, "I meant every word and I do want you to be my girlfriend, if you will have me. I feel something for you, and it is so strong. I hate that we even have to be apart. I haven't figured out what it is yet. I would like to really explore this feeling I am having with you."

Before I can say anything, he reaches to cup my face tenderly and kisses me with so much passion that my legs almost give out on me. He pulls me closer so I don't fall and kisses me like a starving man. I kiss him right back the same as he does me. Never have I felt this in my life. I never knew that a guy could make you feel like this. I can feel the heat building in the kiss and I don't know if I will be able to stop. We kiss like this for what seems like forever.

Behind us, someone loudly clears his throat. We stop kissing and step away from each other to see who it is. I am blushing when I look up. Standing next to us is this guy, who is smiling at Phillip.

He says to Phillip, "Some study session, I see." He winks before heading out the door.

Phillip laughs. "Well, I see Jack liked our public display of affection. *Wow!* That kiss was intense. After that kiss, I believe you have to say yes to me. I don't think I could ever accept you kissing anyone but me. I am sorry for the way Jacob acted. It was uncalled for. Please be my girl. I promise to take care of you and I love you in my t-shirts." He pulls me close to whisper in my ear. "Keep this shirt so you can think of me today. I hope you wear it all day. Maybe when you get to our biology class you will still have it on." He kisses me under my ear, making tingles run up my spine. How will I be able to say no to him?

I smile up to him. "*Maybe*, I will wear it all day. I will think about your question and then *maybe* by biology class I will answer." I smile, turn, and walk out the door. Before I get too far, I hear him chuckle out loud.

I get in the car with a smile on my face. I want to say yes to him really badly. He turns me into mush inside and out. This has me scared to death. How can I feel this way, knowing that I shouldn't bring him into this mess that is my life? I am selfish for even considering this at all. As I drive to my dorm room, I am in deep thought about this. My phone starts ringing. I usually don't answer while driving, but I see that my mom is calling. I need to talk to her. Maybe she will help me with my answer.

"Hi, mom. How are you and Dad?" I ask first thing.

"Hi baby. We are both doing well, but we're missing you really bad. I had to call so I can hear your sweet voice. Tell me how school is going. And how is your roommate? Are you and her getting along? I know it's only been a few days. I need to know you're doing well so I don't worry about my precious girl."

"*Oh.* Mom, I know you worry. I am doing really good. So far classes are going fine. Kristen and I are getting along, when we see each other. She stays with friends sometimes. We went out the first night I got here and I have already been to the beach every day. You have no need to worry about me.'

"You know I will always worry about my baby girl. That is what mothers do. Are you taking your medication and is it working like it is supposed to? Do you feel tired or anything?"

"No, mom. Everything is going really well and I'm taking my medicine. I have been making a few friends already. I really shouldn't though. What if something happens to me?"

"Baby, you know that you need friends no matter what happens to you and you can't focus on that all the time. Even if it does, they would have felt honored to even get to know you, even for a short time. I know you are a true fighter. You will be around for a long time. You need to live your life and not be afraid. Just let people get to know how wonderful you are, my darling. Anyone could die at any time. You will live a long life because you got a miracle five years ago. This world isn't ready to let you go, so quit being afraid to live life. Just live it the fullest every day." She is such a wonderful mother and I am lucky to have her.

I ask her how she met Dad and how she knew he was the one.

"I knew he was the one the first time I talked to him, sweet girl. I know that seems fast to most people, but I knew and he did too. He even told me two weeks after we met that he loved me. I was scared and didn't tell him until later, even though I knew, I did. We met through a friend who thought we would be good for each other. It turned out that my friend was right. Why all the interest in this subject, Alexia? Have you met someone and you're afraid you might get sick on him? If you have, don't let that get in your way of happiness."

"Well, mom, I think I have met a really good guy. He wants me to be his girlfriend already and I am scared. I hate the thought that I might break his heart, if my heart gave out on me and I died leaving him all alone. I don't think I should do that to anyone. I know you and dad will have broken hearts. Why should I put anyone else in that pain? It kills me to think about you guys hurting."

"Sweetheart, we love you and wouldn't ever want to live without you. If that happens, I know that I will be honored to have what time we had with you. This guy would feel the same. If he already wants you in his life, he would be honored to have just a little while with you rather than no time at all. Live for the now, my sweet Alexia, and take care of yourself so you can live a long, full life. Don't forget to be honest with him about your condition and what might happen up-front. That is only fair to him." She makes me happy, and now I might let things happen naturally with Phillip.

As I get to school, I thank Mom for her advice and let her know that I have to get ready for my class.

I get to my dorm and find Kristen there getting ready for her classes. She looks up at me and smiles. "Well look at you. You must have been out all night. Looks like you had to do the walk of shame in a guy's t-shirt. Where is your shirt? Or did he rip it off you in the heat of the night?"

"I didn't have sex last night, but I did stay over at a guy's condo on the beach. We were studying and it got late. He let me borrow a shirt to sleep in. He didn't want me to drive late because he worried I'd be too tired to drive." I smile.

Kristen gets up and looks me over. "Who is this guy? Seems like a good guy if he was worried. Or was he hoping you would want more?"

I smile. "Yes he is a good guy and didn't ask for anything more. His name is Phillip Ryan."

"*What?* Phillip Ryan? He is model gorgeous. You better watch out for him. I hear he plays girls. Uses-them-and-leaves-them type of guy, if you know what I mean. Sometimes I don't believe it. Megan has been throwing herself at him forever and he seems like he doesn't like her. She can be trouble for you if she sees you around him even if you and Phillip don't get involved. She's usually determined to have what she wants and will hurt and step on anyone who gets in her way," Kristen says.

I frown at what she just said and think about the look Megan gave me last night. "I guess Megan already has it out for me. She saw me with Phillip last night, when we went to pick up his friends at her party. She gave me this look, like if she had a knife she would stab me."

"Wow! This is bad." She paces back and forth in our little dorm room before looking at me again. "What exactly did you and Phillip do in front of her? Did you kiss or something? If you were just next to him, you'd probably be okay, but if something else happened, you might need to worry." She frowns.

This can't be too good. Sounds to me that Megan may be obsessed with Phillip. "He held my hand while we were at her house. We were on the beach. His condo is close to her house, so we walked over to pick up Jacob and Tyler. She tried to get him to stay with her and even offered to sleep with him, but he wouldn't have it. He even told her he wasn't interested in her. He left with me, holding my hand."

"*Darn*! I must have missed the best party ever. So much drama at that party and I had to stay here to do homework. I hope she doesn't try to cause you trouble over Phillip. Megan can be a drama queen and she likes trouble. Well, I have to go to class." She gives me a smile before leaving.

I decide not to think about it. It is too much to stress over right now. I really need to get a shower, so I hurry to the bathroom. I take a quick one. If I don't hurry, I will be late for biology. I think about biology and smile. Who knew biology could make me smile? Maybe it is who is in my class.

That makes me think about putting his shirt back on. Now that I'm clean, I don't want to put it back on until I wash it, but after all, I did just sleep in it last night. I finish getting ready and see Phillip's shirt lying on my bed. I say, *what the heck*, I'm going to wear it.

Putting on the shirt, I notice I only have about twenty minutes to get to class, so I gather my backpack and books. I head out the door to my future and hope that I am doing right by him with my answer. I am smiling all the way to class. I have a bounce in my step too.

I get to class a few minutes early and head to my seat. Since we have assigned seating, I know who will be sitting next to me soon and I can't wait. I get my books and paper out of my backpack to be ready for class.

I look up and see Phillip walk in. I smile at him, but he doesn't smile back at me like I thought he would. I wonder if he has changed his mind about me already. I wish now that I hadn't worn his stupid shirt. He sits down beside me and looks ahead like he doesn't know me. *Well,* I guess that answers my question. It's over before it has even begun.

I frown and turn my attention to the teacher, attempting to pay attention. It is hard to do with this new Phillip sitting beside me. This Phillip is cold and stiff. He doesn't even seem like the same guy I just left a little while ago. I wonder what happened since I left. I have to pay attention today. I focus on the professor to keep my mind off Phillip.

Fourteen

PHILLIP

*A*lexia is the cutest thing when she is waking up. Her hair is messy, but it still looks sexy while she is lying in my bed. I could keep her in my bed all day, and her in my t-shirt isn't helping matters much. I better get us out of this room or my hands are going to start touching her all over. I tell her that I made her breakfast and coffee. We needed to hurry, so it doesn't get cold. I believe she is amused that I did that for her since she is smiling at me.

She throws back the covers and notices that the shirt has risen up to her belly button. Seeing how red her face is lets me know she is embarrassed by it. I tell her that she is beautiful and doesn't have to be embarrassed. Seeing more of her body has really gotten me turned on, so I have to get out of this room before she notices. I believe she needs to go to the bathroom. I remind her that I will go get breakfast set up for us. I head out fast. I don't want her to see how much I wanted more of her.

I go to the kitchen to gather our food and drinks to put on the table. I look out at the balcony, where I usually eat, and decide that we should eat out there. While I set the table, I finally calm myself down. Being around Alexia gets me so worked up and I don't know why I can't behave around her like I can around every other girl in the world.

I just sit down at the table and take a sip of orange juice with my medicine as Alexia comes out. She still has on my t-shirt, and even out here, she takes my breath away. I ask her to sit and join me, and she does. I can't believe that this amazing girl is here with me. How did I get so lucky? We talk and eat together like we have done it all of our lives and this feels like home.

Suddenly, I hear something inside the condo. *Oh no.* I forgot that Jacob and Tyler are still here. How did I forget those two? I asked Alexia if they will scare her off, I hope they don't. They will be hung-over and grumpy, but she says no. This girl has amazed me every minute I have known her.

We finish our food and take the dishes to the kitchen. I watch her while she puts the dishes in the dishwasher. She gets done and turns around. I pull her to me but act like I've accidently done it.

She doesn't pull away and I get ready to kiss her when Jacob comes into the kitchen smiling. He makes a rude comment about us being together or just hooking up? I look at Alexia, and she stiffens, like she is getting mad. I let him know very quickly that we are not hooking up. I have asked her to be my girlfriend. Instead of this satisfying him with my answer, he starts badgering Alexia about why she hasn't answered me. I get ready to tell him off, but Alexia surprises me and does it herself.

One thing about her - she takes nothing from anyone and isn't afraid.

She does say something that surprises me though. She says that she really doesn't know if I meant it when I asked her to be mine. How could she not see how I feel already?

She storms out of the kitchen and I give Jacob a dirty look. I hear the front door slam and I know that she has left. I can't let her leave like this without knowing how I feel. I run out the door. As I get to the elevator, I see the door close. *Ugh*! I run over to the stairs and go down them two at a time so that I can beat the elevator. I get to the bottom floor just as the elevator does. I make sure I am standing right in front of it as it opens up so that she can see me.

She sees me as the door opens. I reach and pull her to me. I let her know how I feel about her, that I meant every word and would like to see where this is headed. I tell her that I have never felt this before. I can't help myself. I kiss her. I meant to lightly kiss her, but when my lips touch hers, I feel something inside me explode. I kiss her like I am never going to kiss another girl again so that she would never want to kiss another guy again. The passion between us is like a fire growing every second that we kiss. I can't stop kissing her. I kiss her for what seems like forever before I hear Jack behind me. I know who it is without needing a glimpse of him, especially after he says that it must have been a good night of studying. He winks and walks on. I look at Alexia and see her blush a little. I continue to ask her to be mine and even tease her about wearing my t-shirt.

She tells me that she might give me an answer by the time she gets to biology class and *maybe* she will wear my shirt all day. Then she turns and just walks off. I laugh at her. Maybe she is the real tease to walk off like that with no answer after that kiss that set me on fire. I think I have to go take a cold shower now. I turn around and see Jack coming back around the corner grinning at me.

"Well boy, looks like the studying took longer than a few hours. What did you do study all night?" He laughs.

I know he is joking with me, that he knows me better than that, so I say, "A man can't tell all his secrets. I don't kiss and tell. Really though, Alexia isn't that kind of girl. It got too late for her to drive and she stayed over. Jacob and Tyler did too."

"Well you must have been crazy to have those guys around that pretty little woman. I wouldn't let any guy around her. She is just too pretty and little." He smiles at me.

"Don't you worry. If I have anything to do with it, I plan on making her mine only," I say proudly.

He laughs at me. "Boy by the looks of that kiss, I would say she is already yours." He walks off after that comment.

I want to ask what he meant by that, but now I will never know. I sure hope she says yes today. She is driving me crazy already.

I head to the elevator to go back up to my room. When I get there, I see that Jacob and Tyler both have made themselves right at home. They better not get used to it. If Alexia says yes, I plan on having her around more, and that means the guys will have to behave.

Tyler looks up from the food he has made for himself. "Hey. Thanks for letting us crash last night. I really didn't think I could have made it back to the dorm. Jacob said Alexia stayed too. Are you getting serious about some girl you just met? You have never brought girls here before."

"I know I haven't brought girls here, because no one has made me feel anything about them. This is my private place. I really like Alexia, and she makes me feel things I haven't before. I would say yes that I am serious about her. I even asked her to be my girlfriend," I proudly tell them.

Tyler looks stunned for a minute. "Wow. You are serious about her, and I have never seen you actually have a girlfriend since you started school here. How did she do that so fast, man?"

"I don't really know. When I met her on the plane trip here, we just connected, and every time I am around her, I feel more and more connected to her. I just want to see what we have going on. I feel like she might be worth all the work I have to do for a relationship. Just to see how it goes."

Jacob decides to jump into the conversation, "Man, you know you can't give up on having all the girls you want. No girl is worth that. You are too young to be with one girl already. Play the field like you have been and test all the waters before you get too old to enjoy life. Look at Megan! She has been after you forever and I think she'd do anything to get a little piece of you."

Why does Jacob have to think he knows it all? Sometimes he doesn't seem to have a brain or feelings at all. One of these days they both will understand what I am feeling. They even think I am a player but I am not. That is something they have made up in their minds. "Jacob, why do you think I want to go out with someone like Megan? She only thinks about herself and she treats everybody badly. I believe the friends she does have only have her as a friend because of her partying and her money. They really can't stand to be around her unless they are drunk. She isn't worth the trouble to be with."

"I didn't say marry her," Jacob defends. "Just go get some from her and go on to the next girl. You need to enjoy life and not settle down yet. You're young still. And don't forget, you can have any girl you want."

"I don't want any girl and I'm not like you either with being a man-slut. I am ready to see more of Alexia and see how it goes. Maybe there might be something that will last for a lifetime. I don't know yet, or even if she will say yes, but I sure hope so."

Tyler speaks up for me. "I think it is great. You have already found someone you might be interested in. Sometimes it is hard to find a good girl out there these days. I say if she is what you want, then go for it. Alexia seems like a really nice girl and she is very pretty. What she did last night to save Jacob's butt was amazing. She has some guts to get between Jacob and James while he was angry at Jacob."

"What did she do for me last night? I was so out of it that I can't remember half of what when on," Jacob says.

Tyler speaks before I get to. "Yeah, you were wasted last night. You were flirting with James's girlfriend and he was going to beat you up for it. Alexia jumped in between you guys and stopped it by acting like she was with you and looking for you. All she had to do is bat her pretty blue eyes at James and he believed her. I know she was brave for doing that when he was angry. He was going to beat you up."

"Well now she has my vote for being awesome, so I guess Phillip should go for it. If you two don't work out, let me know and I will take her off your hands," Jacob kids.

After he says that, I see red. Tyler notices that I am getting mad and stands up. He yells at Jacob. "Are you serious, man, or are you still drunk? Phillip will kick your butt out of here if you talk like that about his girl again! I wouldn't blame him either! If I had a girl like her, I would kick your butt too. Straighten up and apologize to Phillip now."

Jacob looks up, "Sorry man, I think, I am still a little bit drunk. I must have drunk way too much last night. I didn't mean anything by what I said. If you like this girl, then go for it, and I wish you the best of luck. Maybe I am jealous you found such a beautiful girl." He frowns and drops his gaze down at the table.

Maybe he is jealous, I think. "It is okay for now Jacob, but don't treat her bad. I like you, and you have been a great friend to me. Don't make me feel bad for having feelings for a girl. I can't explain it, but I believe she is the one. At least I hope so. Really, Jacob you know you shouldn't be drinking like you have been. If you're drunk still, you need to stop drinking so much. Don't you care about your classes?"

"Darn it! I think I need to go now, Tyler. I believe I have a class soon. *Oh! No*! I can't be late for this class again. If I am the professor will kick me out. Can you take me back to the dorm, now?" Jacob is starting to freak out.

"Yeah, man. I'll take you back now, if you're ready." Tyler agrees.

"I'm ready now. Thanks, Phillip, for letting us crash and everything. Sorry I am so much trouble for you. You are right I need to cut back on the drinking and partying. See you later, man," they both head out the door.

I am glad they are leaving, because when I look at the clock, I see that I have to hurry to get ready to leave so I can make it to my biology class. I head to the shower and take a quick one. Throwing on some clean jeans and a t-shirt, I am ready to go out the door.

As I get off the elevator, the security guy yells at me. I stop to see what he wants. He says that a girl wanted to go up to see you and I ask him who she was. He tells me her name is Megan, but she isn't down on the list so he didn't let her in. I told him not to ever let her in and then head out to my car. Now I needed to hurry to school.

As I am driving, I think more about Alexia. Maybe I shouldn't pursue her. I have been okay for a long time since I had the surgery, but it was touch and go for a little while at first. The doctors had a hard time keeping me alive with my brother's liver, and they had to try different medications to help my body to accept his liver, even though I was a perfect match for it.

I still hurt for my brother who died. I am grateful he signed his donor card on his license. When the accident happened, my parents were shocked by it too. They had no idea he'd done that because he never told anyone, but I am blessed by his last gift to me. Maybe he knew something was going to happen and that when it did he could save many lives by doing that simple thing.

Alexia should have a guy she could count on at all times. Not one who has to survive by taking medicine every day to stay alive. I should at least tell her what could happen and let her decide if she wants me or just move on. This scares me just to think she might not choose me.

I finally get to the university and find a parking space. I get out of my car and as soon as I do, I hear someone calling my name. Why couldn't it be Alexia calling for me and not Megan?

"Phillip, why have you been ignoring me? I even went to your condo building and that guy at the desk wouldn't let me in. I would have loved to see your condo. I bet it has a perfect view. Come on, Phillip. Walk me to class. We need to go out and do something special together. I think we should go out on a date tonight. How about it, Phillip? Will you take me out tonight?' She asks. Boy, she is persistent.

"No, Megan. I can't take you out tonight. I have plans. No. I can't walk you to class because I am seeing someone. No, you can't come into my condo or building because that is against the rules. Please leave me alone. I don't want to date you or spend time with you," I explain hoping she will get the hint and leave me alone. Knowing I have to be hateful to her, but she asks the same thing over and over. I keep saying no. When will she learn?

She looks at me angrily. "Who are you seeing Phillip? Is it that girl Alexia that was with you at my party last night? I thought she was with your friend Jacob? I bet he won't like you going behind his back and stealing his girl from him."

She has some nerve to ask these questions. "It is none of your business who I am seeing, and you need to leave Alexia alone and not bother her. Jacob isn't seeing her, so leave it alone now," I angrily walk off, but she grabs my arm.

"You will be sorry you turned me down Phillip. I could give you everything. Now that you are being this way, I guess we will see who will be seeing whom. I will make your life and Alexia's life miserable. Just wait and see." Finally she leaves me.

I yell and tell her to leave us alone, but she keeps on walking. I am worried even more about Alexia now. First, the problem was my possibly getting sick on her, and now crazy Megan thinks she owns everyone around her. Megan better leave Alexia alone, that is for sure, or she might get a taste of her own medicine. I won't stand for her picking on my girl. *My girl*, I like that saying. If only I knew what she would do, when I ask her how she feels about my possibly dying on her. I can't think about this anymore. I am going to be late for class. I hurry to the classroom and barely make it in before class starts.

I know Alexia is looking at me and wondering what is wrong with me. I can't tell her now because I need to think some more about what I need to tell her. This day started out as the best day ever, and now look how it has gone downhill so fast.

Then I remember what Alexia was wearing when I came in. She didn't notice me looking in the classroom before I came in, but I saw that she still is wearing my t-shirt. That made me stop a second and think that maybe she is going to say yes to me. What have I done to this girl? I need to focus on class and think a bit. I have to try to ignore her awhile.

Seeing her in my shirt is driving me crazy. How can I ignore her? I need to let her go, but I don't think I can. *Just ignore her. Just ignore her. Just ignore her*, I think over and over all during class, *and maybe she will get mad and leave.* Then I won't have to explain to her how I might destroy her life one day if she fell in love with me and I ended up dying on her.

This is harder than not wanting to be with someone because I feel so close to her already. I know I should just talk to her. I am so scared that she might up and leave me because of my weakness. I try to be strong around everyone, but I know I am on borrowed time that my brother gave me.

Class is almost over and I still don't know what I am going to do. I haven't even listened to the teacher and now I probably will have to ask Alexia what I have missed. I am going crazy over this woman and still don't know why or what to do.

Fifteen

ALEXIA

*T*his class is a waste of my time today. I haven't paid attention one bit to the professor, and now Phillip is ignoring me. I will have to find someone else in class to tell me what I missed. I really don't know what is up with him. He is like a different person. It is crazy.

The way he kissed me before I left made me weak in the knees and I wanted more of that with him. Maybe I am thinking about this too much, and maybe his mood isn't about me. Maybe someone made him upset before class. Perhaps it was the friends who were still at his place when I left. Maybe they don't think I am good enough for him.

I'm really not good enough for him. I am broken and just fixed for a little while. If we did get together, I couldn't even give him kids. I have to live by taking medicine every day. Maybe his ignoring me is for the best. He needs a girl who could give him everything he needs. As soon as class is over, I make a beeline out the door. I am out the door in a flash and so glad to be free.

A tear slips out of one of my eyes. I quickly wipe it away and head out of the building. My goal is to go straight to my dorm and not come out until I get my head straight.

Just as I get out of the building, I almost run straight into Megan. I look up at her to tell her that I am sorry, but she asks, "Why are you in such a hurry and where are you going?"

"I was headed back to my dorm. I have homework to work on." I tell her this big lie so I can get moving on. I don't want to be out here when Phillip comes out of the building, and I know it will be soon but she keeps on talking.

"You should come hang out with my friends and me because we are going to the beach for a while," she smiles.

"Sorry, I can't. I have another class soon." Trying to get away from her.

"Oh skip it and come to the beach. You're so pale. You look like you need a week at the beach and then maybe and you might get a small amount of color. I know Phillip likes his girls tan" she hatefully tells me this. Now I know she is jealous of me because Phillip turned her down last night. Kristen warned me about her this morning.

I am now upset with her and her rude comments. "I really don't care what you think or what Phillip thinks about me. If I go to the beach, it will be by myself. I don't care to have a tan. I don't need one. I will be me the way I want to be me and not for anyone else. So go and leave me alone."

I try to get away, but she steps right front of me and stops me, "I bet Phillip was late to class today. He told me he had to go but couldn't leave me. He kept me in his king-sized bed for way too long this morning after you left. He said all he wanted was to be with me, but you wouldn't leave so I could come over sooner.

Leave him alone so we can get on with our lives without you trying to get in the way." She smirks her smile at me.

"You can have him. He is just my study partner," I leave as fast as I can. I want this day to be over with.

How could I be so stupid to even think about saying yes to him? He said that everyone thought he was a player, but he also said that it wasn't true. He must have been lying to me. The first time I open myself up and let someone in I get hurt. What a fool I have been. Never again! I want to live my life and not have to worry about anyone else.

I get to my room and sit on my bed just to relax for a few minutes. I have another class soon. Having a minute to myself is wonderful. I hope Kristen doesn't come back right now. I don't want to talk to anyone.

I take my medicine. I almost forgot to take it. My mom would be unhappy if I forgot.

Before I know it, I wake up about an hour later. *Oh no!* If I don't hurry and leave I will be late for class. I shouldn't have fallen asleep, and now I will miss eating which isn't good for me. I hurry to my class, and before I get there, I buy something from a vending machine. I arrive at the next building and have a few minutes to spare. After this class, I will head out somewhere to find myself something extra good and I don't care how many calories it has. I need comfort food.

Class goes by super fast and I am glad. I don't go back to my room, heading straight to my car instead. I drive to my favorite burger place. A day like today, I need a good burger and maybe some fries too. I decide to get it to-go so I can head to the beach. I love it there, and a picnic on the beach is what I need. I always carry a book with me, so I can read, relax, and eat in peace.

I don't drive far because it doesn't matter where I go to the beach. I do like the more private areas, and I just found a nice place. I get my chair, food, and book and make my way to the beach. This is why I wanted to go to school here.

I set everything up and eat while I read my book. Yeah, this is what I needed. I want to forget about today and relax. I know I will have to finish my biology project though so I think I will do it all by myself. As I get into my book, I relax even more. I don't realize it is getting late until it is almost dark. I guess I need to head back to my dorm room.

As I finish packing up my things, I get a text from Phillip. He wants me to come over and work on our project tonight. I don't feel like it. I text back and tell him not tonight, that I am busy. He texts back several times trying to get me to come over, but I tell him no. I turn my phone off and head to my dorm.

I realize once I get back to my dorm that I finally am relaxed for the first time today and that makes me smile. The beach and a good book, plus an awesome burger and fries, was just what I needed. I go in my room and see that Kristen isn't here. I'm sort of glad for that too. I decide to get ready for bed. When I go to take off my shirt, I noticed that I still have his t-shirt on. How did I forget that I was still wearing it all day? Must have been all the stress. Oh well. Now off it goes, and on with my pajamas. I brush my hair and teeth then get in bed. I am restless, so I get my book out to read for a while. I set my clock so I will be able to get up in the morning. Sometimes I fall to sleep when I read and tonight I might do that. Best to be prepared.

My clock goes off and I smack it to hit the snooze button. Today I get to snooze and I like it. In between my sleeping, I start to think about yesterday, waking up with Phillip. Yes it was nice, but I don't care for all his stress and drama. Today, I plan on ignoring him in class.

I get up to get ready. While in the shower, I think about how I will dress extra nice today and make him appreciate what he is going to miss out on. I put on my sexy short shorts and really cute top that hugs my body in all the right places. I even take extra time to fix my hair and makeup. I look in the mirror and think, *Wow,* who is this woman looking back at me? I go to grab my things and backpack.

The dorm room door flies open and in comes Kristen. I smile at her. I know she has been out all night. She was just kidding with me about that yesterday. Now it is payback time. "

I see who really is doing the walk of shame." I laugh.

Kristen grins wide at me. "Yeah, you know it all, girl. Yes, I am doing it and proud of it. Look at you! You are super hot with that outfit on, and look at you hair! It is gorgeous. Who are you dressed up for?" Is it Phillip?"

"I haven't dressed up for anyone, just for me only," I lie. "You are right about Phillip, being a player, by the way. Megan told me all about him and her getting together after I left yesterday. How dare him to ask me to be his girlfriend and then turn around and screw around on me as soon as I get out the door?" I tell her all about yesterday, and she seems surprised about Phillip.

"I can't believe he would do that with her. He always stays away from her no matter what or where he is. I saw him just the other day go out a different door because she was coming in the way he was headed out. He actually ran out that other door to get away and it was that obvious to anyone around. She is like the plague that won't go away," Kristen tells me.

"Well she knew a lot about when I left and what was in his bedroom. How would she know that if it weren't true? He was even late for class like she said and he didn't speak to me during the whole class. I think that is suspicious of him so it seems to be true."

Kristen looks like she still doesn't believe it. "I don't get it. I have known both of them and have been to a lot of parties with them both. All I have ever seen is that Phillip blows off Megan every time. This doesn't add up to me unless he finally caved into her advances. Still I don't believe it. Maybe she told you a big lie to get you to stay away from him."

"Maybe she did. That doesn't answer why he didn't talk to me in class yesterday." I say this, but I remember him coming in late and then I ran out the door so fast he couldn't have said anything.

"No it doesn't, but you should ask him about it and he will probably tell you. Did you stay after class and ask him why he wasn't talking?" Kristen asked.

I frown. "No. I was upset, ran out the door, and then ran right into Megan."

"See? You didn't even give him a chance. I bet he was wondering why you ran away so fast. Has he called or texted you since then?"

"Yes. He has texted me to come study. I told him no and turned off my phone."

"Well turn on your phone and let's see what you have missed," she suggests.

I grab my phone and turn it on. As Kristen predicted, it has several texts from Phillip. He kept texting me to come over and that he was sorry about not getting to class early enough to talk to me. Maybe Kristen was right and Megan was lying. How did I get into so much drama with Phillip and Megan? I don't need this stress.

"Okay, it looks like he is sorry and I now believe Megan was totally lying her face off. When you get to class, ask him what his problem was yesterday and ask him about what Megan said. Just plain and simple, use your mouth to ask questions. Do not hide out and think the worst until you know for sure what is going on. How did you get into this drama so fast? Megan will probably make your life worse if you date Phillip. Don't let her know she can bother you because that will make her worse. Phillip must really be interested in you since he has texted so many times. You are the first girl I know of who has caught his attention for more than a few minutes, and that makes you a lucky girl. I say hear him out and if you hear the right answer go for it. Who knows he might be the one for you." Kristen smiles.

"You make it sound so simple. Maybe he is the one, but I don't know if I'm good for him. I sure hope he wasn't screwing around with Megan as soon as I left the condo. I think that would break my heart a little just knowing he was that bad of a person. What if I ask him and it is true?" I look up at Kristen and she is still smiling at me.

"I see it and it is so clear to me now. How could I have missed, what was right in front of me? I am usually good at reading people, but I missed it," she says, like she knows a secret.

"What do you see so clearly?" I ask, wondering what. I'm a little bit scared to find out.

Kristen jumps from her bed and walks over to mine. She sits down beside me, puts her hands on my face, and looks right into my eyes. "You are already in love with Phillip. That is what I see and that is why you are already afraid he might break your heart. What if he tells you nothing happened and he had a good reason to not talk to you yesterday? Maybe he was afraid that he was already falling for you too and might be as scared as you about these feelings. Just talk to him and see what he says. I know you love him already. If he is seeing Megan then get out of it now before there will be no going back. As I see it right now, you would still be okay if he doesn't feel the same. Listen to your heart and you will know if things are right between the two of you."

"I do have feelings for him. Not sure what they are yet. I guess I will talk to him. I am not as confident as you are though. I don't know if I should get involved with anyone. My life hasn't been the perfect one, and I'm afraid to bring anyone else into it." I tell her hoping she doesn't ask what happened in my past. "What is going to be your major anyway? You seem to be so smart about everything and give the best advice.

"Well my major is going to be psychology because I plan on being a marriage counselor, so I am already getting good at helping people. I believe Phillip would be lucky to have you in his life, so don't ever think you're not good enough for anybody. I am glad to have you in my life and I have just met you. You bring life into this world and light up everyone around you. Now I have to go to shower or I will be late for my class. You look beautiful today. Go knock Phillip's socks off." She hurries to the bathroom.

I am smiling by the time she gets to the bathroom. I look at the clock and find out now I only have a little bit of time to get to class. I grab my things and am out the door. I think all the way to class. How can I be brave enough to ask Phillip if he slept with Megan? He may get mad at me and tell me that it isn't any of my business who he sleeps with. I sure hope he didn't. Every time I think about him and her together, my stomach feels queasy.

I get to class with barely a minute to spare. I see Phillip has already made it before I did and he seems happy that I made it to class. Wondering if he thought I wasn't coming or hoping I wouldn't be here. I get ready to say hello to him, but the professor tells everyone to be quiet and have a seat.

The professor starts class right away and I barely have time to think about anything but the notes I am taking. I look over and see Phillip taking his notes. I know I have to wait until class is over to talk to him.

As soon as class is about over, Phillip tosses a folded-up paper on my desk. I pick it up and bring my gaze up to his. He smiles at me, and it takes my breath away. I look down and unfold the paper. What I see is a letter to me, and I think, *Why write a letter?* I stop listening to the professor and read my letter.

Alexia,

I want you to know that I am sorry about my bad mood yesterday and it had nothing to with you. I want to talk to you about it when we get done with all of our classes today. I hope you don't have plans for this evening. I want you to come over to my place and I will even cook dinner for you. I know I can't cook much, but I will cook something. I really would enjoy cooking for you. So please don't say no.

I did follow you out of class yesterday and I heard what Megan said to you. So you know, I never did anything she said. I have never had her in my condo or any other girl. That is my private place and I don't let people in unless they are special to me. She did come by my condo yesterday and she must have seen you leave. The security guard wouldn't let her in and I told him to never let her in. As I got to school yesterday, she cornered me as soon as I got out of my car. She told me she came over and kept on hitting on me. I told her to leave me alone. She got mad at me and told me I would be sorry. Even told me she would make you sorry for knowing me. I just wanted you to know she is very selfish and will try to make you upset with me. I wanted to tell you all this yesterday, but you wouldn't answer my texts or calls. I am so sorry for any hurt she may have caused you, and I wish I could take away any pain she may have done. Please forgive me for the pain you might have felt. I never want to cause you any kind of pain or suffering ever.

I thought you looked really nice in my t-shirt yesterday and planned on telling you that. I hurt you with my bad mood and you left before I could tell you. As much as you looked great in my shirt, today your beauty takes my breath away. When you walked in class, I just couldn't breathe. You looked like an angel sent from heaven. I mean it. You are the woman for me and I hope you will be mine and only mine. I sure hope you are really taking notes in this class. I can't take notes when my mind is only on you. You will have to tutor me in this class. I will be waiting to hear from you whether you're coming over tonight, so please say yes.

XXXOOO

Phillip

P.S. I can't get your kiss and your sweet lips off my mind.

I get done reading his letter and I can't believe what he wrote. I sit in my seat in shock for a few minutes. I look up to see what Phillip is doing, but I am sitting in the class all by myself. Everyone is already out of the class and it is over. The teacher looks up at me and asks if I am all right. I say yes to him and get up to leave. I am still in shock.

I decide to go get some food and think about everything Phillip told me in his letter. I decide to head to my favorite place to eat and think. Yep. The beach is calling me, so I must go to my happy place and ponder on my letter.

Sixteen

PHILLIP

*A*lexia is out the door before I can say a word to her. I get up quickly and try to catch up with her. As soon as I get closer to her, I see her wipe her eyes. Now my heart is broken for sure. I did this to her, with my bad mood and not telling her why. I will catch her and make things right. But before I can, I hear that voice that gets on my nerves, and it stops me in my tracks to avoid it. She seems a little bit louder than usual. I ease closer so I can get to hear what Megan is saying but keep out of sight. She is talking to Alexia and asking her to the beach. Why would she do this?

Then I think about what Megan said about making us sorry. Is she going to do something to her at the beach? I hear Alexia tell her that she is busy and has class soon. I think, *Smart girl*, but Megan keeps on and Alexia keeps telling her no. I get ready to go to help Alexia, but Megan starts saying other things to Alexia. My ears can't believe what she is saying to Alexia. How did she know what size bed I have? Megan is relentless as she keeps running her mouth. This has to stop now or I am going to have to beat up a girl.

Then Alexia stops my heart, by what she says back to Megan. She tells her that Megan can have me and that she isn't interested in me before she turns and hurries off toward her dorm. I step closer to watch her go, and then Megan turns and sees me.

She comes over to me and says, "I just did you a favor. She isn't interested in you at all, so now we can be together."

I think about what Megan said to Alexia. Now I'm more furious with this girl in front of me. How can she even think she just did me a favor with that huge lie she told Alexia? Did she think by running Alexia off that I would be interested in her? How many times do I have to tell her that I'm not interested before she gets that into her head? Megan has to be crazy.

I look at her with my face straight at her. "What is wrong with you Megan? Do you think with those lies you just told I would go out with you? I will never go out with you. You are the most appalling person I have ever met. A person who thinks they can lie and steal their way into another person's life. You and I are never going to happen. Never in a million years will I be with a girl like you. Oh by the way, I told the security guy at my condo to never let you in," I yell and quickly turn to leave. I am getting far away from this crazy sicko girl. If I don't, I might punch her.

Megan grabs my arm before I can get away. She gets ready to say something, but I shout, "Stop right now! I do not want to hear another word out of your mouth now or ever." I leave without another word from her. I am glad, because I don't know how much longer I could have kept my fist off her face.

I walk to go to my car. I stop and wonder if I could find Alexia at her dorm room. No, she told Megan that she didn't want anything to do with me. Maybe this is my out before I get too serious about her. I think I will go surfing so I can think about what I need to do. Surfing the waves always makes my mind clearer. This day isn't going so well. Not like this morning at all. Waking up next to Alexia this morning made it the best day ever, and now it has been turned upside down. Surfing is really calling to me, so I head to my car.

As I get closer to the condo, I can smell the ocean. When I get out of my car I take a deep breath to really smell the salty air, and I am relaxed a little bit. Yes, this will do as my therapy for a while. I head inside to change my clothes and grab a small bite to eat. I head to the elevator and who do I see getting on the elevator? Jack. That guy always is coming and going. I wonder what he does with himself. Does he work or is he retired?

"Hi, Jack. How have you been since I left?" I smile.

"I'm fine boy. Have you captured that girl's heart since you left?" he jokes with me. This is how he usually is every day I see him.

"Not yet. Another girl told her a big lie about me and now I may never capture her heart," I sigh.

"Cheer up, son. Girls like to cause a fellow trouble now and then. If that girl really is into you, she will come to her senses soon and figure out that it was a lie. Have you talked to her about it? Never know what will happen unless you talk to her. Sometimes the best thing to do is to open up that mouth of yours and tell her how you feel and discuss that lie you're telling me about."

"Well, I guess you're right and I should have talked to her. I will try to today if I can get her to talk to me. I will for sure talk to her tomorrow. Thanks for the advice. I will see you later Jack." I head to my condo feeling sad that I didn't try to talk to Alexia.

I go inside and already miss having Alexia here with me. I go to the balcony and see that it is a perfect day for surfing. The waves are hitting the beach with extra force just the way I like them. Yeah, those waves are perfect. I hurry and grab some food as I go change my clothes. Soon I am on the beach hitting the waves and my head is already clearing up. I catch quite a few large waves today and now I am feeling happy again.

I wish I could still do this with my brother. He loved this beach so much. While I'm on my board, I sometimes feel him next to me. Maybe he is with me. At least a part of him is I know that on the inside of me. His heart was always the biggest heart around, and he brought out the best of everyone around him. He made me want to be a better person all the time. If he were here with me, he would give me the best advice about Alexia and what I should do.

I get finished with my surfing and head back to the condo to finish going over my homework I need to do. I think about Alexia and our project for biology. We need to work on it again. This will be a great way to get her here, and then I will tell her about that awful lie Megan told her. I might get brave enough to tell her how I really feel about her.

I text her as soon as I get inside the condo. I hope she comes tonight. I might try to make some food. I think I can do it. Better yet, I might run over to my favorite burger place and grab us some burgers. Yeah, that would be best, because if she says yes, I would have time to run over before she gets here. I get a text back from her and she tells me that she has already plans. I text her back again, but she keeps saying no. Well this bums me out. I try asking few more times, but she never answers me back. I guess she is either really busy or just ignoring me because of Megan.

I think about what she really might be going through and what she probably thinks about what Megan said. I put myself in her place and I can see how she might believe Megan over me. We just met and I told her that everyone thinks I am a player and not to believe them because I really am not. Yeah, if I heard that from someone, I think I would have had a hard time believing that person too. Well darn, I shouldn't have said that to her at all. I made myself look like a player. How will I fix this now?

My stomach reminds me that I am hungry. I decide to get a burger anyway. As I get to my favorite place, I see Alexia going inside. I wonder if she is meeting someone. I go in to see what she is up to, trying to be sneaky because I don't want her to think I am following her. I enter and head to a back table to watch her.

I see that she is only here to get her food and not to meet anyone. This makes me happy and sad at the same time. She is blowing me off. At least she isn't meeting up with a guy. I know I have to tell her about Megan's lie.

She leaves after she gets her food, and I think about following her, but I don't. I stay and order my food. Comfort food is the best when you need to figure things out.

I'm sitting and eating at my table for a while when then Jacob and Tyler come in. Must be that everyone needs a good burger today. "Hey, guys. What are you two up to this evening?"

"Not much. We went by your place to hang out with you, but guess what? You're not there, man." Tyler laughs.

I laugh too. "I had to have a burger, man, and this is the best place for that."

"That is right, and we hoped you would be here when we got here." Jacob speaks up. "I really needed some excellent food to make my head to feel better. I believe, I never want to drink ever again." He rubs his head, and it must be killing him to say that.

"I see that as the biggest lie you ever told man. I will never believe that you will ever stop drinking. You need to take a break from it or your liver will hate you."

Jacob laughs. "You are right, man. I don't want to stop. I am taking a break tonight. I still have a bit of a hangover. Megan must have had some powerful drinks at her party. How about the three of us eat and just hang out at your place for a bit, maybe play some video games?"

"That sounds good to me. I need to get my mind on classes, but we can play a few rounds of Call of Duty. That will help with stress relief." I grin at Jacob, trying not to let them know that I really am stressed about a girl. They would give me crap for that and neither of them would understand.

Tyler hurries and finishes his burger. "Now that sounds like a plan. Hanging out and getting to shoot ragheads, Russians, Germans, and zombies is what I need."

We go pay for our food and head back to my condo. I drive and they follow behind me. I pick up my phone and glance at it to see if I ever got a text back from Alexia. I don't see one. I call and leave a message for her to call me when she gets time. Yeah, I bet she had a lot to do tonight. She is blowing me off.

We play games for a few hours and the guys head back to the dorms. I am glad for the peace and quiet. It is time to get my studying over with. I go to my bedroom and lie on my bed to work. I finish most of it before I fall asleep.

Waking up with one hour until my class starts, I hurry with my shower and run out the door. I should at least try to beat Alexia to class. I want to watch her enter. Maybe this will help me to understand if she is still upset about what Megan said to her.

I get to my seat and I see that I have beaten her. Hurrying, I get my books out so I look like I have been here for a little while, and it is only a few seconds before she walks in the door. *Wow*! She looks amazing today. The way she is dressed is sexy and hot. She has made my heart skip a beat, and she looks like an angel.

She is almost late today, and I wonder if she planned that or not. Alexia sits down and I can smell her perfume. I get ready to say something to her, but the professor calls everyone to his attention and everyone starts taking notes. My mind won't let me take the notes. I can only focus on Alexia and what I need to say. I decide to write what I need to say so I won't forget. I start off writing it and it ends up being a letter. Yeah, I know most people don't take the time to write letters. Once I got started on this, I couldn't stop until it was almost time for class to end.

I see everyone finishing up with their notes and getting their things together. I decide that I am going to hand her this letter and leave without a word. I am too afraid to see her face when she reads it. In a few minutes, I ended up flinging the letter on her desk. She looks at me and she picks it up. As soon as she opens the letter, I see my chance to fall in line with all the people leaving and head right out the door. Why did I do that? I should have stayed and talked for a few minutes. I was sure she wouldn't listen, so I left because I am afraid she doesn't feel about me the way that I feel about her.

How do I really feel? I think about this for a few minutes as I walk to my car. I stop dead in my tracks. It hits me like a ton of bricks right on my head. I am in love with her. This realization about freaks me out. When I calm myself down, I am happy about it for the first time. Never have I felt love for a girl before. Why didn't I stay and talk to her? I should turn around and go find her.

As I go to find Alexia, I see her heading out the door and straight for her car. She gets in and leaves. I hurry to my car. This time, I am following her. I follow her through the drive-thru as she gets food and heads somewhere else. It isn't long that I figure out where she is headed. It seems like she is going to have a picnic at the beach. I am afraid to approach her because she might be meeting a guy. She parks at a private public beach area that most people don't even go to. She gets out a chair, her food, and a book, and she has my letter too. Alexia takes everything to the beach, and I hope no one is going to meet up with her. I wait a few minutes and watch her from the distance.

I watch her for a while as she sits in her chair. You would think, she would start to eat right away, but she doesn't. Now I really think she must meeting someone. Then she pulls out the letter, reads it, and smiles. That does something to my heart. It is like for the first time my heart beats, and it is for Alexia. I know she is the woman, I want to be with and I hope that smile means she might feel the same. If not, I will prove to her that she can trust me and even love me.

It is time to stop stalking her and make her mine. I get up and head over to her then sit down right beside her. She jumps when she sees me but smiles at me like I'm supposed to be here. *Yes*, I think to myself, *I am supposed to be here and nowhere else*. She is my sweet angel and I plan on making her mine.

T.R. LYKINS

Seventeen

ALEXIA

I leave the school and head to get my food before I noticed someone following me. Yeah, he thinks I haven't paid enough attention to what is going on around me. I play along and let him follow me. I order my food and order double. If he is going to follow me, then he probably is hungry too. I head to my favorite spot at the beach and get everything out of my car. I know he will wait to see if I am going to meet someone, because that is what I would do too.

I put up my chair and get relaxed. I noticed that he is still waiting. I leave the food in the bag and lean back in my chair. He still hasn't come over. *Why?* I wonder. How can I get Phillip to come on over? *I know.* I pull out his letter and start reading it again. Yeah this has his attention, and it is working. I even smile at myself for my trickery.

I get excited as he comes over, and then I start blushing. I can't wait to have him next to me. Yes, I do believe Kristen is right about my being in love with this man. *Oh boy*, what a man he is!

Phillip walks sneakily over and flops down beside me. I can't help but smile at him when I look at his eyes. Yes, he thinks I didn't know he has been around me the whole time.

I smile at him. "Well it is about time you got over here. Your food probably is getting cold. I don't know about you, but I am starved, and I ordered you the same thing as I ordered for myself. I hope you like what I got us." I grin big at him.

"You are sneakier than I am. Here I thought I was being a good private eye. You knew the whole time I was behind you? Well I guess I better not become a private investigator. I am starved. What did you get us? Looks like we are having a picnic on the beach." Phillip grins at me, and my heart melts as soon as he does.

"Well let's look in this bag and see what I got." I open up the bag and pull out two grilled chicken sandwiches and fries I got at Chick-fil-A. I look up at Phillip and he is still smiling at me. "What?"

"You amaze me, that is what. I love this place and love this sandwich. It seems to me like we both like a lot of the same things. My stomach thanks you for this food and I thank you for thinking enough about me to feed me. I truly appreciate it," he says before he grabs his sandwich and bites into it.

"Well you're welcome, Mr. Not-So-Private-Investigator. Looks like we have this whole area at the beach to ourselves for a little while, and that makes it nice place for a picnic," I start eating too.

We sit there for a while enjoying each other's company and it was nice to be able to have Phillip beside me. I feel relaxed for the first time since I left Phillip's condo. He must really be the reason I feel comfortable around him.

He gets my attention by grabbing my hand. "I hope you believe everything in my letter. Megan was horrible to you yesterday. I didn't do anything with her, I promise you. I don't know how she knew about what size bed I have at the condo. She probably guessed and got that right. I have never had a girl before you in my place. You can ask the guys and they will tell you that. She knew you left my condo yesterday and tried to get Jake to let her in. I told him to never let her in and to not put her on my list of visitors. So she got mad at me. When I got to school, she was waiting on me. I told her to leave us alone. She told me she would make us sorry. I couldn't believe she would just come out and lie like that. Please stay away from her. She must be crazy or insane - maybe both. I told her off yesterday after you left about her deception and she made me so angry that I almost punched her. I would never punch a girl. She kept on and on about how she and I should be together. She wouldn't listen to me. Stay away from her, please, and I told her to stay away from us. All I can think about is you and only you. Alexia, you make me come alive and I hope you will be my girlfriend. I know I don't want to be without you. I wanted to tell you all this yesterday, but you wouldn't come over and then you stopped answering my texts. I knew you were still mad at me. Please don't be mad at me for something I didn't do."

"I was mad at you. I came here yesterday to think and I wanted to be alone to do it, so I turned off my phone. Kristen told me this morning that you always stayed away from Megan no matter where you were. Megan must be crazy or obsessed with you to act the way she does. The only thing I still don't understand is why you didn't talk to me in class yesterday and gave me the cold shoulder." I frown at him.

"Well, I don't know how to talk about this. It might change your mind about me, and it is even harder now that we seem to be getting along." He looks sad.

"Don't be afraid to talk to me, Phillip. If you can't talk to me about it, then we shouldn't be together," I say, but now I am terrified of what he might say. I am also remembering that I have been keeping something big from him.

"Okay, you are right. We can't keep things from each other if we are going to be together. This will affect you and maybe hurt you, if not now, later." He sighs.

"Okay, out with it and now please. I have to know what it is. You are making me scared by not telling me what it is. " Now I am really afraid.

"Well you know about my surgery. When I first got my brother's liver, I had a hard time accepting it. The doctors had to put me on a lot of different medication and I have to take it every day or I will die. I didn't want you to have to be without me, if we were together. Who knows, if my medicine will stop working? And I might die from it. I didn't want to put you into that situation. I was debating the whole class how I was going to drop that bomb on you, only to have Megan to drop hers first. You should be able to be with someone who is healthy enough to be with you forever. I don't want to put you through the pain of losing someone."

I am in shock. Not because I am afraid of him dying, but because it is the same with me. I could be the one who could possibly die. He doesn't even know this yet, and now I feel guilty for not telling him about my heart transplant. I have to think on how to do this, but not today. I really need to do it soon before we get more involved in our relationship. Yes I am being a coward today.

"Phillip I know all about that, so don't be afraid of it. I will never, not choose you, because of that. Everyone can die at any time, and you know this. Trying to stay away from one another because you are afraid I will be hurt is not going to happen. I could be hurt at any time or you might get hurt. We should never think of the awful things that can or could happen. By the way, if I choose you, it will be because I want to be with you, and I won't let anything like that get in my way." I say this, but still I feel like a hypocrite for not telling him about me. Why am I holding back? I don't know yet. I have to wait until I'm ready, and maybe that will be soon, but not today.

He smiles at me and my stomach does a flip-flop, "Well I hope I didn't scare you off because I want to live every day to the fullest and be with you."

"Okay," I tell him.

He looks confused. 'Uh, What are you saying okay to?" he asks.

"Do I have to spell it out for you, Phillip? I said *okay* to us. Unless you changed your mind about me being your girlfriend?"

As soon as I get those words out, he has me pulled out of the chair and on his lap. Phillip holds me close to him and kisses me with everything in him. I feel the intensity of the kiss all the way down my back to my feet. While he is kissing me, he keeps running his hands all over my body, and I can feel the passion rising in the bottom of my tummy and down between my legs. As the passion is heating up inside of me, I begin to really kiss him back and I even straddle his lap. I have never even been this close to a guy before, and I can feel that he is getting really turned on. This makes me more excited.

I keep at him like I know what I am doing, but really I don't. I am letting go and letting nature takes its course. I love the way I feel in Phillips arms, and he kisses me with fervidness that would set the world on fire. I know that if we don't stop soon I think I will let him have his way with me, and I noticed that I have begun rocking on him while I'm still on his lap. He lets out a moan. I am moaning right with him.

Suddenly, we hear someone one behind us and stop to see who it is. Now I feel extremely embarrassed, about what I was doing right here on a beach for whoever to see. My face feels really flushed, and I bet it is blood red.

The person who interrupted us begins to talk. "You two know this is a public beach right? If you keep acting like that, then you should leave. There are kids right over there playing, and they even could see you. Now stop or leave. I would hate to have to call the cops on you two," the guy says and walks away.

Phillip looks into my eyes with all the emotion I am still feeling. "I'm sorry about that. I shouldn't have done that to you here. I meant to kiss you. Once we got started, I couldn't stop. You make me feel alive inside for the first time in my life. All could think about is how I could get you closer. Please forgive me for embarrassing you in front of everyone. It won't happen again. By the way, thank you for saying yes. I now have a girlfriend for the first time of my life and it feels wonderful."

"You have nothing to be sorry for. I was enjoying your kisses, as you were mine. I felt everything you did and I am as much to blame. I wanted to be closer to you too. I am a virgin though, so this is something I have never done before. I never wanted to be with a guy like that and I am embarrassed with my actions. I have never had a boyfriend. You are my first everything, and I will have to keep more control on my raging hormones. I didn't mean to give you the wrong impression to think I would go further with you this soon. I want you extremely bad. I want to get to know you more before that next step happens. If you can wait, that is. Can you?" I look up at him hoping he will be able to.

"I want to take it slow with you too. You are my first girlfriend and now I wished, I had waited so you could be my first also. I wish I could have taken that back and kept it for you. You are a terrific girl and I can't wait until we have many more firsts in everything else. Like our first date, for example, which we haven't had. We seem to have skipped that part. How about you, my girlfriend, go and get ready for your first date with me?" He is asking me out on our first date. Wow, we did skip many steps.

I grin at him, "Well, being that we already slept together, why not go out on a date? Sounds like fun to me. Where are you going to take me and what time?"

He laughs at me. "You are right, we have slept together, but really not what your smart butt was meaning. The place I am taking you to is a surprise. You will have to dress up casually for it. How about seven tonight? That will give you a couple hours to get ready and I will come pick you up. If you would like, pack an overnight bag and your books. We might as well study after we finish our date so we can keep our hands off each other," he says, but I can see passion still in those eyes.

"Overnight bag? You mean you want me to stay all night? I'm not ready to go further with you, Phillip. You will have to keep it PG-rated if I stay. Can you do that?" I ask, batting my eyes up at him.

"I will. I promise. You will make it hard for me though. Having you with me will make it worth it. I miss you when you're not with me. You better hurry and leave so I can come get you. You are already running behind as we speak."

He gets up and gathers all my things. He even carries everything back to my car. Such a gentleman he is. After we get everything loaded he pulls me close and gives me another fiery kiss that lights up my insides. Maybe not too much of a gentleman as he runs his hands down my back and grabs my butt.

I laugh at him when he does this. "You sure you can keep it PG tonight, sweetie?"

He grins wickedly. "Yes of course I can. I didn't say I would keep my hands off what is mine." He laughs and grabs my butt again then turns and heads off to his car. What have I gotten myself into? I don't know if I can keep my hands off him either.

I drive back to my dorm room with a smile on my face. I actually hope Kristen is in the room. I can get her to help me pick what I need to wear tonight. As I drive, my phone beeps with a text, and when I stop at a red light I glance at it to see who it's from. It is from Phillip, saying that he is already missing me and can't wait until tonight. This makes me smile even more. I wonder if everyone who finds someone to love feels this way. I feel like I'm floating on a cloud. I hurry back to my room so I can finally get ready for my first date.

I open the door and see Kristen relaxing on her bed reading. She looks up and smiles really wide. "Well, it looks like someone had a great day with that happy face you're making. How did it go with Phillip?"

I sit down and tell her everything that happened today, from my letter, to him following me to the beach and our talk while we were there, but I left out the part about our make-out session.

"You have to help me pick out a nice outfit to wear tonight. I don't know where we are going. I think I need to dress up. Will you help me?"

"Of course I will help. Let's get you all dressed up and I will even fix your hair. He will be wowed with how beautiful you will look."

She gets up and goes through my closet to pull out my clothes before she picks out an outfit I didn't even know I had. It looks awesome together. I go take a shower and get dressed. By the time I get my hair done, it is almost time for Phillip to arrive.

I hurry and put some of my things in my overnight bag and I even throw in Phillips t-shirt. When I get done, I go take a look at myself in the mirror to see how I look. I can't believe I can look like this once I get dressed up. I look pretty good for a girl who almost died and I frown at myself for not telling him about my transplant. Now I know I have to tell him, because he was worried about the same thing as me. He doesn't even know I am worried about the same thing.

Kristen looks at me. "Wow! You look amazing, and you will not get any studying done tonight. Don't even take your books." She laughs.

"We have to work on our project or we won't get done. Yes studying will happen." She laughs again at me like she knows better. Maybe she knows me better than I do.

Before I even get to think more about it, there is a knock on the door. I freeze and look at Kristen.

She answers the door. "Well, hello, Phillip. Do you want to come in or are you ready to take my girl out now? You know, you better not hurt her or I will come looking for you and hurt you worse than you ever could be hurt. You understand what I'm saying? She looks right into his eyes for a few seconds before turning to me and winking.

"Yes, Kristen, I understand you clearly and I don't plan to ever hurt Alexia. She is too special to me. I'm ready to go whenever she is." He looks at me for the first time. "*Wow!* Alexia, you are the most beautiful woman in the world." He smiles at me and my heart starts beating faster. "Are you ready to go or do you need a few more minutes?" He is already being a gentleman.

"I am ready to go now." I turn to Kristen. "Thank you for helping me this afternoon."

"You are welcome, and I loved doing it." She gets close to me and whispers in my ear, "Girl, you are in trouble. This guy is in love with you as much as you are him. Don't be scared. Go with it and enjoy each other." She gives me a hug and turns us toward Phillip. "Now, you two... don't do anything I wouldn't do and have fun tonight. Please use protection if you start having extra fun tonight," she tells us both. Then winks at us and pushes us right out the door.

I turn toward Phillip and see that he is blushing as much as I am. Kristen is blunt about what she says and knows how to embarrass everyone around her. That is why I like her so much. Phillip grabs my bags and my hand. We head out to go on our date.

Eighteen

PHILLIP

I can't believe she knew I was following her. I really thought I was doing a good job. Even thought that maybe I should be a private investigator. There goes that plan really fast. Oh well, I'm glad she is happy to see me and she even bought me food. Yeah, a girl after my own heart for sure. *Wait!* She already has it. She doesn't even know it yet, but still she got me food. Wow! What an amazing woman she is and she keeps getting better. She even has one of my favorite sandwiches. She must be a mind reader. That's what it is. That reminds me of a movie I watched while I was in the hospital. It was a chick-flick movie but I was too bored and tired to change the channel. The one of the main characters could read minds.

She hands me my food and we eat in peace. Like we were meant for each other and enjoy each other's company, even while sitting quietly together. We finish our food. I grab her hand and I tell her everything about what the letter said was true and how sorry I am about how mean Megan is. I even tell her about what had me in my bad mood yesterday. That I was scared that she would be in pain if anything happened to my sick body. That still makes me sad to think about that if something happens to me, I won't be there for her and she will have to go through the pain I would cause her. I know this will have to be her decision. I had to tell her so that she can decide if she can be with me. Her decision scares me the most. What if she doesn't choose to be with me? Which would be best for her? I know it would hurt me horribly if she chooses not to pick me.

She tells me that it doesn't bother her about my possibility of dying and that we need to live our life to the fullest each day. She is the smartest girl in the world. Holding her hand and sitting on the beach with her makes this day the best ever. My heart keeps growing with love for her with each word she tells me. She seems to know about loss and what it means that we could die any time, when our time is up. She looks sad when she talks about this and I wonder why. I decide to ask her to live life to the fullest every day with me. I really don't think she will tell me yes, but a guy can hope for the best.

Still holding my hand, she turns and smiles and says yes. I think for a minute and wonder what she is really saying yes to. Is she really saying that she will be my girl? I ask her and that is what she meant. *Yes!* She is going to be mine.

I grab her out of her seat and sit her in my lap so fast that I even surprise myself. I start kissing her and I lose control of myself. I kiss her like there is no tomorrow and I don't even want to stop, but I know I should. We keep kissing, and the more we kiss, the more I get turned on right here on the beach, but I can't stop. She sets me on fire as she starts rubbing herself on my lap. I know if she doesn't stop soon that I think I am going to explode.

She keeps kissing me, and *oh,* do I love the way she kisses me, and she even moans. Good grief, I can't stop myself. I want to strip her of her clothes right now. She has me even moaning with those lips and her rocking on my lap. I can feel the passion all the way down my body and definitely in my lap. When I can hardly take much more, I hear someone clear his throat behind us.

That makes us stop really fast. I look into her eyes and see that this has embarrassed her. I smile at her to let her know that it is all right. The guy let us know that kids were watching us, so we should stop making out on a public beach before he leaves. Thank goodness. If he'd seen how turned on I am, he probably would call the cops. I tell her that I'm sorry for acting that way here on the beach. I thanked her for being my girlfriend, which makes me the happiest guy ever.

I ask her to go out on a date with me since she is my girlfriend now. I at least should take her out on a first date seeing as we already skipped the first date and went straight into a relationship. Really it seems like we have known each other longer and it feels right to have her be mine. *Mine.* I love the sound of her being mine.

She tells me that she is a virgin and I'm not surprised. I tell her that I wish I had waited for her. I really mean that too. Having sex isn't the same if you don't love the person you're with. When Alexia and I do go down that road it won't be sex, it will be making love. Making love, because I'm in love with Alexia.

Alexia jokes about already sleeping together and being in a relationship before going on a date. She sure is funny, this girl of mine. I tell her to pack an overnight bag. I'm not going to bring her back once she is at my condo. I let her know that we won't go any further than she wants to and I will keep that promise even if I have to go take several cold showers just to have her next to me.

I help get all her stuff back to her car, but I can't leave until I kiss her once more. I even grab her butt and pull her close to me. She laughs at me and asks me if I can keep it PG tonight. She even calls me sweetie, and I hope I can keep it PG tonight. I tell her yes and that she better get going so I can pick her up tonight.

Alexia leaves me first and I can't help the smile that comes across my face. I am so far gone and head over heels in love with her. I climb into my car and send her a text. I hope she waits and reads it when she gets back to her dorm. I don't want anything to happen to her by reading my text and driving.

I head toward my condo when my phone rings. I see that it is Tyler, so I answer it, "Hey, what's up Tyler?

"Nothing much. Jacob and I are thinking about going to a football game tonight and thought we would ask you to come along. Do you want to come with us?"

"Any other night I would. I am going on a real date tonight with Alexia," I tell him.

"What? I thought you just hooked up with girls to get what you wanted and didn't get tied down to them. You never take them out on a date. She must be special to get you to go on a date."

"You are right. That used to be me until I met Alexia. I never took a girl on a date before. I don't know, man. She is really special. So special that I even asked her to be my girlfriend. She even told me yes. To make it official, I'm taking her out to celebrate tonight." I smile while saying these words. I know the guys think I am a player but I never was.

"I can't believe my ears! Phillip is off the market. That is good for the rest of us guys. Now we have no competition for the girls. I know one girl who will be mad at you, and I really wouldn't want her mad at me. Megan is going to be furious with you and Alexia. She has been waiting for you to ask her out. She keeps coming to me and asking if I could get you to go out with her."

"I really don't care about what Megan will do. She already tried to get in between Alexia and me, but it didn't work out for her. I told her to leave us alone and not to even talk to either of us."

"Wow, Megan must have it bad for you or she is crazy. I believe she must be obsessed with you to keep at you the way she has over the past year. I wish you luck with your girl tonight. Hope you don't mess it up with her either, being that she is your first girlfriend. Jacob and I will miss you at the game. Have a good time with her."

"I hope I don't mess it up with her either, because I really like Alexia. She is different and special. I will keep her as long as she will have me. I plan on taking her somewhere nice and then we have to study. If you guys drink tonight, don't drink and drive, okay?"

"I won't drink anything tonight because knowing Jacob he will be plastered by the time we get to the game. Don't worry. I will be his driver. Have fun and talk to you tomorrow, Phillip."

"Bye, Tyler." We hang up as I pull into my condo garage.

I hurry to my condo so I can make reservations and straighten up around the condo. I have to make sure everything is perfect for my girl to stay with me. I check out my food and make sure I have everything she might need while she is here. I wonder if I should try to make her pancakes in the morning. I look to see if I have everything to make them, but I notice that I need a few things. I make a list of what I need and so I can stop at the store. Now time to get ready to pick up my girl.

I shower and shave because I want to look nice tonight for Alexia. I put on my dress slacks and a button-up shirt. As I button up my shirt, I notice my scar and it reminds me of how really lucky I am to be here and how lucky I am to have Alexia in my life. No more guilt between us because she understands more about me than anyone. It seems we connected from the first day we met. I'm out the door quickly. I can't wait to see her.

I get to her dorm room and knock. I hope Alexia opens the door. If she does, I will grab her up in my arms and kiss her. The door opens, but it is Kristen and she is smiling up at me. Darn, no kiss yet. I smile back at Kristen. She starts off wanting to know if I'm here to take out her girl. I almost laugh at her. *Her girl?* Then she finishes by telling me not to hurt Alexia ever or she would hurt me. I tell her that I don't ever plan on hurting Alexia.

I look up from Kristen to see Alexia behind her, smiling at me. *Wow! Breathe Phillip.* I tell Alexia how beautiful she is. She is the most beautiful girl I have ever laid eyes on. I ask her if she needs a few minutes, but she says that she is ready now. As she gets her things together, Kristen whispers something in her ear that makes her smile. Before we leave, Kristen starts telling us to use protection and have fun. I look at Alexia and notice how flushed her face is. She is really embarrassed, and it is time to leave now.

I grab her bag and we head out to the car. I open her door for her to get in. As she starts to enter the car, I brush her hair up off her neck and kiss her under her ear. She moans when I do this and I know that tonight is going to be hard. I want her with me more than anything. I close her door without further teasing and walk around to get in the car. I hope I don't mess up our first date. All I want is to have our many firsts of anything together to be special - like our first date tonight.

T.R. LYKINS

Nineteen

ALEXIA

When we get to the car, he opens the door just like a gentleman does. As I get in the car, he raises my hair and kisses my neck. This makes me moan; I can't help it. What in the world is he doing to me? He finally lets me get in and closes the door. This date is really going to be hard for me to keep my hands to myself if he keeps that up. I am already blazing inside from that kiss. He makes his way into the car and we are off.

"Where are we going to eat?" I smile wide and bat my eyes at him, hoping my eyes will get an answer out of him.

"I can't tell you, my beautiful girl, and stop batting those big, beautiful eyes at me. Most of the time, eye batting would work. I am going to be strong and keep it a surprise because I don't want to spoil a minute of our first date. I will try my best to make tonight special for you." Phillip smirks at me like he has a big secret.

"It already is special for me, so you can tell me now if you'd like to. It was special as soon as you told me I was beautiful."

He grabs my hand and kisses the palm of it. Kissing my palm makes me feel loved. I have only ever read about that happening to the girls in books when a guy loves her. I keep holding his hand as we drive. The place he is taking me to must be close to the beach because we are getting closer to the beach area.

We arrive at the restaurant too quickly for me. Now I have to let go of his hand to get out of the car. I notice the restaurant and then instantly fall in love with this place. It looks like it used to be a house on the beach a long time ago and now it has been turned into a cozy restaurant on the beach. I hope we get a seat close to the window so I can look out at the ocean.

Phillip grabs my hand as we walk into the restaurant. He goes up to the hostess and tells her that we have reservations. She looks up at Phillip and smiles really wide at him before saying that we should follow her. We do, but the looks she keeps giving him are upsetting me. I start to think that she better quit or I might have to tell her off.

Wow. How did I become so jealous this fast? Maybe because he is mine now and no other girls can have him anymore.

As we get to our table, Phillip lets go of my hand, so that he can pull my seat out for me to sit in. He smiles at me. "Have a seat my, beautiful girlfriend and look out the window." I sit down and look up to see what he is talking about. What I see is the most spectacular view, and it takes my breath away. He must have asked for this table so that I can see this. The sun is glistening over the waves, and they sparkle like diamonds.

I look back at Phillip, who is only looking at me. "Phillip, this is the best first date a girl could ever have and we are just getting started. I love this view, and this place is perfect. I haven't even tried the food, but I believe it will be the best ever."

"I am here to provide you with best date ever, my beautiful girl. I have eaten here with my parents and my brother. The food has always been the best. You are the first person I have ever brought here. No girls or even my friends. This is another first for us. I requested this seat, because when I was little, I remembered how the sun setting over the ocean always looks like sparkling diamonds. To a little boy, I guess it was magical, but now with that smile and the brightness in your eyes, I will always remember your sparkle and not the ocean's sparkle. Every time I see you I will remember this look on your face and see how magical you can be. I am officially under your spell and I like being under your spell. Let's order and enjoy our evening together." He reached over, grabbed my hand, and kissed my palm. Phillip kissing my palm here makes me blush, because his doing that feels so intimate.

I gaze into his eyes and see a man who could be the one I could love forever. He has this passion and absolute caring about him that I never want to let go. I smile at him and bring his hand to my lips to kiss his hand - the same as he did mine. We never take our eyes off each other the whole time we do this. Our waiter soon interrupts us to take our order. We order our food and take a minute to catch our breaths. I believe we both have been holding them in for a while.

I decide that I need to know more about Phillip. He has told me some things about himself, but not enough. "You know, Phillip, we hardly know anything about each other. Let's talk while we wait on our food. Tell me, where are you from?"

"That is an easy question. I'm from Cleveland, Ohio. It is easy flying from Cleveland to here, being that it has a direct flight. You were on the plane with me. Are you from Cleveland or did you drive to that airport?"

"I am from Cleveland too. Wow. What a small world? All this time we have been talking and we were even on the plane together, but we didn't even find this out. That should have been the first thing we had in common, but we keep doing everything backwards. I live in a suburb close to the city about twenty minutes away. Where in Cleveland are you from?"

"I live in the city. It is easier for my parents to be closer to their jobs. We used to have a house when my brother was alive. I think they just missed him, so we moved to a condo in the city. They really work extra hard since he died and I think they do it because they haven't accepted that he has died. I miss him too. I know he wouldn't want them to be in pain because of what happened to him. Are you and your parents close?"

"Yes, I'm very close to them. They stay by my side no matter what, and I can tell them anything. Maybe it is because I am an only child. They work hard too and they truly spoil me so much, but I'm not going to complain. They didn't want me to drive from Cleveland to here by myself. They even had all my things and my car delivered. All I had to do is just pack my last bag and get on the plane we flew together on. See what you're getting into with me?"

"I don't mind that you're spoiled, and I will do my best to help them out by spoiling you while you're here with me. What was high school like for you?"

"High school was fine, and I had no problems until I was a sophomore. I had to take off for a year because of a viral infection that made me very sick. I had to skip a year. Then I went back and all the friends I had had moved on without me. I just kept to myself and studied extra hard so I could get into college. What about your high school days?" I change the subject quickly. Our first date isn't going to be the day I tell him about my heart transplant. I don't want to spoil it.

"I was a popular guy who played football up to the car wreck that killed my brother and when I received his liver, I had to stop. I didn't want to take any chances of getting hurt. At first, I was angry with everyone and blamed whoever came my way because I didn't get what I really wanted. I really was being selfish at the time. All I really wanted was to play football for a college team, only now I am good with being an average guy. It was hard not being the popular football jock that everyone wanted me to be. Instead I went from popular to everyone feeling sympathy toward me. I was glad I was a senior or I really would have been a grouch. Did you ever play sports?"

"No sports, but I wanted to be a cheerleader. Well, actually I was going to try out before I got sick. The week of the tryouts I found out I had a viral infection and wasn't allowed to try out." I need to stop talking about my sickness; thank goodness the waiter brings our food. That was convenient for me. We thank our waiter, and I realize how hungry I am and dive right in. "This seafood is the most amazing seafood I have ever had." I smile at Phillip and shove another bite into my mouth.

He smiles back at me. "That is what my brother always said and I agree. What are your favorite things to do?"

I grin and think about this. "Well, I am a book nerd mostly. I love going to the beach even when it is cold outside. The ocean seems to be always calling me, which it continually calms and relaxes me. I really don't have much I like to do, except I love going to the movies. More so if I have read the book before the movie comes out. I like action-packed movies the best and I am always willing to try new ones. Walking on the beach is my favorite exercise. If you give me a beach chair and a book, that can be my next favorite exercise. I guess, I really don't do much and I bet that sounds boring to you."

"Sounds to me like we have to get you to try surfing because you love the ocean and beach. I can teach you sometime. I love to ride the waves. When I am out in the ocean it seems like the whole world is peaceful and that relaxes me. You at least have to try it once. You know tomorrow is Saturday and we don't have classes. If you want to try it, we can go out. Have to try it soon before the water gets too cold in the fall. How about you let me teach you tomorrow?" he asked.

"I don't know if I can learn to surf. Maybe we need to let me think about doing that first. I am sure you're a great teacher. However, I'm not too coordinated. If you want to surf tomorrow, I will be glad to sit on the beach and watch you. I would love to watch you surf." I know I am not ready for him to see my ugly scar on my chest from my surgery. I can wear a one-piece bathing suit, and it usually covers it up. I smile at him and hope he doesn't try to convince me to surf.

"You wouldn't mind to sit and watch me surf?"

"No I wouldn't mind at all. I would enjoy watching you and spending time on the beach. I think it will be a blast." I smile and finish my food.

"That is another date we are going to have tomorrow. We will hit the beach when we wake up in the morning. It is easy at the condo to just walk down to the beach and grab the condo's cabana. Do you want dessert?"

"No dessert for me. I am way too full on this food. Next time I will not eat as much so I can save room for dessert. You know the date isn't over until you take me back to the dorm, so tomorrow at the beach will be a continuation of our first date. Looks like this date keeps on going. You may never top this first date though." I look into his eyes and see that he seems to be enjoying our date. The waiter comes over and hands us the bill. "Do you want me to pay for my meal?" I think he will say no, but I wanted to ask to be polite.

He looks at me to see if I am joking then shakes his head. "I asked you on a date and that means I will be paying. Every time I take you out, I expect you to accept that I will be paying. Believe me, I will be taking you out a lot from now on, so expect to be spoiled and pampered."

"You don't have to pay all the time. I should be able to pay from time to time. We are both still in college, and I don't want to break you."

"You forgot that my parents gave me a large budget for food, and believe me I can't eat that much by myself. You will not be breaking me, and I will enjoy feeding you. It gives me another way to be with you. I will take every moment you will let me have. Are you ready to go? We should head back and work on our assignment so we can spend all day tomorrow at the beach. What do you think? Is that a good plan for you? We could do something else if you want." He gets up from his seat and pulls me up after him.

"That sounds like a wonderful plan. One thing I would like to do before we go inside the condo is take a night stroll on the beach. I need to exercise because of all the food I just ate." As we head out the door, Phillip keeps my hand in his.

"Yes that does sound like a great plan. I like walking on the beach at night and I believe the moon will be out because the night is clear."

We walk to his car and head to Phillip's place. This night has already been fabulous and I can't wait for the rest of it.

Twenty

PHILLIP

We head out to my car and I get a whiff of Alexia's scent. *Oh my*, she smells like heaven, and I want to taste her skin before we leave. I open her car door but before she gets in I reach to pull her hair to the side. I bend down and kiss her neck to tease her. She moans. I know if I don't hurry and get us to the restaurant we both will be in trouble.

I picked a special place for us to eat at for our first date. I don't know why I have never brought anyone else to this restaurant before. Maybe it's because the last time I ate here it was with my parents and my brother before the accident. I grew up eating at this place, and I always thought it was magical when I was little. It used to be a house on the beach about forty years ago. When the owners passed away, the family didn't want to live in it. When they sold it, the new owners turned it into a restaurant on the beach. I love sitting by the big windows overlooking the ocean. I made reservations so we can sit by the windows, and I know how much Alexia loves the ocean. I can't wait until she sees this place and the view from the windows. This place brings back memories I sometimes forget. How my brother and I would always try to outdo each other, even if we were just coloring a picture. I miss him and I know he would have been happy that I am bringing Alexia to our special restaurant.

Just as we pull into the parking lot and park, I turn to see Alexia's face and what I see is what I felt the first time I came here. Now I know why I haven't brought anyone else to this place. It had to be the special girl I love and I know right now that she is the one.

I grab her hand when we get out so we can hurry inside to get to our seats. I can't wait to see her face light up when she sees the ocean from the giant windows. As soon as I tell the hostess my name, she takes us straight to our seat. Alexia hasn't noticed the view and I point it out to her. She looks out the window and I see her eyes sparkle like I know the ocean is right now. I picked this time of day because the sunset is on the water right now. She knows how I felt the first time I came here. I can see it in her eyes.

I don't even take my eyes off her because of her beauty at this moment I want to always remember this day, our first date, with my first girlfriend, the one I'm in love with. Yes, I am in love with the most beautiful girl in the world and I can't help myself. Look at her sitting across the table with those bright blue sparkling eyes and a face of an angel, how could I not be.

Alexia finally turns back to see me watching her and tells me that this is the best first date ever and it just only began. I tell her all about how I use to love it here when I was little and that she is the only person I have ever brought here. That this was a place that I grew up in with my family and now I wanted to share this special place with her. I let Alexia know that I am under her spell that she magically has me captured. I kiss the palm of her hand, and it starts to feel so intimate, but I really don't want to stop. Fortunately, the waiter comes and takes our order before things get too heated, between us.

Alexia starts asking questions to learn more about me and I start telling her everything about me that she asks. It is about time we learn more about one another since we are already dating. I know we have been doing everything differently, but I like how we have ended up together. This makes us a unique couple. We soon find out that we both live in the same city, and I like that. I wished I had met her sooner, before everything turned bad for me after my brother's death. I went into a darkness for a while, and I believe Alexia could have helped me with that pain. I was angry at the world after my brother died. I made everyone around me unhappy, and even got into trouble at school because I didn't care about my grades. If I was unhappy about life then everyone around me at the time should be unhappy too. I hated waking up and not having my brother in my life. Maybe I had to overcome that period in my life just so I could be here with Alexia now.

We keep talking about our pasts, and I find out that Alexia was sick her sophomore year with some kind of viral infection and had to take that year off. I want to ask more about what kind of viral infection she had, but she seems so sad just to mention it. I will ask more about it later. I don't want her to be sad tonight. The waiter brings our food. Time to get our moods back to now and our special place.

She loves the food and says the same things about it that my brother used to say. I tell her this and she smiles her beautiful smile at me. We talk more about the things we like and her love of the ocean and the beach. She makes this warm feeling come over me. This stunning woman sitting here with me is mine and I would have loved for my brother to have had met her only because they both have this love of the beach.

I tell Alexia that tomorrow is Saturday so we should spend the day at the beach. I even try to convince her to let me teach her how to surf. She seems to be afraid to try it. I won't push it on her. I will show her how it is done and how much fun it can be. My brother taught me how to surf and I have never taught anyone. It would be fun to teach Alexia. Maybe the next time she will be on a board beside me in the ocean. I find out that she doesn't mind sitting on the beach and watching me surf. How lucky am I with my girl?

The waiter comes back to see if we need dessert, but we both are too full. I get the check and start to pay. Alexia asks if she needed to pay for her part. I let her know fast that that isn't going to happen. She says that she should at least pay for food sometimes and I reminded her that my parents have me well taken care of for food. It won't be necessary for her to use her money. My parents used the money they got from the insurance company to finish paying off the condo and the rest went into a fund for my school and other needs I may have. I don't tell her this.

We get up to leave and I ask her if she wants to go back to do homework so we are free to spend the day at the beach tomorrow. She says that she wants to take a walk on the beach first. I think this will be perfect before we start working on the assignment. I see the moon out so we have a perfectly clear night for a walk. This first date is much more than I could have ever dreamed of and now I hope, I don't mess things up with Alexia in the future. Sure hope Megan isn't having another one of her parties tonight. If she is, we will go the other way. Megan seems to always be having parties lately.

T. R. LYKINS

Twenty-One

ALEXIA

*T*he drive back to Phillip's place is quicker because the traffic is less hectic at this time of the night. We pull up to his condo building and I ask him if we can go in so I can use the restroom before our walk. He tells me, "There is a restroom on the first floor unless you want to go up first."

"No, this restroom will be fine, and then we can get on the beach faster." I smile and go to the restroom.

I hurry and freshen up while I'm inside. I look in the mirror and see a glow on my face I have never had before, and I wonder if being around Phillip has this effect on me. If it does then I really like being with him even more. I didn't even know that it could be possible to like a person more. He said that I have him under a spell. I believe he has me under his spell as well.

I am smiling as I come out the restroom and see Phillip talking to the security guy. He sees me and smiles back "Are you ready for our walk? Mark is taking up our things to the condo so we can head straight out to the beach."

"Yes, I am ready and can't wait." He grabs my hand and we head out the door. "That is nice of Mark to take our things up. I didn't know security workers did that."

"Mark is like security and a doorman all wrapped up into one person. The condo association pays him well to do both. I think he is a really nice guy and does things like that more than he has to."

Phillip never lets go of my hand as we walk to the beach. I am happy that the moon is going to be out and bright over the ocean tonight. It may not be a full moon yet, but it lights everything up over the usually dark water. When we get close to the sand, I take off my shoes. I have to put my toes in the sand when I'm on the beach, and the warmth from the day has the sand still warm. I have to let go of Phillip's hand so he can take off his shoes. As soon as my hand leaves his, I feel lost without it. There is a connection when we touch, which makes me tingle through my whole body and without his touch I seem desperate to get it back.

"So you are like me and have to have bare feet in the sand?" Phillip asks.

"I've loved to have my feet in the sand ever since I was a little girl. I would play all day on the beach and make sandcastles. I wasn't very good at making them when I was small. I really didn't care what they looked like. I wanted to play and pretend I was a princess in my castle waiting on my Prince Charming to come. I know that was silly. I was about eight when

I used to be a princess, and don't laugh at me for telling that story."

"Why would I laugh at your story? I think it is cute just like you are. Keeping telling me more of your stories please." He smiles so wide that his dimples appear and melt my heart. How could I resist that face?

"Okay, I will tell you another one as we walk. Then we need to get back to do the homework that is waiting on us. I remember another time my parents brought me here for summer vacation. I guess I was about eleven and I started noticing boys. I was enjoying a nice sunny day when this boy came over to where I was. We hit it off really quick and started building a huge sandcastle. This castle was bigger and better than the ones I use to make by myself. We even made a moat around it and collected shells to decorate the castle. I can't remember the boy's name. Every day that summer we played on the beach. I think I might have had a little crush on him. I knew he didn't feel the same, because he was a bit older than me. That was a really great summer and I hated that I had to leave. It was always hard for me to leave this place and go back home. I guess we need to hit those books." I notice that we've walked a different way than toward Megan's house and I'm glad. It looks like that girl has parties every night. Her parents must neglect her or something, because she seems like she needs to have people around her every night. Who knows she might just be lonely.

Phillip gazes at what I am looking at, and I believe he might have just read my mind, "Megan must be at it again. I wonder how she gets away with so many parties. I think she has had one every night since school started. I hope Tyler and Jacob haven't ended up at her party again. They told me they were going to the football game."

We ended up back at the condo and Phillip looks a bit worried. I try comforting him. He must be thinking about his friends.

"I'm sure they went to the game. Who could party every night? It has to be rough on the body."

"Jacob could party every night and that scares me. I hope he never drinks and drives. If that happened, something bad could happen either to him or others."

"Why don't you give your friends a call and see what they are doing? That way you won't worry while we are studying."

"How did you get so smart, my girl? You wouldn't mind if I called first, would you?"

"No. Go ahead and while you are on the phone, I'll get in the shower, if that is okay with you."

"That would be fine by me. If you need some help, let me know I will be glad to help out." He winks at me as I head to the shower.

I giggle. "I think I can manage, but I will keep you in mind if I happen to need some help." Smiling at him, I close the door.

Wow, I now remembered, how hard tonight will be. I hurry and shower. I want to spend every minute I can with Phillip. By the time I finish, I head back out to the living room and see Phillip sitting outside on the balcony. He looks like he must have showered and changed into comfortable clothes. I walk out on the balcony to join him. It feels so natural being here with Phillip, and I know how fortunate I am to be here.

"Did you talk to your friends?"

"Yes, and they are fine. They knew about the party but stayed away tonight. Jacob even surprised Tyler with not drinking or wanting to go partying. That surprised me too. I'm glad he has taken a break tonight. I want to spend every minute with you and not be a designated driver for my friends. Don't get me wrong I would go pick them up anytime but tonight I want to be selfish and spend the rest of our first date together without interruptions though."

As soon as he says this, he pulls me down onto his lap. Phillip reaches up with his hand and caresses my face. He gently pulls my face close to his and kisses me. The kiss is passionate and intimate. I'm glad that I'm sitting while he is kissing me or I would have been on the floor. Can you say weak-in-the-knees kind of kiss?

We finally come up for air and we both are having difficulty breathing. He looks into my eyes and I can see desire in his beautiful brown eyes. This makes me melt into his arms and kiss him again. He interrupts us because we are getting too excited and our hands have been roaming in places they shouldn't go unless we want to go further. Tonight we are not going there.

"Alexia, my beautiful girl, if you want to keep tonight a PG rating we need to stop now," he says, barely breathing, and I notice that I'm barely breathing too.

"I'm sorry. I got carried away and couldn't help myself. I do want to make love to you, but not tonight. I think we should wait until we get to know each other better and I am new at this. I should get off your lap, so we don't get carried away." I try to get up, but he doesn't let go of me.

"It is my fault as much as yours. Don't be sorry. I truly enjoyed myself, and when the time is right, we will make love when you are ready. I will wait as long as it takes. I don't want to rush our relationship. You are too special to me not to wait. Take as long as you want. I will be right here when you're ready, and no pressure." He kisses me softly this time and I know he meant what he said. I hope my hormones don't get the best of me and I can wait until I am truly ready. Being close to Phillip makes it so hard.

"Thank you for understanding. You are special to me, and I want our relationship based on getting to know each other first, not about sex. We can't rush this. So far we are off to a great start in our relationship, although we have been doing things backwards. Making love is a big step and I have to truly know you and know how you really feel about me before that happens. I have been saving myself for that one person who loves me the way I want to be loved, and that is with all of his heart. That no matter what, he will take care of me and be there for me when I need him to be." I look into his eyes, and I believe he understands me.

"You deserve all that and more, my sweet girl. I plan on being everything I can be for you. To show you that kind of love. And I will be there for you as long as I am able. Hopefully my liver will last a lifetime. I need to prove to you my feelings and earn your trust so we have to wait for this before the next big step. Now let's see if we can work on that homework we planned." He gets up and goes and grabs our books.

I notice that he seemed a little sad when he talked about his liver. Hopefully it will keep him alive for a long time. I know I have to tell him soon about my heart, and maybe he will accept me the way I do with him. We may not have perfect bodies, but we can live for the now and enjoy each other while we can.

We study for a while and get a lot done. I start yawning before too long and Phillip says that we've done enough. We head to the bedroom like a real couple does and get ready for bed. *Wait.* We are a real couple. This sets in that this sexy guy I am going to bed with is mine. Yeah, I'm thankful. Who knew five years ago when I was on my last heartbeat that I would be here with Phillip?

Phillip sees me smiling. "What is that beautiful smile all about?"

"I am thankful to be here with you. It is crazy that it has been just been a week since we met. Now I am your girlfriend and going to bed with you, even if it is just to sleep. Maybe we'll kiss for a while and snuggle before we sleep." I smile and bite my lip after saying that.

"Well I'm thankful too. I have made out the best in this deal. Look how beautiful and sexy you are. Every guy will be envious of me. Even getting you in our bed for your kisses and snuggling will be my dream come true. You know, if you bite that lip again. You may get more than what you bargained for. That is hot, and it makes me want to lose control. I want to throw you on our bed and kiss you all over, so you better stop biting your lip." He gives me his sexy smile that shows off his dimples.

I wonder if he is telling me the truth. Yeah, I am biting my lip and smiling at him, daring him to do it.

"I warned you, Alexia. Now be prepared to be kissed," he growls and grabs me. We fall on the bed.

Wait. Did he call this bed *our* bed? Maybe I heard that wrong. He looks into my eyes smiling and starts kissing me all over my face before he starts moving to my neck. I really like this too much and never want him to stop. He keeps going down to my shoulder, and I shiver with each kiss. I feel his kisses it all the way to my toes. This makes me wonder how it will feel if he keeps kissing me farther down, and I welcome it because I want to know the feeling. He knows what he is doing that is for sure.

He starts to pull my shirt down around my chest to kiss me there and I am so into it that I almost forgot about my ugly scar. I quickly jump up from him and pull my shirt back up. I hope he didn't notice my scar. Tonight I am not ready to tell him how I got it.

"Sorry, Phillip, I got carried away and I shouldn't have let that happen. You make me want to do things I've never even thought about before. Please forgive me for teasing you like that. I will try not to do it again." I look at him with a little smile, hoping he really didn't see my ugly scar.

"You have nothing to be forgiven for. I was as into you as you were me. We will have to stop now before I won't be able to stop. Let's get in bed and snuggle. It is getting late and we do have a beach date tomorrow. I need to go to the bathroom. I will be right back to snuggle." He gets up and heads to the bathroom.

While he is in there, I go to the other one and wash my face to cool down. I look in the mirror and pull my shirt down to where he was last kissing me. *Oh no!* He had to have seen my scar. I hope he doesn't ask about it tonight. When I get done, I head back to the bedroom and Phillip is already waiting on me. He gets under the covers and pats a spot for me with a smile on his face.

I smile at him and get in the bed. Then I snuggle up to him. "Goodnight Phillip. You have given me the perfect date today. Thank you for this amazing day." I smile and kiss him.

"Goodnight, my sweet girl. I hope to make everyone of your days better than this one. Thank you for being you and for being mine. Now go to sleep and dream of me." He laughs.

"Why would I dream of you when I have you already in my arms? My dreams have already come true." I really think I have found my Prince Charming. I kiss him once more and fall into a deep sleep curled up next to Phillip.

T. R. LYKINS

Twenty-Two

PHILLIP

I'm so glad the traffic is much lighter than before we left. I really want to get back to my place so we can spend more time together and take a walk on the beach. Since the moon is out, it will be a spectacular view of Alexia when it shines on her. I can only imagine what she will look like, and I bet it isn't even as close to how beautiful she will actually be.

We arrive in no time, and Alexia is in need of the restroom. I let her know there is one on the first floor. She decides to use that one instead of heading up to the condo first. While she is inside, I walk over to see Mark.

"Hey, Mark. How is everything going out on the beach tonight? We plan on taking a walk and I wanted to make sure nothing wild is going on."

"Everything is clear out on the beach around the condo area. I took a walk outside right before you got here. I did see a party at one of the private beach houses and it seems a bit loud. I wouldn't head that way if you want privacy. Is that the girl you had me to put on your list the other day?" Mark smiles at me.

"Yes, she is that girl, and her name is Alexia. I asked her to be my girlfriend and I got lucky when she said yes. You will be seeing her around a lot more, I hope. I am going to take up these bags before Alexia gets finished. If she beats me, will you tell her where I am?"

"Looks like you did get lucky with that girl. She sure is pretty and you better be good to her or she will drop you fast. I will take up your bags for you so you can be here when she comes out. I don't mind. You can head out for that walk while the moon is still bright," Mark says. He is such a really good guy.

"Thanks, man. That would be awesome." I get done saying those words when out comes Alexia with a beautiful smile on her face. All I can do is smile right back at her.

Before Alexia gets close enough to hear, Mark says, "Looks like the both of you are already in love. Congrats, man." I turn and smile at him. I believe it is true that I love her. When I see her look at me like she is right now, I think maybe she feels same thing for me.

I tell her that Mark is taking up our things so we can hit the beach. I grab her purse because she won't need it and hand it to Mark. I thank him again. I take Alexia's hand and we head out to the beach.

I love her hand in mine and I don't let go until I have to take my shoes off before we get to the sand. Once the shoes are off, I put them in our cabana so we won't lose them. I hurry so I can hold her hand again and as I reached for it, I notice the moonlight shining through her blond hair. I was right. I couldn't have guessed this picture-perfect moment. She looks like an angel sent from heaven with a halo around her head.

I noticed that she had her shoes off before I did and that is something else we have in common. I ask her about it and she starts telling me about when she was little she would make sandcastles and pretend she was a princess looking for her Prince Charming. I hope I will be her Prince Charming. I almost laugh out loud at myself at that thought. How did I get here with this girl and fall hopelessly in love with her so fast?

I ask her to tell me another story and she does. The next story is amazing, and it sounds like she loved spending time here at the beach growing up, as much as I did. This story seems a bit similar to a memory I had when I was around thirteen. I broke my leg that year and couldn't get in the water or do much. My brother was upset about me not being able to do stuff with him. All I could do is make it out to the cabana and read, which I did a lot that summer. My brother found this girl who he would make these huge sandcastles with, and that made him happy that year. He would even blush when he would tell my parents and me all about his day with a girl making sandcastles. Maybe tomorrow when we are on the beach we should make sandcastles. She will have a memory with me building them. My brother used to be really good at making sandcastles and would teach me how to make them. We'd build giant sandcastles when we were younger.

She reminds me about getting back to finish our homework. She looks toward Megan's house, and I know what she must be thinking, '*Another party*'. I'm glad we went the other direction. I wonder if Tyler and Jacob ended up at the party. I sure hope they didn't. For once, I want to be selfish and not leave Alexia tonight to be a designated driver. She notices that I am worried and suggests that I call my friends as we get back to our condo. She is smart to pay attention to me, and how I worry about my friends. Especially Jacob, since he has already started this year off partying every day.

She says that she is going to shower. I can call my friends while she is gone. I joke with her and asked if she needs any help showering, but she giggles and says that she doesn't. I will wait until she is ready and not push her because that would be a big step in our relationship. While she is in the shower, I call the guys to see where they are and I am surprised that they didn't go to the party and only went to the football game. The biggest surprise is that Jacob didn't even drink one beer tonight or any hard liquor. That is shocking, but I am glad. I get to be selfish and spend the rest of my night uninterrupted with Alexia.

I decide to jump in the other shower while she is taking hers. I am back out on the balcony and getting comfortable for a few minutes before I hear Alexia coming out of the bathroom. I get a whiff of her scent before she arrives outside and I suddenly remembered how hard it would be to keep tonight at a PG rating. I have to get a hold of myself and not scare her off because I can't keep my hands off her. She comes out looking so sexy in her tank top and short pajamas, I barely can think straight. She walks over to look over the balcony and leans against the rail then turns toward me with a smile. The moonlight is still shining on her and I barely can concentrate on anything but her beauty.

She asks if I called my friends, which brings me back to my senses, and I tell her that I did. I tell her that I was even shocked about Jacob. While she is standing next to me, I get another whiff of her amazing scent and lose it instantly. I pull her down on my lap and kiss her like I am a starving man. She is kissing me with everything she has and she definitely knows how to kiss. I am getting so turned on, and my hands have started roaming her body. She is touching me the same way. I know I have to stop before I can't, but I need a few minutes longer. Alexia tastes like heaven and smells sweet as a breeze. I have to stop now and force myself to do it. I tell Alexia if we don't stop now, I won't be able to.

She tells me that she is sorry for her behavior. Apologizing for kissing me like that is something she should never do. I enjoyed it way too much. I let her know, I was part of that to blame and not to be sorry. Alexia tells me about saving herself for that special person and I want to be everything she deserves and more.

I get up to get our books. I have to take a breather before I take back what I said to her and take her right out on the balcony. When I get back out on the balcony, I have calmed down enough to study. After a while, I notice Alexia yawning a few times and I tell her that it is time for bed. I hope I can control myself when we get to the bed better than when we were hot and heavy on the balcony earlier. I must not think about her kissing me on the balcony and keep myself in check.

We get ready for bed like any other couple would. Watching her do this makes me happy to have her as mine and she doesn't even realize she is turning me on by doing this normal thing. She turns and smiles at me. I ask her what that smile is for, and she surprises me by saying that she is thankful to be with me and being my girlfriend. Alexia bites her lip as she smiles at me. Biting that lip makes me want to grab her and throw her on the bed so I can have my way with her. I tell her this and to stop but she bites it again teasing me and testing to see if I will do what I said I would. Now she will believe me.

I tell her that I warned her. I growl like a predator ready to devour its prey. I grab her up and we land on our bed. Kissing her with a passion I have never felt before, I get so caught up with what I'm doing to her that I forget about waiting for a second. I start kissing her down her neck and she moans likes she is ready for more. That makes me even want more. I keep kissing her neck and then slowly move down to her shoulder.

Alexia's taste is intoxicating causing me to release a kissing frenzy on her body. She is moaning and grinding her body into mine making me want even more of her. I keep moving down her body, getting closer to her breasts. All I can think of right now is that I have to taste her breast so I start to push her shirt down and keep on kissing her. I am close to my destination and we both are into the moment. I don't think we could possibly stop if we keep this up. I don't stop, and Alexia hasn't stopped me yet. I keep kissing and push her shirt down even more. I am kissing between her cleavage and headed over to the nipple. I open my eyes so I can see how beautiful her breasts will be and notice a scar on her sternum. I pay no attention to it because I have another destination in my mind.

All of a sudden Alexia jumps up and pulls her shirt back up telling me once again that she is sorry for teasing me. She asks me to forgive her. I tell her that there is nothing to forgive her for, but we need to stop now before I can't. I tell her that we need to get in bed so we can hit the beach in the morning. I excuse myself to go to the restroom. I really have to go splash cold water on my face and cool down before I get back in bed with Alexia. I dry my face off and look in the mirror. I see a man who has to calm down and now. Then I remember the feeling of her body and how beautiful she is and that is keeping me from cooling off. I have to think of something else, but what?

Wait. What kind of scar was that on Alexia's body? How did she get that long scar? She must have had to have a lot of stiches and have been hurt extremely bad to have that big of a scar. Is that why she took a year off for school when she was younger? Should I ask her about it? Is that why she stopped me from going further? Why has she not told me about what happened to her? So many questions unanswered, but I'm not going to ask her about it tonight. I will wait until she feels that she can trust me enough to tell me, and I hope that will be soon.

I hurry back out and notice that she is gone. Did I scare her off? I look into the hall and hear her in the other bathroom. I go back to our room and get the bed ready. I decide to get into it and wait on Alexia. Not long after I get in the bed, she walks in and smiles. I pull the cover back and pat the bed inviting her to join me. She comes right over and gets right in beside me. She tells me that today was perfect and I let her know that I plan on making every day even better. I mean that.

She kisses me, and I tell her goodnight and to dream of me, which makes me laugh. Alexia tells me that her dreams already came true, because I am already hers. She curls up next to me and goes sound asleep.

I watch her sleep for a while and I feel peace for the first time in a long while. I still wonder though what she had to go through to get that scar. I know one thing it had to be bad, and she had to be strong to overcome that kind of pain. I will ask her about it soon if she doesn't tell me. I want to be the one to take care of her and protect her from now on. While lying with Alexia curled up next to me, I am content. Today with Alexia has been amazing. I soon fall into a deep sleep.

Twenty-Three

ALEXIA

I wake up still curled up to Phillip. He is still in a deep sleep, and I watch him for a little while until I have to go to the bathroom. I ease out of his arms without waking him. I hurry to the bathroom to do my business and brush my hair and teeth. I decide to treat him to breakfast since he is always treating me like a queen. I can't cook much. I will see what is in the kitchen and figure something out.

When I come out of the bathroom, I look to see if he is still a sleep and he is. I quietly exit the bedroom and close the door so I don't wake him. I head to the kitchen and see that the sun is shining through the large windows and glistening over the water. It is extremely beautiful out today and I can't wait to spend it on the beach with Phillip. I check to see what we have to fix and decide on pancakes and bacon. I hurry to fix everything before Phillip gets up and when it is almost finished,

Phillip walks in the kitchen. He smiles sleepily at me and kisses me on my cheek. I kiss him back on his.

"Wow, you fixed me breakfast. Everything smells good and it looks amazing." He snags a piece of bacon.

I playfully smack his hand. "You better not spoil your appetite. I worked hard to make you breakfast. We can eat as soon as the coffee is finished. I hope I didn't mess up the pancakes. I'm not a real good cook. Do you want to eat on the balcony? It is a perfect day out."

"A piece of bacon won't spoil my appetite. I'm a growing boy and need lots to fill this tummy." He pats his rock-hard abs. "Outside will be a perfect place to eat. What do you need me to do to help?"

"You can go have a seat and relax. I am treating you this morning. How do you like your coffee? What else do you like to drink in the morning?"

"I take my coffee with sugar and no cream. A glass of milk would be great with those pancakes. Are you sure you don't need any help carrying anything?"

"No baby I got it today. You just go out and relax." I smile and wink at him.

He laughs before kissing my cheek and heading outside. I get the plates and silverware out. I stack everything up and take it to the table outside. Phillip grins at me and I hurry back to get the rest. It doesn't take me long to have everything set up outside and then we are ready to eat. I am glad because I have worked up an appetite.

Phillip starts filling up his plate as soon as I sit down. I laugh at him. "I hope this food will be good enough to eat. You sure have piled your plate up high."

He takes a bite of the pancakes and moans. "Baby, these pancakes are delicious. And you said you couldn't cook. I believe you lied. Take a bite and see for yourself." He keeps digging into his plate like they are good.

I take a bite and can't believe I made good pancakes. That hasn't ever happened before. Maybe we are just hungry, and that makes them better.

"Well how do you like them, Alexia? Am I right?"

"Yes they are good. These are the best I have ever made. I think it has to be that we are hungry and anything would be good. I am surprised with these. How did you sleep last night? I slept really good and didn't wake up once." I notice Phillip thinking about something for a few seconds and smile. He must be trying to make me feel good about my cooking. That is how he is, always making me happy.

"Well I slept like a baby curled up to this sweet, beautiful girl. Then I woke up and she was gone. I was hoping she would be there when I woke up so that I could kiss her awake. Then I started to smell the bacon and I knew she hadn't run out the door early to leave me. Thank you for this sweet surprise. No one has cooked for me since I left home. I usually grab something easy. You keep surprising me, Alexia. How can one person be so thoughtful?" He reaches over and squeezes my hand.

As I squeeze his hand back, I can feel the tingle I always feel when he touches me. "What time did you want to head out to the beach? We slept late this morning and I needed the extra sleep. You must have needed it to. You slept later than I did."

"I was tired once I fell asleep last night. I had to watch you sleep because you are my angel and you were curled up next to me. I slept the best sleep for the first time in a long while. You know what that means don't you?" He grins and winks at me.

"No, I'm sorry I wish I did. What does it mean?" I asked, and he squeezes my hand looking me in the eyes.

"It means you have to stay with me every night so I can sleep. Since you're my angel, I need you with me to protect me while I sleep."

"You would get tired of me if I stayed with you every night. What would my parents say about paying for my dorm room if I don't stay in it? Kristen might not like me leaving her alone every night either." I actually think he is kidding about me moving in.

"Since the semester just started, I'm sure you can withdrawal from your dorm room. I am sure they have a waiting list of students waiting on a room. I will even go with you to registration to check it out. That would save your parents a lot of money and you can spend that money on when we fly home. I hope you'll go with me when we get a break. Kristen can come over here to see you and you can spend girl time with her too. I don't want you to feel like I have taken away any space from you to do your things. I hope you will take me up on my offer and move in with me. We will take our time and get to know each other that way. Take today and think about it. There is no rush. I would love to have you with me. Don't answer now. Just think about it okay?" He looks serious about this and I believe he means it.

"Okay. I will think about it and it also depends on if I can get a refund on my dorm room. I will have to talk to Kristen and see if she will be mad at me for leaving her when we are becoming friends." I also should speak to my mom about this first to make sure she will not be angry with me.

He kisses my hand. "I will wait on you until you're ready to give me an answer. Now let's get ready to head to the beach." He pulls me up and gives me a heated kiss. Right when I can hardly take much more, he stops and starts gathering the dishes. I help take the rest in and we put them in the dishwasher.

"You can take the bathroom in our bedroom and I will grab my clothes then hit the other one. That way we can change into our beach clothes. Are you sure I can't get you on a surf board today?"

"Not today and maybe never, I would be too scared. I will sit on the beach and watch you. I will enjoy watching you. I have a really good book I want to finish too. Let's see who can change first, I bet I can beat you." I tease him.

He grabs his clothes out of the dresser and smiles. "I will win this bet." He is already headed to the other bathroom. I grab my things and run into the other one. We both come out of each bathroom at the same time.

I smile at him and take a good look at what I will be seeing today at the beach. He is something out of a magazine, even with his scar. I twitch my eyes at him. "Looks like we have a tie. We both must really want to hit the beach soon. Let's get out of here quick so I can work on reading my book."

He looks at me like he is hungry and grins. "I think I might have beaten you by a little bit because I had to cross the hall. I will let that slide for a tie for now since I get a treat and seeing you in this cute bathing suit. This one-piece is sexy on you. I was hoping for a bikini. A teensy one."

"I'm sorry to disappoint you and for not wearing a bikini. I don't like wearing them. I feel more comfortable like this. I don't own a bikini either." I give him a smile. I am sad to see that he is disappointed. I have to wear a one-piece suit to cover my ugly scar and it is too long to cover it up with a bikini.

"It's okay. I think you are perfect in this bathing suit. All your curves are in the right place and keeping them covered up makes me want to see what is under the suit. Mystery is what makes my blood boil. Let's hit the beach before I want to put my hands all over your sexy body. I will grab the beach bag that is in the hall closet that has the towels and lotion in it."

Phillip kisses my cheek and walks out to the hall. I still need to tell him the truth and the real reason I can't wear a bikini. Who would want to see my ugly scar? I have learned to appreciate it because of what it means to me. It means a second chance at life, and I am grateful, but most people would look at my scar like I have a deformity on my body. *Quit feeling sorry for yourself and go have fun with Phillip*, I think to myself. I go out in the hall and Phillip looks up from the bag.

"Looks like everything is still in here and ready to go. Do you want me to grab some bottles of water and snacks to take with us?"

"Yeah, that would be great. Can I put my book in the bag?"

"Sure. We have plenty of room. Here is suntan lotion. You might want to put it on now before you get sand on your body." He hands me the lotion.

"Thanks. That is a great idea. I will need help with my shoulders and back. Will you help me? I will do yours too."

"Of course I will help you. Any time I get to touch you, I look forward to it. I will grab the snacks and then rub you down."

I lotion up while he finishes up putting things in the bag. As I finish with my second leg and start to put it down, he grabs it. "You missed a spot here." He begins rubbing my calf. I know I didn't miss that spot, but telling him to stop is out of the question. It felt so good. I might have moaned a little and I blush.

He grins that sexy grin at me. "Does that feel good that I am putting lotion on your leg?"

"It does when you do it. I've never had anyone rub my leg with lotion before and I believe you covered it." He keeps rubbing and smiling. "I think my shoulders need lotion on them."

He lets go and puts lotion in hands, goes straight to my shoulders, and starts rubbing them. I lean closer to him, and I can't help myself for enjoying the moment. He keeps on rubbing, and I lean even closer to him so that my butt is right against him. Then I feel how much he likes it too. I move away quickly and he laughs at me.

He pulls me back to him so I am touching his body and whispers in my ear. "You do this to me every time I am around you. Don't doubt how you make me feel. I want you really bad. I am being a gentleman and will wait on you to be ready. Remember you do this to me. Let's get out of here before I lose control." He lets go and moves away from me. I feel lost and miss him already. What is happening to me? I never have felt this way before around any guy.

I walk over and kiss him on his cheek. "Come on big boy and show me how you ride those waves." I walk toward the door and hear him growl. I smile to myself and I don't turn around because I might not get out the door. I want him as much as he wants me and I better get outside now. I'm still smiling when I get to the elevator. Phillip catches up to me as the doors open.

He pulls me up next to his body and whispers in my ear, "I will show you how I ride the waves. You can see how smooth I can be." He lets go of me and I giggle. The doors open up on the ride down and Phillip's neighbor gets on the elevator. Phillip smiles at him. "Good morning, Jack. How are you on this fine day?"

Jack smiles, "Oh I'm doing good. Looks like you're doing better than me." The doors open and out Jack goes, smiling and shaking his head.

I look at Phillip as we get off and he has the biggest grin on his face, "He is right, I am doing better than him." He grabs me and kisses me in the lobby. Then he takes my hand and out the door to the beach we go.

I put my sunglasses on as soon as the bright sun hits my face. Today at the beach is going to the best ever and I can't wait, until I see Phillip out over the water riding the waves. I doubt that I will even get to read my book. We stop at the same cabana we used last night when we walked on the beach. "This is our cabana and we can leave our stuff here and go do whatever we want. No one will bother our stuff here." He lays out our towels on the chair and pulls his shirt off. *Holy Wow*! The sun shining on him and that makes Phillip look like a God. His body is ripped and tanned all over. How in the world am I going to keep my hands off him? What has gotten into me all of the sudden? All I can think of is this sexy guy and his body on mine. Glad I put my sunglasses on or he would know I am staring at him. I am even enjoying the view.

"Well if you don't want to hit the waves with me, how about I take a chair next to the water so you can be closer to me?"

"Yes that would be great. I would like that." I walk behind him and fan myself so he doesn't see how worked up I am.

Phillip puts a chair close to the water and I go claim it. He has his board in his other hand and hits the water as soon as I'm settled. He paddles out and soon he is up riding that board like a pro. He must have been doing this for years because he is really good at surfing. He surfs for a while then comes in, flops his board beside me, and sits on it.

"Wow! The waves are awesome today. Alexia, you should try it just once. I will go out and help hold the board so you can get up on it. How about it, my girl?"

"I don't think I could do that even if you held the board for me. The only thing I probably could do is lie on my tummy on the board and hope I wouldn't turn over." I laugh.

"How about I go out and hold it and you ride on your stomach? That would be fun too. Look at all these other people out riding that way. You should try it once." He smiles at me, and that makes me feel brave.

"Okay. I will try it once. Don't laugh if I fall off."

"I would never laugh at you. You're going to have a great time. Let's go. The water is really warm today and that makes it perfect."

He pulls me up from the chair and puts my chair back where the tide won't carry it out into the ocean. Phillip lifts the board up and we head out into the water. The water does feel good on my skin, and I like being in the water with Phillip. I hope I don't make a fool of myself or drown us both.

"Okay this should be far enough for you to ride out a little ways." He holds the board still as he can and I can get on it.

First, I sit on it, to get the feel of the waves, and they are awesome. I get brave enough to lie down on my stomach, and as soon as I do this, Phillip lets go. I am riding my first wave ever and it feels great. I am almost back on to the shore when another wave hits me and I fly off the board. Phillip must have been right behind me the whole time, because he catches me before I go under the water.

He looks at me with concern on his face. "Are you okay Alexia?" He pulls me close to him.

I start laughing. "Phillip, that was awesome and I loved it! Thanks for catching me before I went under. I think I will give it up though. You look like I scared you to death."

"You did scare me. I almost didn't get to you in time. Girl, you're going to be the death of me. You really want to stop now after your first time and liking it so much?"

"Yes. Once is good for me. Now I can say I rode the waves. I think my spot is on the beach. That wore me out." I smile and go to my chair. "You go ahead and ride the waves as long as you want, Phillip. I will be here watching." That really did make me more tired than I put on. Maybe my body isn't up for such hard physical exercise yet.

"I think I will ride a few more times. Then we will make a sand castle. You up for making a sandcastle with me?"

"Yes, that would be great. Take your time and I will wait here until you get back."

He comes over and kisses me on my lips. "I will be back soon."

Then he is back to surfing. How does he do that so long? Once wore me out and I didn't even stand up. I guess the waves are too rough for my fragile body. I need to work on that so I can keep up with Phillip. He makes it look so easy.

Before long, Phillip comes back in and sits beside me. "Let's make a sandcastle and make it the way you want to."

"I told you that I'm not too good at it. We can make one if you want to."

"I saw some buckets by the cabana. I will go grab them and be right back." He kisses my cheek and takes his board with him. He is back in a minute and looks like he is excited to get started. "Look what else I found! Some shovels too."

"You are going to spoil me with this shovel. I would use my hands when I was little. This will make it much easier. Time to get this castle built."

We start building the sandcastle and before we know it, it has grown into a huge castle. Watching Phillip work and the way he moves his body makes my heart skip a beat. The sun and sand on his body are stunning to look at and his muscles move like a mass of perfection. I think my mind may have gone to the gutter because all I can think of is how wonderful those muscles would work with my body. I think this princess has found her real life Prince Charming. I start collecting some shells to put on the castle to finish it off. Once we've covered the castle with the shells, we step back to admire our work.

"Alexia those shells make it perfect. We made a castle for a princess to live in. You, Alexia, are the princess of this castle. I hope you can find your Prince Charming." He grins at me.

I look up at him and smile. "I might have already found him, Phillip." I take his hand in mine and we step closer to the castle. "You are my Prince Charming. Would you like to share this castle with me?"

"Yes, I will be your Prince Charming. You will have to share my other castle with me too. Move in with me, my beautiful princess." He stares into my eyes and I can see love in his.

"You make it hard to say no, my prince. I am not going to say no, but yes, I will."

He pulls me close to his body and kisses me beside our sandcastle. He doesn't stop kissing me until we hear someone coming up behind us.

"Get a room Phillip." We look up and see Megan standing right behind us with her arms crossed, smirking at us. "You know Phillip, I could give you a lot more than she can. Looks like you're going to mess up and miss your chance with me. I will give you one last chance. If you say no, I won't give you another."

Wow. Did she ask Phillip that in front of me right now? This girl has some major problems.

Phillip looks at me and then back to Megan. "I'm sorry Megan. I already have my princess. I don't need you and I won't ever ask you to ever be with me. Alexia is my girlfriend and we are going to be together for a long time. Please leave us alone so we can spend the rest of our day together."

"I see you really don't know what you're missing out on. Before you make your mind finally up, I can give you a taste first." She stands there looking at Phillip and she even licks her lips at him. I really want to punch her face in and right when I make my mind up to do it, Phillip hugs me closer. He must have read my mind and knew what I was going to do.

"Megan, leave now. I don't want a taste of anything you have. Nor do I want anything else from you. I have already told you no and I would advise you to leave now." Phillip looks at her like he is getting angry.

"Fine! I will leave and you will regret this." Megan storms off back toward her house and I am glad.

"I'm sorry for that princess. She messed up our date. I wanted today to be perfect. You know I have never wanted anything from her and I never would." He kisses me tenderly on my lips and smiles, showing off his cute dimples.

"She hasn't messed up our date. She can be a bit dramatic. I have heard you each time turning her down and I'm glad you have chosen me over her."

"Baby there is no comparison between you and her. You are the best thing ever for me and I never want to be without you. Thanks for being mine and saying yes to moving in with me, my princess is going to be in our home every night." He pulls me close with a gentle but loving hug. "I don't know about you, but I'm beginning to be starved. Hitting the waves and building our castle has made me hungry. Let's go in and get food for our tummies." He smacks his stomach.

"I am getting hungry too. All this hard work has made me famished."

We get all of our things and head back up to the condo like a normal couple, but I know I'm not a normal girl. This girl has been broken and pieced back together. I have to tell Phillip soon. Maybe I should tell him before I move in with him. I have had such a wonderful day and I would hate to do it today and mess it up. I will wait a little longer and then I hope he will forgive me for not telling him sooner. I will call my mom soon to talk to her about how I feel about Phillip and let her know my plans about moving in with him. This decision makes me scared and happy at the same time. I hope waiting on telling him doesn't come back to haunt me later on.

Twenty-Four

PHILLIP

As soon as I woke up, I could feel that something was off. I haven't slept that well in a really long time. The car accident did a number on my sleeping habits. Sometimes I would wake up as soon as I would go to sleep or other times I would wake up in a cold sweat. Today is different and I have to figure out why. It comes to me with a whiff that smells just like bacon and my tummy starts to growl. I look over to the pillow and remember that Alexia had slept next to me. That is the reason I had slept well, and I pick up her pillow and smell it. *Yeah*, I know that sounds *creepy*. I wish I could smell her instead. That would have made this morning perfect. I get another whiff of food cooking and my tummy growls again. I get up and go to the bathroom. I hurry to brush my morning breath away so I can see what my woman has cooked me. My woman is already making me grin this morning. I am lucky to have her in my life.

I enter the kitchen and see the bright sun shining through the huge windows. Normally that would make me happy. What I see standing in my kitchen is heaven-sent. The most beautiful girl, my woman, is making me breakfast and I never knew having her here would make my heart grow bigger, because I keep filling it with more love for her. I suddenly know how the Grinch who stole Christmas felt when he realized what love was and his heart grew. Right now at this moment, I can feel my heart growing.

I smile at her and kiss her on her cheek. She tells me that it is almost ready, and to go have a seat on the balcony and she will bring the food out. I steal a piece of bacon and she smacks my arm telling me I will spoil my appetite. She will soon find out how much I can eat and I let her know it won't be spoiled. Alexia asks how I like my drinks in the morning and I tell her. I kiss her and head outside.

I sit there for a few minutes and think that this is something I would like having every morning - waking up with her. Not the cooking, but that is a nice perk. I like waking up and having her around. I like that she is learning what I want to drink, and I want her to learn everything about me, as I want to learn everything about her.

When she brings out the first of the food, I smile at her. Not because of the food, but because I know I want her here with me every morning. I wonder if I asked her this soon to move in with me if she would. Maybe I should wait. I don't want to pressure her because this morning is perfect.

She finally sits down beside me, and I know she is my home and I need her with me. I start piling up the pancakes, and Alexia tells me that I should taste them first. No way will I do that. I'm going to eat these pancakes even if they are horrible because she wanted to surprise me with them. I take a bite and I am so glad that they are delicious. I tell her to eat and see how good they are and she does. I see this surprised look on her face. She should have known they would be good.

Alexia keeps asking little things like how I slept, and I let her know that I slept like a baby. I love that she wants to know stuff like this. I even ask her if she slept well, and she did. That puts a smile on my face, and I know I have to ask her to move in. I tell her that I slept the best I had in a long time and even threw a joke in saying that she knows what that means.

She looks at me and says that she doesn't know. I squeeze her hand to give myself some courage to ask her. When I get done asking she tells me that I would get tired of her, but no way would that happen, and I let her know it wouldn't. She asks about her dorm cost and Kristen. I tell her that she would probably get her money back, because the semester just started and I would go with her to ask. I let her know that Kristen can come over and they can have girl time whenever they want. I know the guys will be around, so why can't she have friends over? I decide to tell her to take her time and think about it. I hope she says yes.

Alexia wants to go to the beach and tells me that we slept late. That is another surprise. I usually get up early every day. She bets me that she can get dressed faster than I can and I let her know she can't. The bet is on. I get up and grab the dishes to take back in and hurry to put them in the dishwasher. I am dying to see this girl in her bikini. I hope I can keep my hands off her or we may get into trouble.

We head to the bedroom, and I grab my trunks and t-shirt then head to the other bathroom. It doesn't take long to throw them on, and as soon as I get into the bedroom, out comes Alexia. She doesn't have a bikini on, but her bathing suit is gorgeous on her. The way it hugs her body is amazing and takes my breath away.

I'm not disappointed that she has a one-piece bathing suit on. I might be a little, but I tell her that she is beautiful in her bathing suit, which she is. Maybe it, will keep my mind out of the gutter this way. Who am I kidding? With her moving around the bedroom and the way her body moves, I feel my trunks growing tight. I have to think about something else, but what? I wonder why she doesn't like bikinis. She makes a point to say that she never wears them. Is it because she is afraid to show her scar? I have a scar and I don't care about mine. Maybe she thinks it is ugly, but it's not. Soon I will have to ask her how she got it. I hope she will tell me before I have to ask.

I tell her that I am going to grab the beach bag, which is always ready. I hand her the sunblock so she doesn't burn. I don't usually put much on myself. She looks like she will burn with her beautiful fair skin. I even start rubbing some on mine so she will. While I watch her apply the lotion, she makes it hard for my mind not to go back to the gutter. She rubs it so delicately all over her exposed skin. She has one leg up rubbing lotion on it. I grab it and rub her leg like she didn't apply enough lotion to it. A guy has to touch his girl any chance he gets. Then she asks me to get her shoulders and neck. I step closer to her and grab the lotion for her shoulders. How can I refuse that kind of request? I start applying the lotion to her shoulders and get a bit carried away. I am so turned on that I pull her next to me and let her know that is what she does to me. What does she do? Well she just wiggles that butt and that makes me crazy. She is lucky I don't throw her over my shoulder and take her to the bedroom. She tries to wiggle and get away. I pull her close and whisper in her ear that this is what she is doing to me and that we better get outside.

You would think this girl would run out the door, but no. She is a *vixen*. She tells me that she wants to see how I ride the waves then turns and heads out the door without looking back. I may have growled when she said that. Now I have to take a few seconds to calm down before I can follow her. I have to run to the elevator to catch up with her, but at least I am calmer than before.

She is smiling when I get on the elevator, and this is going to be the longest ride down ever. I can smell her sweet scent because we are so close to each other. We stop, and Jack gets on the elevator. Jack can tell by my grin that I must be thinking of things, I shouldn't. I ask him how he is doing right when we get to the bottom floor. He tells me that he is doing fine as he steps off. Then he smiles a wicked smile and says that I'm doing better than him.

I laugh at that old man as we get off the elevator. I pull Alexia into my arms and kiss her right in the lobby. I don't care who sees us. I had to kiss her right then. I put her hand in mine to lead her out to the beach before I hit the elevator button to take us back up to the condo.

Finally getting outside, I take her over to our cabana so we can leave our stuff. No one bothers things here because of security. Plus this area is private for the owners. I lay out the towels on the chairs and pull my shirt off. I glance at Alexia and I see that she is blushing. I straighten up and I might have flexed a few stomach muscles and arms. She thinks that I'm not noticing her looking at me through her sunglasses; her blushing gives her away. I have to put on a really big show for her. It really is her fault for making me growl before we came down to the beach. I have to tease her like she does me.

Okay I better get in the water to clear my nasty mind of Alexia. She does deserve better than that. I really don't want to leave her up here at the cabana. That seems too far away. I suggest taking a chair down next to the water and she agrees. Now she will be closer to me. I grab a chair in one hand and my surfboard in the other. I have to hit those waves fast and get some space between us, but not too much space. I like that Alexia will be close by me.

Once she is in the chair watching me, I hit the water. Surfing always clears my head and relaxes me. I have been coming out here and hitting the waves since I was little. It keeps me fit now. When I was little, it took me a while to learn to get up on the board. I was on a boogie board one day when I first saw some guys surfing. I knew that day that I had to learn to surf. My brother was much faster at learning than I was, but now I can do it as well as anyone around.

I stay out for a little bit and I can still see Alexia in her chair watching me, which I like. One last wave and then I am going to see if she will try it. As I am riding the wave in, I noticed Megan and some friends are out on the beach, and I'm glad she hasn't noticed us yet. I hurry to get to Alexia because I know Megan will start if she sees us together.

I set the board down beside Alexia and ask her if she wants to ride some waves. She seems a bit scared to try. I let her know that she can ride the board on her tummy and then she finally says she will try it. I take her out and hold the board as still as I can so she can get up on it. Finally she does and she rides a really big wave, but she doesn't even know she is on a big one. I get a little scared for her. I follow her as fast as I can in the ocean water.

Oh no! She is going to go under. As she starts to go under, I get close to her and grab her up in my arms. I think she is scared, but when I see the smile on her face. I am happy and relieved. I ask if she wants to go again. She says no quickly and that makes me happy. That was such a great ride for her that I don't push her to do it again.

I get her back to her chair and she sits down fast. Maybe that wave was too rough for a beginner. She looks happy but a little tired. I worry about why that wore her out. I remembered that my first time out made me tired, so I don't ask her about it. I tell her that I am going out for a few more times and she tells me to take my time. Really I wanted to make sure Megan is gone. I ride a few more times and noticed that Megan has left. I am glad for that. Now I can spend the rest of the day with Alexia.

I get back to the beach and ask Alexia if she is ready to make a sandcastle. She nods her head and I tell her that I saw some buckets at the cabana. I go get them and luckily I find shovels too. I know that these buckets and shovels have been at our cabana for a long time because my brother and I use to use them. I make it back and hand her the shovel.

She surprises me again by saying that she always used her hands as a shovel. My brother did that when he was little too. We get started on our castle and it is looking really good by the time we are done. She goes to find some shells to put on it and I remember what she said when she was little that she would think about finding her Prince Charming. I tell her that I hope she can find her Prince Charming someday. I hope that I'm the one she is looking for.

She looks up at me with those big blue eyes and tells me that she already found him. Yes, my heart grew again, and if it keeps this up, it won't fit into my chest soon. She even asks me to share her castle with her. I tell her that I will, only if she says yes to share our other castle with me. I really thought she would turn me down, but then she surprisingly agrees. I pull her close and kiss her right beside our sandcastle. I had to make it official with an amazing kiss from my princess.

We are really getting into our kiss when I hear that squeaky voice interrupt us. Megan is standing beside us, and she looks like she is mad. For what reason, I have no idea. Who knows with Megan?

"Get a room Phillip." Megan is standing right behind us with her arms crossed and smirking at us, "You know, Phillip, I could give you a lot more than she can. Looks like you're going to mess up and miss your chance with me. I will give you one last chance but if you say no, I won't give you another chance"

I look at Alexia and then back to Megan. "I'm sorry Megan. I already have my princess. I don't need you and I won't ask you to ever be with me. Alexia is my girlfriend and we are going to be together for a long time. Please leave us alone so we can spend the rest of our day together."

"I see you really don't know what you're missing out on. Before you make your mind finally up, I can give you a taste first." Megan just stands there looking at me and she even licks her lips. I can feel Alexia tense up, and I hug her close so she won't leave me. Megan is very strange and annoying.

"Megan, leave now. I don't want a taste of anything you have. Nor do I want anything else from you. I have already told you no and I would advise you to leave now." I start to get angry with her because she is trying to mess up what I have with Alexia. I won't let that happen.

"Fine! I will leave and you will regret this." Megan storms off and I couldn't be happier.

I turn to see if Alexia is all right and I tell her that I am sorry for that. I didn't want Megan to mess up our date. I kiss Alexia on the lips and smile at her. Alexia tells me that Megan hasn't messed it up even though Megan can be dramatic. I agree with Alexia about that, and I can add to that by saying Megan is wacko. I let Alexia know that she is the only one for me.

Alexia tells me she is hungry so we gather our things up so we can go eat. While we do this, I look around for Megan. She said that I would be sorry for turning her down. I have to make sure she doesn't do anything to mess this up for Alexia and me. I want this relationship to last, and I don't want any girl's drama messing up our good thing we have going. Now that Alexia has said yes to move in with me, I look forward to spending each day with her. My tummy growls and I pick up our pace so we can eat. Got to feed my princess so she doesn't starve on my watch.

T. R. LYKINS

Twenty-Five

ALEXIA

The rest of the weekend flew by and we spent it talking. Yes kissing too. Maybe some hand roaming, but that is all. We keep saying we need to get to know one another before we take the next step and I need to tell him my secret before that happens also.

I haven't officially moved in yet because we don't leave the condo until Monday to go to class. It was hard to leave Phillip's arms on Monday. They make me feel special and I was still afraid if I left that somehow he would find out about my secret. I know this weekend would have been the perfect time to tell him, but every time I thought about doing it, something made me change my mind.

So now, on this Monday, I have to leave him early, because I don't have many clothes with me. As soon as I pulled out of the parking lot of the condo, my phone rings. I look at the number and smile. I bet you thought it was Phillip, but really, it is only my mom.

"Hello, mom."

"Hi, baby girl. How was your weekend?"

"My weekend was perfect, Mom. I spent the whole weekend with my boyfriend, Phillip." That must have made her drop the phone. There was a thumping sound that wasn't from my mom. Yes, I tell her everything. She has been by my side for so long, and she deserves my honesty.

"Alexia, did you forget to tell me something? Like when did you get a boyfriend? You barely have been in school and you didn't mention a guy to me the last time we talked. Wait a minute, is this the reason for the conversation the last time we spoke, when you wanted to know about Dad and me?"

"Yes, Mom, it is about our last conversation. I fell for this boy so quickly it scared me and I didn't know what to do. He feels the same way as I do. It still scares me. When he asked me to be his girlfriend, I couldn't say no to him. He treats me like a princess and even calls me that."

"This is a big step for you Alexia and if you're happy then I will be. You have always known what you wanted and your judgment has been incredible. I hope you don't rush this relationship and take everything slow. I'm glad he treats you good. The only thing is that you make sure he knows about your past so he can be prepared if something happens to you. Have you told him yet?"

"No Mom, I haven't told him. We have something in common though. He has had a liver transplant. I am sure he will be able to accept me with my borrowed heart. I have been waiting for the right time to tell him. He is also from Cleveland.

He has asked me to travel with him when it is time to come home. You will like him Mom, and I can't wait until break so you can meet him. Maybe we can come for Labor Day weekend."

"Alexia, you have spent the whole weekend with him. What kept you from telling him? He told you that he has a liver transplant. That would have been the perfect time to tell him about yours."

"I know Mom. I met him on the plane coming here and he told me about it then before I really knew him. I didn't feel comfortable to tell him then, so I kept it to myself. Now I can't get it out and I am afraid of how he will act once I do. By the way, he has asked me to move in with him at his condo and if I do, it will save you and Dad money. I need to tell him first though. You won't mind if I do move in with him?" I don't tell her that I already told him yes. This is a first for me. Why am I all of a sudden keeping things from Mom and Phillip? I must be a coward. This relationship thing is so new to me.

"Well you are full of surprises today Alexia. You know you can't get pregnant with the medicine you're taking, right? You need to talk to your doctors about birth control when you come home. Please use protection if you do have sex, okay? I wouldn't mind about you moving in with him, but you have let dad and me meet him, and tell him your past first. If you don't that will make this relationship fall apart and you don't want to start out with secrets this big in the way. He is from Cleveland and his name is Phillip? What is his last name?"

"I will tell him today. I know I can't get pregnant and we aren't having sex. Phillip's last name is Ryan. Do you know any Ryan's in Cleveland?"

Mom is quiet for a minute, and this is so unlike her. "Yes Alexia, I do. When did he have his transplant and where did he get his liver donated from?" The way she asks me this sounds off a bit.

"He got it when he was seventeen about five years ago I guess, because he is twenty two. He took off a year from college. He was in a car wreck with his brother, when a drunk driver hit them. His brother died but had signed his driver's license to be a donor and Phillip ended up with his brother's liver. Phillip said he had a hard time accepting it although he was a perfect match. Oh, I just thought of something. We must have had our surgeries about the same time. Now that is a coincidence, don't you think, Mom?"

"Yes dear. Do me a favor and talk to him about this tonight okay. Don't wait another minute. As soon as you tell him, let him know about the time frame of both of your transplants. I want you to be happy, and don't keep this from him. It might hurt him or you down the road. Promise me that you will do this today?" she pleads with me.

"Okay, Mom. If you think it is that important, then I promise to do it today. I have made it back to my dorm and I need to get ready for class. By the way, we aren't doing anything that will get me pregnant so don't worry. I love you and talk to you later."

"I love you too Alexia. Please tell him today. I will call back tomorrow to check on you. Bye." Mom hangs up.

I felt like she was keeping something from me, and calling me back so soon seems a bit strange too. Now I will wonder what it is. I open the door to my dorm room and see Kristen getting ready to go to class.

She smiles at me. "I can see that the date was a good one. So good it happened to last all weekend. Tell me if Phillip is as good as his reputation says he is?"

"It was a really awesome date that did last all weekend. I still don't know if he is as good as his reputation says. We spent the weekend together and that is all for now." I smile at her.

"Now you have to give me more details than that. I know you can't hang out with a guy all weekend and not have sex."

"I promise we didn't have sex. We kissed and made out a bit, but that is it. We are waiting until we get to know each other better. I can tell you one thing though. I am now Phillip's girlfriend and he has asked me to move in with him. I don't know if I should leave you. I know this relationship is happening fast and it is scary. I love being with him."

"You better leave me and move in with that hunk of man. If I were in your shoes I would have moved this weekend. Tell him yes, but you have to keep in touch with me. Now that you have a boyfriend, you better not forget me."

"He told me you could come over anytime you wanted to. I am sure his friends will be over. Do you really think this isn't happening too fast? It is scary. My mom told me her and Dad knew as soon as they met. Who does this at this age and time? Isn't that something that would have happened years ago and not now?"

"If you're both on the same page about really liking each other this quick and not even having sex it means you are special to him. No guy would keep you all weekend and not try not to have sex unless he likes you a lot. Have you already told your mom about this? Just asking because you mentioned her."

"Yes, she called me on the way here and I told her everything. I don't keep secrets from my mom. She told me I was good at making my decisions, only I needed to tell him about my past and told me to do that before moving in with him.

Even made me to promise to tell him today. I thought that was a bit weird, making me promise."

"What is it about your past that she wants you to tell him? Do you happen to have a shady past Alexia?" She grins up at me.

I tell her everything about my transplant and I even tell her about Phillip's because we have so much in common. I happen to tell her when and where we both are from. When I get done, she just sits there looking at me.

"Oh no. You think he will be mad at me and break up with me because I didn't tell him sooner?"

"No. I think he will figure out what I just did." She sort of looks pale when she says this.

"What did you figure out?" I am worried now by the look on her face. She is looking at me with sympathy and I am scared of what she is going to say.

"Think about what you just told me Alexia, and focus on the time frame. Your mom knows people named Ryan from where you live and you both had surgery about the same time. What if you and Phillip had your surgeries on the same day?"

Is she saying what I think she is saying? Does this mean I may have Phillip's brother's heart? That can't be possible, can it? Is this why I kept this from him unknowingly? Does my mom know whose heart that I have? I thought the doctors aren't supposed to tell you who the donor is. Everything happened so fast that day when I got my surgery. The doctors had said I wouldn't make it until the morning. Then I got a heart at the last minute. I was even on my last heartbeat.

I have all these things running through my mind and I am wondering what I am supposed to think about all of this. I look up at Kristen, "Do you think that it is possible that I have Phillip's brother's heart? What do you think he will say about that, if he finds this out? He has had a hard time getting over losing his brother. What if what I am feeling for Phillip has something to do with that? I am so confused right now, and I don't think I can go to class." I sit down on the bed and put my hands over my heart because it is hurting.

"Calm down, Alexia. All those questions are something you will be able to answer soon, I'm sure. Don't stress over it. You can't be having feelings for Phillip because of a heart. That can't be possible, can it? What did the doctors say about this kind of thing?

"Well they keep saying that once it is accepted in your body that it becomes yours. It is keeping my body alive, but it had a hard time accepting my body. I had to stay in the hospital a long time. Phillip said the same thing about his liver. Maybe his brother knew something we didn't. Maybe we shouldn't have gotten his organs and maybe he isn't at rest because we have them."

"Alexia, you know that isn't true. This was a gift from Phillip's brother to both of you. Maybe he knew you both were meant for each other and knew this would be what brought you together. Who knows about this kind of stuff and if he had some kind premonition? I think you should talk to Phillip and more to your mother about it. Don't stress over this because I'm sure that isn't healthy for you. Think of it as a blessing. I hate to have to leave you now, but I have to go to class. I will skip if you want me to." She smiles and hugs me.

"No skipping for you Kristen. You go on and I will be fine. I will call Mom and talk to her more."

"Are you sure you don't want me to stay?" she asks, and I know she would stay. I probably need her right now, but I can't ask her not to go to class.

"No, I will be fine. I promise. Go ahead and go. I need to get cleaned up for class too." I tell her this so she doesn't worry.

"That is great that you're going to go. Don't let this stop you from doing anything. Talk to them and everything will be fine." She hugs me and then leaves.

I don't think I can go to class. I am so tired all of a sudden. I lie on my bed for a minute and soon I start to cry. This is scary, and I am afraid of what will happen between Phillip and me. I have heard about people getting donor organs and then saying that they feel that person. The doctors keep telling me that it isn't possible though.

What I feel for Phillip is so strong, and it makes me wonder if I am feeling this way for him because of me or because those are his brothers' feelings. Right now I can't go to class and sit beside Phillip. He will know something is wrong with me as soon as he sees me. Then he will demand I tell him, but I need to think first and get my head straight. I should get up and head to the beach so I can think. This always helps me when I need to clear my head. I will lie here on my bed for a few minutes before I go to the beach. Before I know it, I have cried myself to sleep.

Twenty-Six

PHILLIP

Spending the weekend with Alexia was the greatest time I have had in a long time. We talked and got carried away a few times when we were kissing. I even had to take a couple of cold showers. I managed to keep my perverted mind straight enough to enjoy Alexia's company. I slept the greatest I have in a long time since Alexia was staying with me. Monday morning we snuggled and kissed for as long as she could before she had to leave me. It was hard to let her leave me. I knew she had to get clothes so we can get to class on time. Today, I'm making her bring her stuff over to really move in. That way we can have more time in the mornings.

Not too soon after she leaves, I get a knock on the door. I go see who it is. Not many people are allowed past security. I am hoping it is Alexia and now I realize that I need to get her a key made.

I open the door and Tyler and Jacob come right on in. "Hey, guys. What have you been doing this weekend? I haven't heard from you two."

"We went out to a couple parties. We didn't drink and drive so we didn't have to call you. That way you could be free to spend with Alexia. I guess since you never called you had a good date with her." Tyler grins.

"Yeah, man. Dump us for a hot chick. Well come to think of it, I would dump you guys for a hot chick if I had one. Hopefully you finally got lucky with her." Jacob winks.

"Guys, what I have with Alexia is more than physical. For the first time in my life, I now have an official girlfriend. I asked Alexia to be my girlfriend this weekend and she said yes." I look at the guys and know what is coming next.

Jacob starts questioning first. "Why did you do that? You barely met her and now after one date, you decide to ask her to be your girlfriend? Who does that, man? Now you will be tied down and can't hang out with us. What about all the girls waiting to go out with you?"

"Jacob, I know you don't understand this. Since the first day that I met Alexia, I have felt something for her. The more I am around her, the more I want to know her. Alexia and I both want the same things, and you guys can come over anytime. Alexia will have friends over too. I don't care about any other girl. Alexia is it for me."

Tyler jumps in. "Wait. What did you mean by Alexia will have friends over too?"

"Well beside Alexia being my girlfriend, I also asked her to move in with me." I grin at them and let that soak in. I can see by the looks on their faces what is coming next.

Jacob looks at me with big eyes. "What has driven you to do that, man? Have you lost your mind? Having Alexia stay with you after one date has made you lose it. This means never hooking up with other girls. I couldn't do that myself."

Tyler jumps in, "You must have got lucky this weekend and it must have been amazing for you to ask her to move in."

Jacob continues. "Wait, does she have any hot friends?"

I look at them for a minute before I answer them, because I can't believe their questions. "Guys, will you listen to yourselves? No, I haven't had sex with Alexia. No, I don't want any other girl. I have fallen in love with her, and yes it has happened fast. Everything between us has happened extremely fast, and for the first time I'm enjoying it. We are waiting to get to know each other before we have sex, as we should. Guys, once you both find that girl who makes you want to be a better person and you fall in love with her, you will understand. Alexia has a friend name Kristen and she is very pretty. Leave Kristen alone. I'm sure Alexia wouldn't want you to hurt her friend. What are the both of you doing here so early?"

Tyler grins at me. "Well, we are going home from a party at Megan's house that lasted all night. We haven't been to bed yet. I guess we should go to our dorm and get ready for classes."

Jacob laughs. "You missed a great party, man. Guess who got lucky with Megan last night?"

"Did you, Jacob? With Megan? Man, she was mad at me Saturday and even practically threw herself at me on the beach. I was with Alexia when she did that. Hope you know she might be using you to get at me. She did say she would make me sorry for turning her down. She is all yours. Hopefully she doesn't hurt you, Jacob." I wonder why she did that with Jacob after I turned her down. I hope it had nothing to do with me. He is my friend and I hope she doesn't hurt him.

"Phillip, you know I was just using her too. I don't have feelings for her, and it was just a hook-up. She wasn't that good either. Don't worry about me. That was a one-time thing with Megan. Come to think of it, she did ask if you were coming last night, and once I told her no, she did start flirting with me until we ended up in her bedroom. I know you don't like her or I wouldn't have taken it that far. Don't worry about me. I'm a love-them-and-leave-them type of guy. Not ready to settle down yet." Jacob grins at me.

"Glad to hear you're still the same Jacob, as always. Guys, I have to go to my class. If I don't leave now, I will be late. I will go down with you. How many classes do you guys have today?" I grab my keys and lock the door.

"I have two today. Jacob has one late one. He gets to go to sleep when we get to the dorm. I might get a nap in between classes. How about you, Phillip?" Tyler pushes the evaluator button.

"I have one today and it is Biology. That is the class I have with Alexia. Glad the professor picked us to do our project together. We almost have it finished." I look at my watch and really needed to hurry. "Got to hurry guys or I will be late. See you later." I hurry to my car and get to school. I have already been missing Alexia and can't wait until I see her in class.

I make it school with a few minutes to spare. I get out of my car and as soon as I close the door, I see Megan coming my way. *No!* I don't have time for this this early in the morning. She must be stalking me or something. Every time I get to school or when I leave each class, she is always around. What do I have to do to get her to leave me alone?

"Good morning Phillip. I wanted to tell you I am over you and I have found someone else." Megan smiles at me with a sneaky smile. I wonder if this someone new is Jacob. "You missed out with me, Phillip. We could have been great together. You chose the wrong girl. Please don't miss me too much." Poor Jacob, I hope he knows what he got himself in for.

"Megan, congratulations. I am glad you finally found someone." I say and start to walk off. She grabs my arm and stops me.

"*Really, Phillip!* I see how jealous you are that I moved on. All you have to do is say the word and I will be all yours." She even has the nerve to try to kiss me on my cheek. I pull myself away from her quickly.

"I'm not leaving Alexia for you, and never try to kiss me again. What if Alexia saw what you did? She would be hurt and I am not going to hurt her. I love Alexia and I am not going to mess this up with her. Whomever you have found, I hope you don't mess that up. Don't follow me around and quit coming up to me every day. Leave me alone and leave Alexia alone too. You and I are never going to be anything." I walk off before I really have to get mean with her. I know saying those things to her that I had to be rough. She needs to know how I feel about Alexia.

She doesn't try to stop me this time. I know now that she only hooked up with Jacob to try to make me jealous. I really don't care or feel anything about that. I would feel bad about Jacob, but he only did it to get what he wanted.

I get closer to the biology building, when I hear another girl calling my name. Now who can that be? I turn and see Kristen, Alexia's roommate coming toward me. "I wanted to talk to you about Alexia. Do you have time right now, Phillip?"

"Yes. I have a minute or two. What do you want to talk about?" I look at Kristen and hope it isn't anything bad.

"I watched what happened between Megan and you a few minutes ago. I know you always turn down Megan, but she can be persistent, and this probably won't be the last of Megan. Whatever you do, walk away from Megan and don't hurt Alexia. If Alexia isn't enough for you, please let her go before you hurt her. She may look strong, but I believe you could hurt her if you did something bad to her. Please don't hurt her or I will have to hurt you. We have become great friends in a short time and I don't want her hurt. Do you hear me, Phillip?" I am looking at Kristen and she is serious about what she said. I am glad Alexia has found a friend with Kristen.

I smile at her. "Alexia is enough for me and I am in love with her. I will never hurt her intentionally. I want to take care of her, and from the time I met her, she has had a place in my heart. It is like I'm drawn to her and she is all I can think about. I am glad she has you as a friend. I see why she was afraid to move out of your room. You know, I asked her to move in with me and the first thing that came to her mind was you, Kristen. She was afraid to lose you. You are free to come over to visit any time."

"Well looks like Alexia has a great guy that loves her, and since you're taking her away from me, you better believe I will be over a lot. I have to get going to class before I am late. You know, I believe Alexia loves you too." After those last words, Kristen walked off leaving me standing with a smile on my face. Does Alexia really love me like I love her? I look down at my watch and notice that if I don't get to class now, I will be late.

I hurry to biology with a smile on my face all the way. I barely make it on time and sit down. I notice that Alexia isn't beside me. She must be late but I wonder why. She left early enough to make it to class and, now I am starting to worry. Did Megan stop her too and harass her? She will be here soon and I will ask her.

Class has started and Alexia still hasn't made it. Maybe it is something else besides Megan. What if she was in an accident on the way back to school? I should have texted or even called her to make sure she got back. I start thinking about Kristen; did she say that she talked to her? I can't remember if she did. This class is lasting too long. I should get up and leave, because I know something is wrong with Alexia for her not being here. Right when I get my books put away, the class ends. I am out the door before anyone else is.

I head toward Alexia's dorm and practically run the whole way. I almost run into Kristen as I get to the dorm. "Have you heard from Alexia today?"

"Yes. She was getting ready for class when I left and talked to you earlier. She said she was going when I left. Didn't she come to class?" Kristen looked worried.

"No, she didn't come to class. I was so scared to death in class and almost ran out of it. I couldn't think about anything but why she wasn't there. I'm afraid something bad had happened to her. Do you think Megan stopped her and said something bad to her?"

"Calm down, Phillip. I'm sure she is fine. She was a little upset after talking to her mom when I left and said she was going to call her back. Maybe the call lasted longer than she thought it would."

"What made her upset? Do you think her mom was mad about us living together?"

"No, I think it was something else. You have to ask her. Let's go see if she is in the room." Kristen opens the door and goes in. The look on her face tells me that she knows more. I hesitate and think that maybe Alexia changed her mind and doesn't want to be with me. What if it is something worse? What could be worse than that? "Come on, Phillip, let's go."

I follow Kristen up to the room. Each step I take makes me feel like my life will change as soon as I get to Alexia's room. I slow my pace as dread starts to take hold of me. I force myself to keep going. When we get to the door, I pause for a minute before entering the room. Why do I have a bad feeling? I do love Alexia and I know I want to be with her. Can I handle what is inside the dorm room? I decide I can and will no matter what. I enter and I am surprised to see Kristen standing in the middle of the room. She is looking toward something. I turn my head that way, and guess what I see.

Twenty-Seven

ALEXIA

I hear the door open to my dorm room, but something is wrong with me. I feel like I am dreaming and can't wake up. I hear Phillip and Kristen trying to wake me, and I want to answer. My body doesn't let me. They both become frightened and I hear Kristen tell Phillip that they need to call 911. I try my best to open my eyes. It is impossible for me to do it.

I start to think what could be going on with my body. I can remember the doctors telling me that if I missed one dose of my medicine my body could shut down. This must be what is happening now. *Think Alexia. When was the last time you took your medicine?* I took it yesterday morning. I was in a hurry this morning, and then when I found out that I might have Phillip's brother's heart. I forgot to take it. Now I am laying here feeling the lethargic effects. I can't even tell them what they need to do. Hopefully Kristen will remember to tell the paramedics when they get here. I hope Phillip can forgive me from keeping this secret from him.

That is the last thing I think before I black out completely

Beep. Beep. Beep. What is that awful noise? Beep. Beep. Beep. I try to move my hand but find I can't because something is sticking in it. Beep. Beep. Beep. That noise is driving me crazy.

I open my eyes to see what it is. When I finally force them open, I realize that I am in the hospital. How did I get here? What happened to me? I look around the room and I see Phillip asleep in a chair next to my bed. I stare at him for a minute and then I remember everything that happened. *No!* Not like this! I was going to tell him after classes. What day is it, I think? How long have I been in here?

I wonder if my parents are here. They are going to be upset with me. I am upset with myself too. Now I am here and have made a mess out of everything. They are going to make me go home after this stunt.

Beep. Beep. Beep. How can anyone sleep with all that beeping? I look to see where it is coming from and notice that I am hooked up to a heart monitor. Did I damage my heart by forgetting to take my medicine? I have so many questions. I wish, Phillip were awake. *No,* I don't. I would have to tell him everything and that scares me. I lie there watching Phillip sleep. He looks tired although he is sleeping. I don't feel as bad as I did, so maybe I will be okay.

I watch Phillip sleep for a little while before he starts to move. Now I have to tell him everything, and I hope he forgives me. He rises up from his chair and looks right into my eyes. He has been here too long. I can tell because his clothes are the ones he had on when I left his condo. He hasn't shaved in a while either. He moves his chair closer to the bed and grabs my hand.

"Princess, how do you feel? You had me scared to death. You have been in this hospital for three days now. The doctors say you will be fine, but you must take your medicine every day without missing a day."

I look into his sad eyes, "I am sorry Phillip. I didn't mean to forget. I had a lot on my mind and forgot. That was the first time I have ever done that. I didn't mean to scare you and I sure didn't want you to find out like this. Can you forgive me for keeping my heart transplant a secret? I wanted to tell you after classes the day I got sick. Before I moved in with you. You should have known from the beginning, what you are getting into with me. I am this weak, sick girl who will never be strong. I can't give you kids if we ever get that far into our relationship. Mostly, I should have told you that I am broken and barely hanging on. You should be with a girl who you wouldn't have to take care of and a girl who can give you kids in the future." A tear escapes my eyes and he takes his fingers to wipe my face.

Phillip looks at me with sad eyes. "Baby, yes, you should have told me. I understand why you might have been afraid to tell me. I did wonder how you got your scar, but it is beautiful on you. I know what it means, and it means another chance of life for you. I don't need to forgive you for anything, but I am mad because you didn't take your medicine. You scared me to death. Kristen and I couldn't wake you up. I have been here the whole three days waiting to see those beautiful eyes open." He gives me a big grin.

"Oh Phillip, you didn't have to stay every day. You need to go home and rest. You look very tired and look like you need to change clothes. You haven't changed your clothes since I got here. Those are what you had on when I left your condo. Did you happen to call my parents?" I give him a weak smile.

"Yes. I called them and they flew down the same day you were checked in. I sent them to our condo to rest and get cleaned up. I didn't leave you because I wanted to see you when you opened those eyes. I never want to leave your side, Alexia." He squeezed my hand, brought it up to his lips, and kissed it tenderly.

"Now that I'm awake, you should go rest and get cleaned up too. Do you know anything about my condition? How long do I have to stay here in the hospital?"

"I will not leave you until your parents are here with you. Since they left about an hour ago, so I would say you get to keep me around for a while. Your parents didn't tell me anything, and they said that was up to you to tell me. I want to hear all about what happened to you, only when you feel comfortable enough to do it. I will wait, but I would love to know since we are together now and I might need to know in case we run into this problem again. Not that I will let you forget to take your medicine again." He looks at me with such loving eyes; I know he means what he is saying.

How long does one mean those words when they have to take care of you? How long until Phillip grows tired of taking care of me? I have so many things going on inside my head, and need to tell him everything. As I decide to tell him more about my heart, the room door opens and in comes Kristen. She looks at Phillip and then over to me.

"Oh my gosh! You are finally awake, Alexia. I have been scared to death. Phillip and I couldn't wake you up and I made him call 911. I am sorry. I had to tell Phillip about your heart. I knew you were going to tell him, but the paramedics and doctors needed to know how to take care of you. Can you please forgive me?" She hurries over and gives me a hug.

"Thank you, Kristen. I'm not mad at you, because you saved my life. I did want to tell Phillip, but it looks like I made a mess out of my plans of doing so. If I hadn't told you right before class, you would not have known, so I am grateful that you knew what was wrong. What all did you tell Phillip?" I looked at her to see if she told him everything.

"I told him you had a heart transplant and that you were going to talk about it that evening with him. Nothing more." Kristen is looking at me with a smile and I knew she didn't tell him that my heart could possibly be his brother's. She saved that for me, I could tell.

Phillip looks between us and smiles. "What more is there to tell me Alexia? Are you telling me that something else is wrong with you?" He stopped smiling, and now concern is on his face.

I look to him and then Kristen, "Yes, I need to talk to you about something else. I have to talk to my parents first to make sure about something, before I tell you. Can you wait until after I speak to them?" I squeezed his hand.

He still has worry on his face when I look into his eyes. "What is it? Is the heart rejecting your body? Please tell me you aren't going to die soon."

"No Phillip. It isn't that. I don't believe I'm rejecting this heart. It feels stronger than ever right now. I missed taking my medicine and I can't do that. But you know right now, I am broken and have been pieced back together. I was barely alive when I received this heart so someday it will stop working. I would understand if you wanted to leave me because I'm not strong enough to be what you deserve. You deserve someone healthy and who can take care of you for a long time. I will never know when my time comes up so feel free to leave before you get too involved with me, the broken girl." I look into his eyes, and they seem to be thinking about what I just said. He is scaring me right now and I am selfish enough to hope he stays with me. I should push him away now, but I can't. I'm not strong enough.

"Alexia, you are perfect to me no matter if you think you're broken. To me you are not broken and never will be. I plan on having you right by my side for as long as you will let me. You are the strongest person I know to have went through what you already have and survived. So what if your heart had to be replaced with another one? You are still you and you're stronger for it. I never want to be without you in my life. I know things could happen anytime, to anyone. That means we need to live while we can and not be afraid of what might happen. I could reject my liver just like you could reject your heart, but don't be afraid of me leaving, because I am here to stay so get used to it, my princess. There's one more thing, I want you to know I love you and I should have said it sooner. I always want you to know that I love you and only you." He smiles and kisses me sweetly on my lips.

As he looks at me, I realize that I love him the same way. I forgot that Kristen was in the room and I believe Phillip did too. We both jump when we hear someone clear their throat. We look up to see who it is. My parents are standing beside Kristen and they all have smiles on their faces. I think my face is blushing because they all witnessed everything Phillip said to me. He smiles like they already knew how he feels.

"Mr. and Mrs. Morgan, if you heard everything I said to Alexia, I want you to know it is true and I would love to have your blessing to date her and please let her move in with me so I can take care of her." He smiled and squeezed my hand.

My mom speaks first. "I could see how you felt about Alexia before I heard what you said. You truly seem to love her, and I appreciate that you haven't left her side since she has been here. Do you realize the task you will have to take on to make sure she doesn't forget her medicine again? What about the future with her not being able to give you kids?" she asks Phillip. I am now scared of his answers.

Phillip squeezed my hand to comfort me. "I do realize how hard it is to have to take medication every day, because I have to take it too. If I had known earlier that Alexia must take it, I would have reminded her to do so. We are still young, and yes down the road we may decide we want kids, but she doesn't have to carry a child for us to have them. We could adopt or find a surrogate to carry our child, but right now we don't need children. For one, we both are still in school, and secondly, we just have found each other so we need to take things slow. I promise to be there for her if you would give us your blessing."

My dad is looking between my mom and me, "Alexia, I will give my blessing for you and Phillip to date. He really seems to love you and he can take care of you. I think your mom has to give her blessing too. If you decide to move in with him, I want both of you to not start a sexual relationship, until you both get to know each other better and be prepared if you do. This is something really serious you both need to think about and discuss further. Phillip, I hope you know what you are really getting into. Having a liver transplant is serious, but a heart transplant is more so. Please don't let her forget to take her medication, and Alexia, don't let Phillip forget his. If Alexia gets put back in the hospital, I will bring her back home for good. I never want to be scared and unable to be here fast enough to get to the hospital if you needed me. So if your mom gives her blessing, I will." My dad just surprised me with his comment and giving his blessing. I wonder what has happened the past three days while I was out.

I look to mom, who seems to be thinking about something, and she looks up at me. "Alexia before I decide, may I speak to you alone first?"

I look at Phillip, and he understands and he gets up to leave. Dad and Kristen follow him out the door without a word.

"Okay, Mom. Everyone is gone, so what do you need to tell me? Is something wrong with my heart or did I damage it?"

"Alexia, the doctors here said your heart is strong, and by the tests they have done, it seems that your heart is stronger than ever. Missing your medication only put your body in shock and you couldn't wake up. Mostly you scared everyone to death, but you will be fine. The doctors told Dad and me before we walked in that you would get out of the hospital tomorrow. Now with that out of the way, let's talk about something I haven't told you about - *how you got your heart*." She smiles at me and sits down in the chair Phillip was sitting in and grabs my hand.

"What haven't you told me about my heart, Mom?" I look into her eyes and she seems sad.

"Well, on that day the doctors said you were going to die, I went down to the chapel to pray. I was praying for a miracle and that you would live. I only had you in my life for fifteen years and hated to have to give you up. While I was praying, another woman came in and sat down in one of the benches in the chapel. She looked scared. I knew something bad must have happened to someone she loved, because she looked terrified. I went and sat down beside her. I put my arms around her, because she really needed a hug. I was afraid to ask her what happened so I kept quiet. While I was hugging her, she decided to tell me what was going on." Mom paused and now I see in her eyes, that she is remembering what happened on that day.

I have this dread that comes over me. "Mom, what did she tell you happened?

"The lady's name was Jennifer Ryan. She came to the chapel to pray for her sons, because a drunk driver hit them and they were in the emergency room. The boys' names were Gabe and Phillip Ryan." She pauses and holds tight to my hand then continues. "While we were talking and praying for her sons and you, her husband comes rushing in to get her. He looked like he was going to pass out, and I knew something must have happened to the boys. They hurried out of the chapel and I didn't see her again until a few days later. I had gone back to the chapel every day while you were in the hospital because it comforted me. Jennifer came in and sat down beside me, and tears were running down her face. She told me Gabe had died, but Phillip had lived, only because Gabe signed the donor card on his driver's license. She was happy to find out that Gabe decided to do that, but she didn't know he had until everything had happened. Jennifer was happy that he saved Phillip and even saved a young girl with his heart that day. I knew she must have been talking about you so I told her everything about you and told her that Gabe was a miracle even though he didn't make it himself. It gave her joy to know a part of him did save many lives that day. She told me not to tell you whose heart you received, because the hospital told them it was supposed to be confidential. Now I could be in trouble that I told you this, but I think you needed to know."

"Mom, do you think what I feel for Phillip has to do with this heart, Gabe gave me? What do you think Phillip will do if he finds out?" Tears start to come down my cheeks, because I am afraid of what will happen now.

"Alexia dear, you love Phillip all on your own. You can't have Gabe's feelings. The doctors say that is impossible because I asked all those questions way before we got to that day I almost lost you. What Gabe did that day, was to give you both a chance to live. That was a miracle. Who knows? Maybe he had a premonition that something was going to happen and he was ready if it did. I do think you need to talk about this with Phillip before you move in with him. I will give you my blessing to date him and move in with him, but only if you tell him first." She smiles at me and rubs my face like she always does when she is worried about me.

"Thanks, Mom. And I know I have to tell him. I will tell him tomorrow when I get out of the hospital. All of this talking has made me very tired and I need to take a nap. Can you do me a favor and tell everyone to go home and get some rest. You and Dad go and take Phillip back to his place. Rest up for a while and tell him to take a shower because he needs one." I yawn really big and she understands I am tired.

"Okay, baby girl. You get some rest and I'm sure we will be back after a while. A good shower for all of us will do some good. I will tell Phillip you are already asleep." She kisses me on my cheek and turns the light off in my room so I can rest. Then she leaves.

I thought Phillip would come back in, but he doesn't. I am glad because I have to go over everything my mom just said to me and sort it all out. I need to tell him tomorrow. I hope he will love me after I do. I yawn again and it isn't long after that I fall back to sleep.

Twenty-Eight

PHILLIP

What I see when I walk into the dorm room will haunt me forever. Seeing Alexia lying on her bed and not waking up scares me to death. It is worse than when I was in the hospital after waking up after my surgery and finding out that my brother, Gabe died and saved my life in the process. Gabe shouldn't have died for me, but I have learned to be grateful for his gift, although it took me a long time to get over his loss.

Kristen jumps in and gets my attention to call 911. I call and the operator keeps asking me questions about what is going on. I don't know how to answer these questions, because I barely know Alexia and if she makes it through this, I will definitely make it my first priority to know everything. I keep asking Kristen questions, but she ends up taking the phone from me. Kristen starts answering right away, and I am surprised that she knows Alexia so much better than me. I am upset and grateful at the same time. What really surprises me the most is that Kristen tells them that Alexia has had a heart transplant.

I am so in shock that I missed Kristen yelling for me to go downstairs to meet the paramedics. Kristen has to slap me to get me moving. I hurry downstairs, and the paramedics are already here when I make it down. We make it back up to the room in a hurry. As soon as they get inside the room, they begin to work on Alexia. While they work on her, Kristen comes over to me and tells me about Alexia. She says that she was lucky that Alexia told her about the transplant this morning and Alexia told her that she had planned on telling me after classes today. I wonder why Alexia hadn't told me before now, since I told her about mine. This is something else we have in common.

The paramedics have loaded Alexia up on the bed to wheel her out to the ambulance and they ask if one of us is going. I tell them that I am and Kristen tells me she will follow us in her car. The drive to the hospital is terrifying and brings back bad memories. I ask the paramedic, if she is going to be all right and he tells me that she is stable, but they have to get her to the hospital and run some tests to make sure. Hearing that she is stable makes me feel a little better.

I text Jacob and Tyler and tell them to come to the hospital when they get done with classes. I don't tell them everything, but I let them know Alexia is stable. I remember that I needed to call Alexia's parents, and I will as soon as I know how she is. Why has this happened to my beautiful girl? She is too precious for this to happen to her. I will tell her how I feel about her as soon as she wakes up; at least, I hope she does wake up.

We arrive at the hospital and they wheel Alexia back into the emergency room. They tell me that I have to stay out in the waiting room until they know what is wrong with her and asked if I am related to her. I let them know that I am her boyfriend and her parents are in Cleveland. They said that they would give me an update soon. Now I have to wait in the waiting room - alone.

I don't have to wait too long by myself because Kristen comes in soon after. She says that she picked up Alexia's phone off the table and hands it to me so I could call her parents. She tells me that it should be the last number she called. I look at her phone but I am afraid that I shouldn't call until I hear from the doctors. I know if I were in their shoes, I would want to hurry and get into town to be close to Alexia.

I call them and talk to her mother. She seems to know who I am. I guess Alexia must have told her about me, and that makes me happy for a minute. Julie Morgan sounds like her daughter. She is easy to talk to, and I tell her that the paramedic said that she was stable. She says that I should tell the doctors about the medicine Alexia is on because maybe she forgot to take it.

I go to the nurse's station and borrow something to write everything down. Mrs. Morgan says that they will get on the first flight out and I tell her that I would pay for her and her husband's ticket. She won't let me and tells me to watch over her daughter until she gets in. I say that I won't leave her side as soon as I get back to her room. Mrs. Morgan thanks me for everything and tells me she'll see me soon.

I hand the medicine list to the nurse and she rushes back to give the list to the doctors. The nurse comes out and gives me an update. Alexia's heart rate has already picked up and her color is back to normal. I feel better upon hearing those words from the nurse, but I am still scared for Alexia. I hope she isn't rejecting her heart.

I go back to the waiting room to find Kristen. "Kristen, I heard from the nurse that Alexia's heart rate and color are much better. Thank you for being there with me when we found her. I would have panicked worse if you hadn't slapped me. I now know, I better not hurt Alexia or I will be hurting bad. You have a wicked slap for a girl, and it is painful."

"Phillip, I am glad you were there too. If Alexia hadn't told me this morning about her transplant, I would have lost it. This experience has been traumatic for you and me. She had told me about it, because she was worried that you would be mad at her for not telling you sooner. She wanted to move in with you but wanted you to know about her past first. Alexia was upset about something her mom had talked about before she got back to the room. I shouldn't have left her when she was so upset, but she told me she was going to class so I thought she was going to be fine. This is my fault for leaving her like that. Forgive me, Phillip, for not saying anything sooner this morning when I saw you. I was worried that Megan was going to cause trouble between you, but never thought Alexia's heart to be the real trouble. Please don't hurt Alexia. She will not be able to take it." Kristen looked worried.

"You didn't know this was going to happen. Alexia's mom told me she might have forgotten to take her medicine and that is what would happen when she forgets. She is already showing improvement. Don't blame yourself for this. I want you to know that I love her and never plan to hurt her ever. When she wakes up, I will tell her how I feel. I have told her that I loved her before this, but I don't think she really believed me. I will make her know for sure. You should go back to the dorm and rest.

Give me your phone number and I will call you as soon as I hear something else."

Kristen types her phone number into my phone and gives me a hug. "Please call me soon, okay? If you need something let me know. I will stay with you if you need me to." She looks at me with tired eyes.

"You go ahead and I will stay. I couldn't leave here if I wanted too. Alexia might wake and be scared by herself. I plan on being here until she wakes."

"Okay, Phillip. Make sure you call me with updates." She leaves, but I can tell she was sad about leaving Alexia here.

After Kristen leaves, I become restless and pace the waiting room. Some of the people who are in here waiting keep watching me like I am a ticking time bomb. I don't care how they watched me. The only thing I can think of is Alexia and why they are not letting me know what is going on. I decided to give the doctors a little while longer and then I will demand answers. Now, I will pace until then.

Every time the doors open to the waiting room, I stop to see if it is a doctor. Right when I finally decide to go ask the nurse if she knows anything more, the doors open and I look to see who it is. This time, it isn't the doctor. It's Tyler and Jacob. They have a bag from my favorite burger place and something to drink. I smile at them, because they knew I would be hungry.

"Hey, guys. Thanks for coming and bringing me food."

We find seats and they started asking me everything about Alexia. I tell them the basics because I really don't know how much she would want them to know. When I get done eating and telling them what I know, the doctor finally comes to find me. He asks me to go with him and the guys say that they wait on me until I come back out.

"Hi, my name is Dr. Martin. What is your name and how do you know Alexia?" He asked and shakes my hand.

"I am Alexia's boyfriend and my name is Phillip. Her roommate and I found her unresponsive. I rode in the ambulance with her. Can you tell me how she is?"

"Well, Phillip, I can tell you that she is fine right now and when you gave the list of medicine to the nurse that helped. As soon as we gave her the medication, we were able to regulate her heartbeat and now she is resting. Her body did start the process of shutting down. I believe she was barely shutting down when you got to her, and that has also helped in this situation. Now we have to wait until she wakes up. If you were family, I could go into detail about the tests that we had to run on her, but I can't tell you. Sorry about that. Just know that she is doing well right now. Did you call any of her family members?"

"Yes, I called her parents and they are getting the first flight out of Cleveland today. They probably are flying here now. Thank you for saving her, Dr. Martin. Do you know when I can go see her?" I hope he tells me that I can see her soon.

"They are getting her room ready right now and you should be able to see her in about thirty minutes or so. I have to get back to my other patients. Ask the nurse for Alexia's room number and have her to tell you when you can see Alexia. Take care, Phillip."

"Thanks again, Dr. Martin." I smile at him and shake his hand. Then he leaves me.

I head over to the nurses' station and ask about Alexia. She looks up Alexia's information and tells me her room number. The nurse says to wait a few minutes and she would tell me when I could go up. I thank her and head to the waiting room. I tell Tyler and Jacob what the doctor said and inform them that they should go ahead and leave because I am staying until Alexia wakes up. Tyler goes gets me some snacks and drinks before they leave me. As soon as they leave, I am allowed into Alexia's room. I head up to see my girl.

I pause at her door before I open it. I admit to myself that I am scared. I don't know what they have done to her. I hope her parents hurry and get here so I can find out. Maybe she will wake up first and then I can ask her about everything.

I open her door and head over to Alexia. What I see surprises me. She looks better and looks like she does when she is asleep. I am glad she doesn't have tubes down her throat. If it weren't for her IV or the heart monitor, I would think she was sleeping.

After seeing Alexia, I relax a little bit. I pull the chair close beside her bed, so I can hold her hand. I talk to her and tell her everything, hoping she can hear what I am saying to her. I wonder why she hasn't woken up yet.

As time passes, I become worried again, but she looks peaceful. A nurse comes in a few times to check her vitals and tells me that everything is fine. I will have to believe the nurse for now, so I just have to wait. I will not leave this hospital until Alexia wakes up and I even tell her this. I continue holding her hand, and I even rub my fingers across her face. I kiss her on her lips and still she doesn't wake up.

I must have fallen asleep while talking to Alexia. I am awakened by voices in the room. I don't move or open my eyes at first, because I am hoping to hear something that will let me know how Alexia really is. I think I hear Dr. Martin talking to a lady. Could Alexia's parents already be here? How long did I sleep? They are talking in very low voices, so I really can't hear everything they are saying.

I am about to rise up when I hear my name being spoken. The lady asks what I know about Alexia's condition and the doctor tells her what he told me. She says that it is good and she's glad they didn't tell me more. I am about to get mad and let them know about it when the lady says she is glad that I am here with her daughter. She goes on saying that it is Alexia who should tell me about her condition and not anyone else that Alexia had told her that she was going to tell me earlier in the day all about it, so I relaxed. I decide that it is time to let them know I am awake by moving like I am now waking up.

I stretch out my arms, pretending to wake. I look over to see who is behind me. That must be Alexia's mom because she looks like her. I smile at her and get up. I hold out my hand to shake hers.

"Hi, I am Phillip. You must be Alexia's mother, Mrs. Morgan?"

She shakes my hand. "Yes, I am her mother. Glad to meet you finally, Phillip. I wish it were under better circumstances. Alexia has told me so much about you. I am glad she has had you with her. How long have you been here with her?"

I smile again. "I have been here as long as Alexia has. I don't plan on leaving until she opens her eyes. I hope it is soon, but if not, I will be here. Did you just get in from the airport?"

Mrs. Morgan nods. "Yes, we did and came straight here. We haven't even found a place to stay yet. You know Alexia would want you to take a break and rest. We are here now if you want to leave and rest up."

"Mrs. Morgan, you and your husband can stay at my place. No need to get a hotel. I have an extra bedroom, but it has twin beds. You can stay there. I really don't need to leave and rest. I plan on being here with her. Did Dr. Martin tell you anything about Alexia's condition and how long she will be here?"

"Phillip, please call me Julie. I wouldn't want to put you out by staying with you. Yes, Dr. Martin told me everything. Alexia must have forgotten to take her medicine today. He said once she wakes up she should be fine. It might take a few days for her body to recuperate from its shock of medication withdrawal. The test shows that her heart is fine. Now we have to wait until she wakes up. I am not telling you anything else about her condition because she wanted to do that herself." Julie yawns and I know she must be tired. When I look out the window, I notice it is already dark.

"I insist, Julie that you stay at my place. I will call the security guard and tell him to let you in the building. Is your husband with you?" I look at her and she really reminds me of Alexia except her eye color is different.

She smiles. "Yes, my husband is here. He just stepped down to the cafeteria to grab us something to eat. I told him to get you something. I hope you will like what he brings. You were sleeping when we got here and didn't want wake you to ask. Thank you for letting us stay with you. I can see why Alexia likes you. You are so good to her. She told me about this past weekend that you two had a great time. She tells me everything and always has so don't be embarrassed. When she told me this morning that you and her were dating and that she wanted to move in with you, I was shocked. Now, meeting you and seeing how much you care for her, I understand."

The door opened and a guy comes in carrying food. I guessed this is Alexia's dad. Yes this has to be him, because he has the same eye color that Alexia has. He hands the food to Julie and comes over to shake my hand.

"You must be the Phillip, I keep hearing about. My name is Steven and I hope you like hospital food because I just got us some chicken sandwiches." He smiles at me.

I shake his hand. "Nice to meet you, Mr. Morgan and yes I am Phillip. I am still a growing boy so chicken sandwiches are good for me. Thank you for bringing me food. I was telling your wife that you two could stay at my place while you're here. I know the both of you are tired and I will stay here with Alexia. You can go to my place and rest. I will call when she wakes up."

"Thank you, Phillip. That is generous of you. We are tired, and the doctor said she would be asleep for a while. Why don't you go with us to rest?"

How could he think that I would leave her?

Julie looks at me and knows I won't leave. "Steven dear, Phillip is going to stay with Alexia. He already told me he wasn't leaving until she wakes up. We will have to leave him here."

He looks at me and realizes that is true. "Okay son. Call us if something comes up. Call me Steven and not Mr. Morgan. Since you're Alexia's boyfriend, we should be on first-name basis."

"Sure thing, Steven. I will write down the address and here is the key to the condo. I have plenty of food so help yourselves." I gave them everything they needed and they left.

It has to have been stressful for them to get the call from me about Alexia. I make sure the security guy knows about

Alexia's parents coming and he says he would let them in and show them which condo to go to.

Now that it is late and I have eaten my food, I have to relax myself. I text the guys and Kristen updates about Alexia and ask Tyler to bring me a phone charger the next day. I don't want to be without a phone. I wash up in the bathroom and realize that I have to ask Alexia's parents to bring my medicine in the morning. I'm glad I already took my dose today. I head back to the chair beside her bed and notice that it reclines. That is nice, so I can sleep. I see a blanket and extra pillow in the closet. Now I am set to stay here with my girl.

This is my routine for the next two days. I talk to Alexia, her parents, and my friends when they all come in. They each try to get me to leave, but I can't go. Thankfully they bring me food, my medication, and a phone charger. I emailed my professors and they email me what I have missed in class. I can make up the work. If Alexia doesn't wake up soon, I will have to request clothes too.

The doctor keeps telling her parents and me that she is still doing fine and improving each day and that she will wake up when her body lets her. I have been here for three days now and I miss her so much. I miss looking into her blue eyes, listening to her talk and laugh, and I miss her in my arms smiling up at me.

Her parents left a little while ago and I am relaxing in my new reclining bed. I fall asleep for a little while and I think I hear movement, but then there's nothing. I go back into deep sleep. Seems like I've slept for about an hour when I wake up. I open my eyes and there is the greatest sight I have ever seen right in front of me. My blue-eyed princess is looking at me. I hurry and move my chair close by her bed and grab her hand in mine.

We start talking about what had happened and how long she was asleep. She keeps telling me that she's sorry, she was going to tell me, and she made a mess of things and how she would understand if I want to leave her because she is broken. I even wipe her tears away.

Not long after she wakes, Kirsten comes in and they talk. Alexia asks her what all did she tell me and Kristen tells her. I wonder what Alexia is now keeping from me, but I decide that it doesn't matter to me. I decide to interrupt them because I have to tell Alexia everything I was feeling. How much I loved her and how I don't care that she has had a heart transplant. That it doesn't matter if we have kids or not because there are other ways to have kids if we decided later we did want some children. She keeps arguing that I don't know what I am getting myself into, but I let her know that I do. I let everything out of my heart to her and forget we were not alone until I hear someone behind us.

It is her parents and Kristen. I tell her parents that everything I said is true. I even ask them for their blessing to date Alexia and move in with me. I am surprised when Steven says yes first but we have to have Julie's blessing also. Then Julie says that she has to talk to Alexia by herself before she will agree.

We all step outside Alexia's room, and now I have to wait until they are done talking to hear if she gives me her blessing. I am wondering why they have to have a secret conversation first. Kristen seems to know more but doesn't say anything. Then says that she had to go. Here I am, pacing the hall. Steven seems as nervous as I am and I wonder if he knows why they are having a private talk. It seems like forever when the door opens.

Julie comes out and smiles at me. "Phillip, while I was talking to Alexia, she went back to sleep. She said for Steven and me to take you home and get cleaned up. You should rest a bit and then come back. She has to talk to you about something when you get back. Go home for a little bit."

"Why do I have to leave? I can wait until she is awake again to talk to her."

"Alexia told me to make you go and she said you needed a shower because you were starting to smell bad. Not to worry. She will rest until you get back." She smiles, and I knew that comment was from Alexia. I want to go check on her again, but I don't.

"Okay. Long enough to shower. I don't want to stink up this hospital." I laugh, and we leave to go back to the condo.

Driving back home after three days in the hospital feels good. It would be better to have Alexia with me. The doctor said that she would get out tomorrow and I can't wait. I hope what she tells me is something good. I have this feeling it isn't.

Could Alexia's mom have talked her out of our relationship? Would Alexia dump me after everything? I decide not to worry too much until I talk to Alexia. I'm glad her parents are driving me home because I really am tired. More tired than I thought I was.

Twenty-Nine

ALEXIA

I must have been extremely tired. I don't wake up until the sun is coming through my hospital window. I feel much better this morning. My body doesn't feel tired or weak. I hope that means they will let me out for sure. I look around the room to see if anyone is with me, but there is no one. I wonder why Phillip didn't come back. Maybe he did and I was asleep, so he left. Hopefully he isn't mad because I had Mom make him leave last night. He really needed to rest and get cleaned up. He looked so tired.

What will I tell him today? Do I have it in me to tell him that I have his dead brother's heart? If I want to be his girlfriend I have to. I can't keep this secret from him any longer. I hope he forgives me when he hears what I have to say. Telling him will be the hardest thing for me to do. I love him and never want him to feel heartache or pain. I plan on telling him once I get out of this place.

The door opens and Dr. Martin comes in. "Hello, Alexia. How do you feel this morning?"

"I feel like my normal self. I slept well last night and no longer feel tired or weak. Does this mean I get out of the hospital today?" I smile at him, and maybe he will let me go.

"Well, with all the tests you had done, everything looks good. Your blood work is normal and the EKGs and echocardiogram show no damage to your heart. You have to promise me not to forget your medication or you will be back here. If you promise me, I will start the process for your discharge."

"Don't worry, Dr. Martin. I promise to take it. I don't want to come back to the hospital again. Nothing against you or anything, but I have had enough of hospitals for now." I smile really wide from knowing that I will be getting out soon.

"Okay, Alexia, I will go tell the nurse to start discharging you. Is your family here to take you home?"

"It is still early. I will call them to come get me. They aren't too far from the hospital."

"It has been nice to meet you, Alexia. You were my first heart transplant patient. Most of the time, the patients I see are not lucky enough to get a donor. Take care of yourself." With those words, he left me.

Yes I have been lucky or maybe it was a miracle my mother prayed about. I will probably never know for sure.

I call my mom and she says that they will come pick me up. They ask me if Phillip is still here. I say that he wasn't when I woke up. I tell her that he probably went to get something to eat. She says that I am probably right. We hang up and now I worried about where he could be.

This time when the door opened in comes Kristen. I love her, but I'm wondering where Phillip is. "You are awake. You were sleeping last night when Phillip and I were here late. Where is lover boy at now?"

"I don't know. He wasn't here when I woke up. Must be out getting food or something. The doctor said I can go home and he already has started the process to discharge me."

"Yay! I am happy for you. Phillip said he was staying last night. I guess he did go for food or something. What did your mom tell you in private yesterday? Phillip is scared that she wanted you to break up with him."

"No, she didn't try to talk me into breaking up with him. After I tell him what she said, he might break up with me. This has me scared to death to tell him. I don't want to lose him. I now know I have to tell him everything."

"Alexia, what is it? Tell me so I can give you my opinion about it." She looks concerned.

I end up telling her everything about who my heart donor is, how my mom prayed for a miracle, and even about Phillip's mom. When I was done she just looks at me for a minute. I believe she might be in shock. I hope Phillip doesn't have this reaction.

"Wow, Alexia, that is a lot to have to tell him. I know he loves you. It will be a shock to him at first and he'd probably have to process everything. In the end, I think his love for you will be greater than the hurt of his lost brother. This has been a shock to you also. Was this the reason you forgot to take your medication? Your mothers keeping this from both of you-- They did it because they had to. You didn't know you would run into Phillip and fall in love with each other."

"Yes, that was the reason I forgot. I didn't mean to. I was upset about why Mom wanted me to tell Phillip and the time frame of my surgery. Then you said what you did about how it could be Phillip's brother who gave me my heart and I freaked out. I ended up crying myself to sleep and didn't take it. I am scared to lose him now. I heard Phillip and you trying to wake me up. I tried to tell you I was awake but couldn't. Then I remembered why I was unable to respond-- because I am broken and have to always take medicine for the rest of my life to live." I look up at Kristen and see that we both have tears in our eyes.

"Oh, Alexia, don't cry. Everything will be okay. I am for one glad to have you alive and in my life. Phillip will be glad too, once he knows that you love him the way he does. I will be with you every step of the way. I will remind you to take your medicine, because you almost gave me a heart attack. You know, I had to slap Phillip. He went into shock as soon as he laid eyes on you in the bed unresponsive." She smiled.

"You didn't slap him, did you?"

"Yes. I did. I had to get him moving to bring up the paramedics to our dorm room."

"Did everyone at the dorm see me being taken out to the ambulance?" I hope not.

"Sorry, but some of the girls did. Megan did too. She was at her friend's room and when the paramedics came, they weren't quiet. Everyone who wasn't in class saw what happened. They have asked me about you, but I refused to tell them."

"How can I face everyone and what should I tell them?" I think about this and I hope these girls don't ask what happened.

"You hold your face up high and don't say anything to them. It isn't anyone's business. Go back to school like nothing has happened."

"You make it sound easy, Kristen. I hope I can do that. I am glad you are here with me. You are a great friend to have." I reach over and squeeze her hand. She surprises me by hugging me, and then I hug her back. She has been such a great friend to me already.

"How much longer until you're freed from this place, Alexia?" She looks down at her watch to see what time it was.

"The doctor left about twenty minutes before you came it. In my past experience, it usually takes about two to three hours. They have to fill out lots of paperwork first. My parents should be here soon if you have to leave for a class. I will have to do a lot of make-up work for my classes." That reminds me, I have to email my professors today when I get out.

Kristen looks at me. "Yes, I need to get to class. I was trying to wait until Phillip or your parents made it here before I left."

"I'm sure they will be here soon. I called my parents before you came in. Go on to class. I will be fine until it is time to leave." I smiled up at her.

"All right, I will leave. If you need me call."

As she gets to the door, I notice that it is open a little bit. She closed it when she came in. When Kristen opens it up further, there stands Phillip. He looks like he heard every word we said. He is pale and in shock.

"Oh, hi, Phillip. What are you doing standing in the doorway?" Kristen asks and she seems to think what I do. She looks back at me and then to him.

He looks up and I see a tear come down his face. My heart breaks into a million pieces. He knows everything and I know he is taking it hard. I want out of this bed to go to him. The nurses still haven't taken out my IV or unplugged the heart monitor confining me to my bed.

I finally find my voice. "Phillip, please forgive me. I had no idea what happened in the past."

He finally looks at me. "I am sorry, Alexia. This is too much for me right now. I have to go. I am sure your parents will be here soon to get you. I will stay with Tyler and Jacob until your parents leave. Leave the key to the condo at the security desk when they leave." He walks over to me and kisses on my forehead. "Sorry, Alexia." Then, before I can say anything, he turns and leaves in a hurry. I see Kristen is as upset as I am.

"Alexia, I am sorry. I shouldn't have asked you about that when Phillip could have come back to hear. This is my entire fault. Let me go talk to him." She has this serious look on her face. She is blaming herself for my mistake. She really is a good friend and the best I have ever had.

I look at her with watery eyes. "No, Kristen, this isn't your fault. It is mine. I kept my past a secret the whole time and I knew I should have told him. Now it is what I knew would happen. I will be fine. You need to leave to get to your class. I need to be alone for a while."

She comes over and hugs me. "I don't want to leave you now. You need me. I shouldn't have left you the other day when you were upset. I will stay here until your parents come. You need me now."

"Thanks Kristen. You are the best friend ever. I wonder if Phillip will ever forgive me. I love him so much and now he is gone. I gave him my heart and now it is broken." I start laughing.

Kristen looks at me like I am crazy, and maybe I am. "Alexia, are you all right?"

"Yes. I gave him my heart. How ironic is that? I can't give him my heart because my heart is borrowed. My real heart is no longer beating. Now I have broken this heart too. It isn't meant for me to have a heart. I must have done something bad when I was little." Tears start flowing uncontrollably down my face. The door opens and I hope it is Phillip. It isn't. Mom takes a look at me and rushes to my side.

She looks at Kristen. "What happened to her?"

Kristen shakes her head. "I asked her about your private conversation last night and when she told me everything, Phillip was outside the door. He heard everything and was upset. He told her he couldn't handle this right now and left."

"Baby girl, look at me." I do and Mom wipes my tears. "You have to stop crying. This doesn't mean it is over for good. Phillip needs time to process all the information, and when he does, he will be back."

"Mom, no, he won't. He said we could stay at his place until Dad and you leave. Then I need to leave the key at security. That means he doesn't want me. It is over. I broke his heart for keeping my past a secret. Mom, can you go check and see how much longer until I get out?"

She looks at me then goes to see.

"Kristen, I will be okay now. You better get to class before you're late."

Kristen comes over and hugs me. "I will go. If you need me, call. I will keep my phone close."

"Okay. Thanks for being here. Go make good grades." I try to smile at her to let her know I will be fine. She looks at me one last time and then leaves.

Not long after Kristen leaves, I am unhooked from everything and heading out the door. It feels good to be outside in the sun. I have been inside for too long. My mom and dad take me to Phillip's. They made their flight plans to leave that day, but Mom is afraid to leave me alone. I tell her that I will have Kristen at the dorm, and once everyone is packed, we leave Phillip's place.

Before I leave, I go to the balcony and look at the beach one last time. I want to memorize this place, even if it hurts to do so. We drop off the key and head back to the dorm. They stop at my favorite pizza place to get me a pizza to take to my room. Once I'm all settled in, they kiss me goodbye, but they hate leaving me. I keep telling them that I will be fine and they finally leave before they miss their flight.

I looked around my room and decide that I need to head out to my favorite beach spot for my beach therapy. I load up my backpack with my books and take my food with me. Once I am at the beach, I will do something I've wanted to do for a while-- read, and relax, forget about my world, and visit another place. I am strong and need to heal myself my way. This is how I will do it.

Thirty

PHILLIP

I go back to the hospital after I showered and rested for about an hour. Alexia is sound asleep. I decide not to wake her. Kristen stops by for a few minutes and we talk a little while. I tell her that I am staying the night and she tells me she will be back early in the morning before classes start. I end up fixing my reclining chair bed and fall asleep soon after. I am awakened when the nurse comes in to check on Alexia. The nurse tells me that she is doing really good and looks like she probably will get to go home today.

After the nurse leaves, I can't go back to sleep. The sun has barely started to rise. I decide to go find coffee and something to eat. The cafeteria should be about to open soon. I stretch my arms and legs out a bit. Sleeping in the chair for the past few days has been rough on my body and it is sore. I really hope that Alexia does gets out today. I look forward to sleeping in our bed tonight. I heard Alexia's parents have scheduled their plans to fly out today if she leaves the hospital. I told them to go ahead and plan to leave, because even if she doesn't, I will stay by her side. I look at my watch and notice that it is time for the cafeteria to open, so I head on down.

Most people hate the food hospitals fix, but if you have stayed in one for a while, you get used to it. They fix healthy foods for the most part. You have to choose the best foods. The smell of food hits me and I decide to stay down here to eat. I don't want to wake my sleeping beauty with the smell of food and coffee. I pay and find a seat by the window. Looks like the sun has risen farther and Alexia will be up soon. I eat fast so I can hurry back up to her room. I think about yesterday and still wonder what Julie had to talk about privately to Alexia. I decide to let Alexia tell me when she is ready.

As I get back to Alexia's room, I hear Kristen talking to her. I open the door a little, but not to spy. I stop because of the question Kristen just asked her. Kristen asked the question that I am wondering about. I really plan on closing the door and then let them know I am there. Alexia starts talking about everything so fast that I have to stop and listen. What I hear floors me, and now I am too shocked to move. My mom and Alexia's mom Julie, both knew who had Gabe's heart. Alexia has Gabe's heart! He not only saved me, but the girl I am in love with. I didn't even know Alexia had been in the same hospital and at the same time as me. I am grateful for Gabe's gift to both of us- yes I am- but since I barely have accepted this gift for myself, how do I process this for Alexia too?

I hear Alexia say something to Kristen that I never would have thought about. She wonders if Gabe's heart is the reason that she loves me so much. She *loves* me? She has never told me this. She knows I love her. What if that is true, that Gabe's heart loves me and not, Alexia herself? That has to be crazy. I mean, we both have Gabe's organs. Gabe isn't alive or has feelings anymore.

Then it hits me. What if our organs have drawn us together? I knew as soon as I met Alexia that there was this pull to her. Does she feel that same pull? My head has so much going on right now that I can't think straight. Alexia even tells Kristen that she forgot to take her medicine when she thought she'd figured this out and that she cried herself to sleep. That is the reason she forgot. How could she do that to my brother? He gave her this gift, and then she didn't take care of it. This upsets me too much and I shouldn't be here right now. I feel like she has betrayed my brother.

I hear the door open, and Kristen is standing in front of me. She is leaving and looks over to Alexia with concern on her face. She moves over so I can come in. I hesitate for a few seconds, but then I go in. I look at Alexia. She has lost all of her color in her face and tears are coming down because she knows I heard everything. I think my heart just shattered when I saw how upset Alexia was. I should turn around and leave before I say something I shouldn't because I am angry. I don't even know why I am so angry. This is all confusing and I don't know how to think straight right now.

Instead, I go over to Alexia and tell her that I can't do this right now. That is all I really meant to say. My mouth had its own agenda though. I tell her that I am staying at Tyler and Jacob's until her parents leave and to leave the key at security. I hear her saying that she is sorry and to forgive her. She didn't know anything about whose heart she had. I hear all this, but I need to leave and think for a while to clear my head with all my confusion. I have to kiss her bye and I do it on her forehead. If I kissed her on her lips, I might have broken down. This is the hardest thing I have ever done, walking out of Alexia's hospital room with tears running down her eyes.

Once I am out of the hospital, I sit in my car for a few minutes. I didn't realize that tears are running down my face. I wipe them off and decide to do what I normally do to think. I head to the beach so I can run. I think about going surfing. Then I remembered that I have guests at my place and I can't change into my swimming trunks. Running will help me just as much as surfing.

The drive to the beach is extremely hard. Once I finally get there, my phone rings. I look to see who it was before I answered. I really don't want to talk to anyone.

"Hi, Mom." I try to sound like I am fine. I don't want to get into this with her until I clear my head.

"Hello, Phillip. How is that wonderful girl you keep telling me about? Is she getting out of the hospital today?" Why did she have to ask about Alexia? Another tear slips from my eye.

I take a deep breath and quickly wipe the tear away. "Yeah, she is getting out today."

"Phillip, what is the matter? You sound like you're sad about something. Did something bad happen to her?" Mom asked, and I realize that I never told her Alexia's name. Now I will see how she reacts to it.

"Mom, I realize that I never told you my girlfriend's name. She is from Cleveland and you may know her family."

"What is her name Phillip?" she asks.

"Her name is Alexia Morgan." I hear my mom gasp.

Once she got her voice, she whispers. "Phillip, I do know her and her family. She is a beautiful girl. What is she in the hospital for? I can't remember if you told me."

"Well she forgot to take her heart transplant medicine and her body started to shut down." I don't know why I am being hateful to my mom. I can't help it. I'm hurting.

"Sweetheart, did that do any damage to her donor heart?" She had to ask that question. Is she even worried about Alexia at all or just whose heart she has?

"No she didn't damage her heart, and it is strong as the day she received it." Mom takes a breath like she was holding it until I answered. The more I talk about it, the angrier I am getting. The next words that come out of my mouth are hateful. "You should be glad about that, Mom. She didn't damage Gabe's heart. How could you keep something like this from me? When she found out by accident, she was so upset that she cried herself to sleep and forgot her medicine. I found about that about thirty minutes ago. I don't know what to do about this information and it is driving me crazy. Should I be mad? What if the connection we have is because of Gabe? I left her in tears because I was afraid I would hurt her. I was more afraid that our connection is because of Gabe and not because we love each other on our own." I realize by the time I've said all that to my mom that I am yelling.

"Calm down, Phillip. You are overreacting to this situation. Gabe is gone and he has nothing to do with the feelings you have for this girl. That is all you or you wouldn't be yelling at me. I did research after giving away Gabe's organs, and what I found out is that it isn't possible. You need to think about leaving the girl you love and go apologize to her. If you left her in tears, then you made a big mistake. What if she did you that way while you were still in the hospital? You would hate her for that and maybe you already messed up with her." Mom had a point. I did mess up with Alexia.

"You're right, Mom and I am sorry for yelling. I am hurt and confused about everything. I probably lost her for good. Mom, I have to go. I need to go run and think for a while."

"Phillip, do that, but remember that every day you put off telling Alexia you're sorry, the harder it will be for you to get her back. I know you love her. Don't blow it over something like this. You have never talked about a girl before. Please don't mess it up over your stubbornness. You need to talk to her soon." She is right. I am stubborn. I will clear my head and then talk to her.

"Thanks, Mom. I will clear my head and talk to her. I do love Alexia and want to make it work. I am going now and I will call later."

"Okay, Phillip. Have a good run and clear that stubborn head of yours. I love you, son. Take care of yourself. Bye." She hangs up, and I realize how much better I feel.

I head over to the beach to run. While I am running, I see flashes of Alexia and tears running down her eyes because of me. She even told Kristen that she loves me but was just as afraid as I felt. Yeah, I made a mess of things. I will try to fix them, but when? Maybe I will give Alexia a few days to not be upset with me anymore. She doesn't need the stress today after getting out of the hospital.

Thirty-One

ALEXIA

Since I went to the beach over a week to ago, I still haven't heard from Phillip. I guess it really is over for good. I emailed all my professors and they emailed me everything I need to work on from that week, plus my make-up work. Maybe the reason I haven't seen him is because I haven't returned to class yet. He still could have come by my dorm room or texted me if he wanted to. I decide it is really over.

I focused on my schoolwork and take a break each day at the beach. Since I finally have my focus on school, my grades have been better. I even finish my part of the biology project I had with Phillip and I email it to him. Maybe he will finish his part and turn it in to the teacher. If not, I will turn in my part of the work.

Every day, Kristen tries to get me to go out with her, but I really need to be alone right now. I don't go with her. I keep telling her that I will soon. I want to heal from my broken heart my way, and I need to do it by myself. I know I should be with people, but every day the beach keeps calling to me. Every day, I go and sit in my chair, not really doing anything. I read some books and try to stay away from the romance ones. Most of the time, I have my special beach area to myself. I am getting good with picking the time of day when no one is around.

Soon, I have to go back to my classes. Dread comes over me when I think about biology class. I have been out over two weeks from classes and still haven't seen Phillip. I really don't want to see him. Why should I? He has made it clear that he doesn't want to be around me.

Forcing myself to go to biology takes a lot of courage I really didn't know I had. I wonder if the professor would let me change my assigned seat if I ask. The closer I get the more strength I find within myself. I can do it and I will. Walking in, I had planned on changing my seat, but I notice Phillip sitting somewhere else. That makes it easier on me. He looks up at me when I walk past him, but says nothing. I won't lie; it *hurts* really badly. Time for real to move on.

A few days later, Kristen begs me to go out with her and some of her other friends. Not wanting her to think I'm not a good friend, I say yes. We ended up at a party. It is at a house beside Megan's and I hesitate about going inside. Kristen says that Megan won't be here, but I am still worried a little bit. Megan has left me alone since I haven't been around Phillip.

Finally relaxing when I don't see her anywhere, I start enjoying myself. Hanging out with Kristen and her friends is better than I thought it would be. We danced, and I watch them play some Jell-O shooter games. Kristen knows I can't drink so when some of the girls handed me shooters, she says that I have to be the driver tonight. True to her word, she never told anyone why I was in the hospital. This makes me believe we will always be best friends, and every day we are getting closer. Kristen is like a mother hen every morning, making sure I take my medicine. I promised myself that I'd never forget again either and set my alarm on my phone to remind me.

Close to the end of the party, I see some guys watching us. I wonder how long they have been watching. Having fun and not paying attention caused me not to notice them sooner. I shake off the look that one of them is giving me and tell Kristen that it is time to go. She asks me why and I whisper in her ear the reason. I say not to look up, which was a mistake because she does first thing. Kristen gives the guys a really mean disgusted look and flips them off.

Grabbing me by the arm, she tells her friends that it is time to leave and we all go. We have to walk by them to get out the door and who do I see standing beside the one, who gave me chills? Megan. She stands close and puts her arm around him. Then she even smiles at me. Kristen pulls me out of the door in a hurry.

"Can you believe those two? They stood there looking like a couple. How is that possible? The other day, I walked by them having a conversation and it wasn't looking like a good one. I guess that slut finally won him over. I am sorry you had to see that, Alexia. If I had known this would happen, I wouldn't have brought you here." Kristen is angry.

"You had no way of knowing who would be here tonight. If someone has a party, everyone has to go to it. I was hurt for a minute and decided it is time to move on. I need to focus mostly on my classes because I fell a little behind. Now is the time to focus and have fun. Let's get out of here." I smile at her and give her a hug.

"If you want to and if you're okay with everything, we will leave. If I can, I will go back inside and kick some butt. Just say the word." She smiles at me, and I believe she would.

"No, I have a better idea. Come on, I'm driving." Heading to the car, I tell her friends to follow me.

She keep asking where we are going, but I keep saying trust me, and she does. I drive to a place, I'd saw on the way to the beach. I wanted to go, but not alone. When we park, I looked at her and she smiles.

"This is perfect place to take out frustration. I better get some extra golf balls in case I see Megan's face." We laugh hard. This is what we all needed.

"Kristen, you know this is putt-putt golf and you can't hit the balls too hard?" I grin.

"It will be only a just in case. I will try to be good, because if this makes you smile like that then I'm happy. Let's get this show on the road." She leads the way into our fun night of putt-putt golf. Then we all laugh hard and enjoyed ourselves.

We plan a weekly putt-putt golf night after that night and we ended up going to every one of the putt-putt golf places in town.

Before long, the days have turned into weeks and then the weeks have turned into months. I give up on the idea of Phillip. Occasionally, it still hurts, and I won't lie, I still love him. I have never seen him out with Megan again. Why has he kept from talking to me? In our one class together, he moved to the front of the class. I wondered how he got out of his assigned seat. For the project we worked on, he turned it in after he finished his part. We ended up with an A on it. That is the same grade I had in all my classes since that was my focus.

I know we must have had fallen in love too fast for it to work. Things like that can't last in the times we live in. I really haven't talked to any other guy since Phillip and I broke up. I really don't want to get involved with anyone else. I am too broken in more ways than most, so why add another guy into my broken life? It would not be fair to that guy.

One day in the middle of November, I go back to my favorite beach spot. I've been doing this every day. I notice where I usually sit, that there is a heart drawn in the sand. It makes me sad to see it. A couple must have been at my spot that day before I got here. I looked around to see if they might still be here, but I see no one around. They must be lucky to have love in their lives and I smile for them, even while I hurt inside. I decide not to let it bother me. I end up reading and relaxing. When I decide to go, I look back at the heart and get a great idea. I gathered some shells and decorated it. Looking at my work, decide that it needs something else inside the heart. I make a cute little sandcastle. It is far enough away from the tide so that if they come back tomorrow, they will have a home to go with their heart. How lucky for them?

Going back to the beach every day, I notice that the heart has grown and more shells have been placed on it. I even believe the castle has grown. Smiling to myself, I believe this couple in love has seen inspiration for their love with my shells and castle. Hopefully they will stay happy for a long time. I always look for them each time I come here. Never once do I see them, and I wonder who they are. They are my mystery couple.

I hate to leave today because tomorrow, I will fly home for Thanksgiving break. What if something happens to this heart and castle while I'm gone? Maybe they are college kids going home on break too. With a heavy heart, I leave to pack my things to head home so I can see my parents.

I really can't wait to see them. It has been awhile since I have seen them. This puts a smile back on my face. They are what I need, and I can't wait to see them for the holiday. Only bad thing about going home is that I have to leave the beach. I have grown up these past few months of college, and I am glad to have been given a second chance to be able to grow. I now thank Gabe every day for his gift. This year at Thanksgiving, I will be extra thankful because now I know who gave me another chance at life. My only wish is that I'd still have his brother in my life too.

Thirty-Two

PHILLIP

Every day, I know I should go see Alexia. I can't bring myself to go see her yet. My mom told me to apologize before it is too late. I have planned many different ways to do so. The only problem is me. I am not ready. I still hurt from everything that has gone on from the past to now. The guys have been supportive and they both tell me every day to get over it. They know I still love Alexia. Yes, I do love her and always will. I even have talked to my mom, and she thinks I may have lost my mind because I haven't talked to Alexia. I am afraid when I go see her that all I will see is Gabe.

Gabe and I were close when we grew up, and it hurt me to lose him. He was only a year older than me and we did everything together. We loved all the same things and hardly fought with each other. We were so close you'd think we were twins; that is why it has been so hard. No one knows how hard it is to lose the one person you looked up to and wanted to be like as much as I do. He was my closest friend, and being my brother was an extra bonus. We would talk about everything, from girls to what we wanted out of life and that we wanted to live beside each other with our families. We had everything figured out, and when I lost him, I lost a big part of myself. When I met Alexia, I was starting to feel whole again. Like my missing part was back in place. That is what scares me the most.

Then she went and asked if maybe that is why we fell in love so quickly, and I can't help, but wonder that also. I saw her look at me the first time on the plane and knew that I had to get to know her better. Maybe Gabe was pulling me to her? That doesn't make this easier to comprehend.

I am afraid when I see her in biology class for the first time that I will have that same pull. She sent me an email with her part of the assignment and I finished it by adding mine to it. I owe her that much to try to get a good grade. I think she is coming back soon, so I asked the professor to move me from my assigned seat. I didn't think he would, but since Alexia was absent and he was giving another two-person assignment he moved me next to a new guy up in the front of the class. Sitting up front sucks, but since I asked to be moved, I had to bear it.

She finally walks back in the classroom. She looks toward our seats and notices that I am not there. It makes me sad seeing her frown. She finds me up front when she walks to her seat. We looked at each other and I have to look away. As soon as I saw those eyes, I knew I either had to let her go or try to get her back. I feel that pull toward her and have a hard time sitting in my seat during that first day with her back. That stupid pull makes me angry. Why do I think it has to do with Gabe? I still can't think straight when she is in the same room as me. I don't think, I hear a thing in class, and when it is over, I hurry out.

I end up back at my home soon after and leave to go surfing as quickly as I can to clear my mind. I believe I need a shrink. I wonder if I can find a good one around here. Does the school have one? I better not go to a school one because someone might find out. I keeping surfing for a long time and when I came out of the water, I see Megan.

"What do you want Megan? I don't feel like putting up with you today," I snap at her.

"Well, Phillip, I was going to invite you to a party I am going to have tonight. Someone must have stuck something up your butt since you're in a crabby mood." She started to walk off, but I stopped her. I know I shouldn't have but I did.

"Sorry about that Megan. I had a bad day at school and I shouldn't have taken it out on you." I smiled.

"Okay, I will forgive you this time, but don't let it happen again. So will you and your friends come to the party tonight?" She bats her eyes at me. Since I was so rude to her, I tell her that I will.

Megan apparently thinks that I said yes, I was going to be her date. She even hung on me all night and I have to try to get away. Every time I think I've lost her, she would find me. Megan tries to get me to go to her bedroom several times. I keep telling her no. I could have easily taken advantage of her. I don't want to though, and knowing Megan, she would never leave me alone after.

Every day, Megan keeps coming up to me and trying her best to get me to go out with her, and every day I tell her no. It got so bad that I would keep an extra eye out and turn the other way so I can dodge her. It is a full-time job staying out of Megan's radar.

Finally one day, Megan catches up to me, and asks me why we keep missing each other. I decide to tell her off and I do. It gets to be a heated moment. Then finally she gets the hint that I am not into her at all. It is depressing that the one girl I want is the girl I am afraid to talk to. Since I haven't talked to Alexia in so long, she probably has given up on me and maybe even moved on.

As I keep thinking about Alexia moving on, I get anxious and jealous. I see her every time we have biology and keep thinking that she has moved on because she pays no attention to me anymore and never looks at me. The more I keep thinking about this, the sadder I become. How stupid of me to let it get this far without talking to the one person who makes me feel something? I love her more every day and I'm scared to tell her.

I haven't gone out with the guys in a while and they keep asking. I put them off as long as I can, but I finally cave to go to a party. I drive us to the place they tell me to drive to, and when I see that it is a house beside Megan's, I almost turn the car around. What stops me is this beautiful girl who just got out of her car with her friends. I decide that tonight, I will find out what she is up to. She isn't a party-type girl, but I have to see what she is doing here.

We go inside the party and the guys hit up any alcohol they can get their hands on. They know I will drive them home so they can do whatever they want. I sit back in the corner so she won't see me. I hope she didn't see the guys either, because that might give me away.

She looks around to see who is here, like maybe she is looking for someone. I hope it isn't a guy. I might have to go grab her up away from him if it is. She almost spots me, but someone steps into my path and she doesn't see me. That was close. I watch her all night, and she is having a good time dancing with her girlfriends and watching them take Jell-O shooters. I'm sitting here watching her and the guys come back over. They are being loud. I hope they don't get too loud. She will notice them.

They keep talking loudly about some hot chicks. I pay them no attention. My eyes haven't been off that beauty who is dancing. It makes me want to go over and put my arms around her and dance with her. She has me mesmerized with the way she moves. She twirls around and then stops. She sees me looking at her and goes over to her friend. Her friend looks up to see what she sees. Then all of her friends stop, and they head over to where we are. *Maybe she wants to talk to me, I think.* I hope.

When she gets close to me, I look into her beautiful eyes. I am going to beg for forgiveness right now and I don't care who sees or hears me. I take a deep breath, and as I do, I feel an arm go around my shoulders. I look to see who it is, and it is Megan. I look back to the beautiful girl, and she looks shocked before she walks right past me and out the door.

I know how shocked she must feel, because what Megan just did shocked me too. I let out the breath I was holding. Shaking off Megan's arm I yell at her to never, ever come around me again. Everyone at the party stops what they are doing and looks our way. I tell her that she better stop stalking me or I will get a restraining order against her. The guys have to grab me and pull me away before I do anything that I will regret.

Megan finally gets embarrassed and says that she will never come around me again. I reminded her if she does, I will get the restraining order. Megan tells me that she understands and leaves in tears. I should feel bad for her for saying that in front of all these people, but all I can think about is my missed chance with that beautiful girl. The look she gave me was a look, like she never wanted me around again.

Before I can dwell much on it, the guys pull me out of the party. They even are still sober and that surprises me. They say we should go do something different tonight, and what they want to do is something that sounds like fun. I haven't done it much since my brother died and I am ready to go.

We end up at a putt-putt golf course that is away from the beach with not many people there. Most people go to the ones close to the beach because at some of them you can see the ocean at certain holes. We end up having a good time and it clears my head. We decide to come to this place more often and we do weekly.

Each day turns into a week and each week turns into a month. I really believe Alexia is over me. She looks good and healthy. I believe she even has a tan now. She never looks my way and she hasn't even spoken to me in biology. I almost give up on the idea of her in my life until one day I run directly into Kristen. We almost knock each other down. Before she notices whom she ran into, she spouts off a few curse words at me. I start laughing at her, and she looks at me.

"Oh, you. Why don't you watch out where you're going? You are too big to run into. You're like a freaking statue and a jerk too." She sounds angry.

"I am sorry. I didn't mean to run into you and I can't help how tall I am. Why am I a jerk?" I look at her.

"Do you really want me to tell you why you're a jerk?" I nod my head yes. "Well it is because you were with Megan at a party. I finally got Alexia out for the night. It took me forever to get her to say yes. Then you went and messed it up," she snaps at me.

"Wait a minute I wasn't with Megan that night. I didn't even know she was there. I was going to beg Alexia for forgiveness right in front of everyone and I didn't care who would see my begging. Then Megan came up behind me and puts her arm around me like she'd been there the whole time. Alexia looked at me liked she didn't care and walked on by. For your information, I told Megan in front of everyone after you left to leave me alone and quit stalking me. Even told her that if she didn't, I would get a restraining order against her. I now have a whole room of partygoers as witnesses and now she finally leaves me alone." Saying this to Kristen, I feel relieved to finally get that off my chest.

She smiles, "Really? You said all that to Megan?" I nod my head yes and smile. "Wow, Phillip, you finally put Megan in her place. And in front of the whole group of people too. I bet she was embarrassed, and now I bet she is afraid to get around you. Just so you know, it did hurt Alexia. She thinks you moved on. She says she is moving on, but I know her better. She still isn't over you."

I can't believe it. Alexia still loves me. What a fool I have been. I've wasted so many days in misery without her. I look at Kristen. "Do you think she will have me back? I still love her, but I was letting her move on. I thought I'd lost my chance with her forever and was afraid to tell her."

Kristen grins. "If you play your cards right, I think you may have her back by Christmas, but you have to take it slow and not scare her off."

So that day, Kristen and I talked about how I can win back Alexia. I realized that day, it doesn't matter that Alexia has

Gabe's heart. I believe it was a gift from him to me. He would be happy for me to have this beautiful girl who I loved and who loves me back. I set out every day to prepare the plans Kristen and I went over. Most of the plans were my ideas, but there was this one she had that was brilliant.

It is about mid-November when I find her special place she goes' to everyday. It is the same one where we met before. I never let Alexia know that I am with her. When she finds a special something I made in the sand beside where she always sits. I think she might get the hint that it might be me. I left her a heart in the sand. She surprises me when she decorates it with shells carefully placed, and then she made a tiny castle in the middle. That makes me smile. I think back to the day at the beach when we built a castle together. *I will win you back my Alexia*, I promised.

By the time it is time to go home for Thanksgiving, I have still been adding to Alexia's heart and castle. She always smiles when she sees it and looks around to see if she can find who has been doing it. It isn't time for her to find out yet. I keep back and try to keep patient.

I have to take this in steps to win her back. The only thing about waiting is that today she looks sad. I wonder why that is. Tomorrow is the day she flies home to see her family so she should be happy. She puts a few more shells on the heart and leaves. I'm guessing to pack.

When she leaves, I go to the heart in the sand. I don't want anyone messing with it. I put '*do not cross*' tape around it with sticks in the ground. Hopefully that will keep off anyone until we get back. Not too many people come out at this spot this time of the year because it is chilly out now. I take a look at my creation and I am happy that it looks secure. Now it's time to get ready for my next step of my plans and the holidays. I have something new to be thankful this year, and it is Alexia. Hopefully I can win her back and I will never let her go, ever again. She is and will be my forever.

Thirty-Three

ALEXIA

The Thanksgiving holiday is a great one. My parents have always showed me love, and that is what I am thankful for in my life. We have lots of family and friends who stop by to celebrate with us. I thought I would be happy to be home, but I miss being at the beach. There is something about it that always keeps me calm and happy. I wonder if the heart in the sand is gone by now. My mystery couple is still a mystery. Thinking about them makes me wonder if they have done some more decorating of their love heart and castle.

My mom notices that I am a bit sad and she tries to comfort me as best as she can. The day before I'm supposed to head back to campus, she takes me to get a manicure and pedicure. What girl doesn't feel better after a bit of pampering? It helps and I like that I will get to show off my toes when I go to the beach.

Once I'm back to my dorm room, I notice that Kristen hasn't made it back yet. I hurry and put my things away. Now is the time to see if my mystery couple left the heart alone or added to it. I am excited and happy for the first time in a while.

Driving to my favorite spot, I keep thinking that the couple is lucky to have love in their lives. Being alone and lonely sometimes hurts. Arriving and unpacking my things, I notice that I'm a bit nervous too. What if something happened to the heart and castle? I shake from thinking that something might have happened to it.

Getting my nerves together to make myself move forward to my spot, I take each step as fast as I can. Soon I can see my place. I stand looking at it for a few minutes because I've found a surprise here. I closed my eyes and open them again just to make sure what I am seeing is true. I felt my face was getting wet and notice I have tears coming down my cheeks. I wipe them as I walk closer to my place. How did this happen? Who did this?

I decided to sit beside this perfection I see, so I can admire what is in front of my eyes. My tears stop and a smile grows on my face. I am glad I came here today to see this amazing creation. Now I wish I hadn't left my phone in the car. I could have taken a picture and kept it always. I sit there looking and admiring it for a long time. My mystery couple has been back and their love must be growing. I feel happy for them.

What they have created has me in awe. They have kept building the sandcastle until it is huge and has perfect shapes. The heart around this beautiful castle is wide and deep. The shells have been placed in perfect spots were the sunshine is on the shells and making them shine like diamonds. I can't take my eyes off it. I look at every detail, so that I can remember everything about it. This has taken them a long time. I was only gone for a few days and how they did this while I was gone is truly genius. I have seen on TV how people make castles like this and it takes them a long time. This one could be on TV, but I don't want anyone to come and spoil my place. I will keep it a secret for my mystery couple and me to enjoy.

I get back to my room and find Kristen there. We hug each other and talk about our holiday. She seems to be really happy and that makes me happy too. I want to tell her about the beautiful castle, but I'm afraid she will tell everyone. I will keep it a secret for now. When I go to bed that night, I think more about this couple who are in love. If Phillip and I were still together, we might have done something wonderful like that. He is a perfect guy and I still love him. I wish he could have accepted that I had this gift from his brother. I fall asleep with mixed feelings, happy for the mystery couple and sad about Phillip and me. Why can't we all have a happy ending?

That night I have this dream and it makes me smile, when I wake up. I remembered every detail of my dream. Could it be possible to dream such a dream and for it to come true? My dream was about Phillip. Maybe I dreamt of him because he was on my mind when I went to sleep. I only wish it weren't just a dream. In my dream, Phillip told me he loved me and accepted that I had Gabe's heart. He wanted me to be with him now and forever. Phillip told me that he'd made the sandcastle for me, his princess. He took me to the spot and showed me how he'd done every detail of the castle.

Yeah, it was just a dream. I shake it off and get ready for my classes. A few weeks from now, I will have finished my first semester. Who knew five years ago, that it would have been possible to accomplish my first of college?

I head out to go to class and Kristen yells, "Have a great day," then she grins wide at me. I wonder what that was about. It is a fairly warm day today, so after classes, I will head back to see the castle, and this time I will take my phone to take pictures of it.

It happens that the class that I am going to is biology. After that dream last night, I am a bit shy to see Phillip. I hope he doesn't look at me today because it may cause me to blush. The door comes into view and as I get to it, someone bumps into me from the behind. I turn around to see who it is. I look right into Phillip's brown eyes. My dream comes flashing back to me in a hurry and I feel my face heated up. I hope he doesn't say anything about my blushing.

He looks into my eyes and with the way he stares I believe I can feel it into my soul. We just stand there for what seems like forever. Phillip finally speaks first.

"I'm sorry to run into you, Alexia. I thought I was going to be late and was hurrying. I didn't pay much attention. Please forgive me." The way he says this, makes me think that he is asking more than forgiveness for running into me. It melts my heart a little.

I find my voice. "You're forgiven, Phillip. How have you been?"

"I am doing better now that I ran into you. You look better than the last time we talked. You even have a tan, which looks good on you. Shows how bright blue your eyes are. I guess we better get to class. We don't want to miss out on biology." He smiles and waves me to go ahead of him.

I don't know what to say to him and that compliment. I walk on ahead into class right to my seat. This is the first time he has talked to me in months and he has left me not able to speak.

I expect him to go to his seat up front, but I am surprised when he comes and sits beside me. What is he doing? Why is my heart beating so fast? I look over at him and give him a look that says, *What are you doing*? He doesn't answer. He only smiles and winks at me. Is he flirting with me? Between his doing these things and that dream last night, I am so flustered. Why now after all this time?

The professor comes in and starts class. I thought he would jump on Phillip, but doesn't pay any attention to him. I try to focus as much as I can on what the professor says. It is too hard to do today.

When the class comes to an end, I gather my things to go. Phillip does the same and looks like he is ready to leave. He turns to me then smiles, "Alexia I hope you have a great day today. Enjoy the bright sunny day." Then he just walks off and leaves.

Is today another dream and am I still a sleep? Why is everyone hoping I will have a great day all of a sudden? Now I wish my next class were already over so I could hit the beach. Off to eat and get to my next class.

Finally arriving to the beach, I remember to put my phone in my backpack. I can't wait to see the castle today. I wonder if anything has changed. Soon as I get close, I look at it. I stop in my tracks, because what I see is breathtaking. Before I know what I am doing, I walk closer so I can examine it further. The mystery couple must be amazing artists. The castle has grown and has even more detail to it.

The sun is setting and I know I should leave. I look at the sparkle coming off the shells as the sunsets. Something else catches my eye. I get up and ease over to it trying not to mess up the masterpiece. I stand before this sparkling thing and my heart skips a beat as I forget to breathe. I lean closer to make sure my eyes aren't playing a trick on me.

I finally get the nerve to reach for it and put it in my hand. It is a note rolled up inside of a diamond ring. Who would leave this on a public beach? Then, I remembered that I have never really seen anyone around here. Tourists don't come here this time of the year.

I look at the ring and note. Should I read it? Maybe I should because I might find out who it belongs to. What if it is meant for someone else to find? I know that this ring is expensive and probably a carat. It is a princess cut, and if it were mine it would be a perfect match for me. I sure wouldn't want to lose it. I decide to open the note to see whose ring it is.

I begin to shake for no reason while I open it. Maybe I'm nervous to see what is inside the note. I begin to read the note and tears start flowing from my eyes. They are happy tears, because of the words on the note. I smile and wipe my eyes. I look up to see someone slowly walking in my direction. I decide right then that he is too slow. I clinch the ring and note in my hand and run to him. When I get close, he stops and opens his arms so I can be embraced as I jump into them. I throw my arms around him and kiss him while tears still flow out of my eyes. We kiss until we can barely breathe.

He sets me down and wipes my tears. Smiling at me, he twirls my hair in his fingers. "I take it with that welcome that you have an answer for that question on my note. I meant every word in the note. I'm sorry for everything I put you through. I never meant to hurt you. I just needed time to heal old wounds so they won't affect us later on in life. I want to start over, but in a big way. I am done waiting on life and now ready to start living with a forever. I beg you to say yes, my princess. I love you and have never stopped loving you. I missed having you next to me. You are the air I breathe and the sun in my life. You make me feel complete. Alexia, please say yes and be my wife." Phillip looks at me and with love in those eyes, which burns into my soul. How could I not say yes to him?

I take a second to stop to think about his note and all he said in it. He has been doing all this work to woo me back and I never knew it was him, the love in my heart. Phillip has never stopped loving me. Most people haven't ever felt what I feel for Phillip, and I know most people wouldn't understand that this answer will change everything, but I do now. Right here today, I understand what I am going to say and what it means- forever starts now. We both don't have time to waste, because who knows what will happen in the future. Why waste more time?

I step closer to him and look into his big brown eyes. "Yes. Phillip I will marry you. I am ready for forever now, too."

He grabs my hand and pulls the ring out of it. Then he places the ring on my finger. He goes down on his knee and kisses the ring on my finger. Looking up at me, he says. "Alexia, I will forever make you happy. Thank you for giving me another chance. I love you and will never leave your side again. I now have forever to make it up to you." He pulls me down onto his lap and kisses me senseless.

Yes, this day is a great day. Could be the best day ever. Let today go down in history as forever, with my love by my side.

Thirty-Four

PHILLIP

*K*risten has given me all the information about Alexia's holiday plans. I thought about surprising her on the flight home but decided not yet. I just need to be patient. I fly up on the later flight and spend a couple days home for Thanksgiving. I talked to my parents about my plans and they are happy for me. Mom surprised me and helped me pick out the special gift I am going to give Alexia. She tells me that I need to talk to Alexia's parents first, and she says that they are great people to have in my life.

Before I leave to go back to school, I meet with Alexia's parents and tell them everything I have planned. I even ask them for their permission to go forth with my plans. They remember me from the hospital and know that I really love their daughter. Giving me the blessing to go forth with the plans makes me the luckiest guy I know. I believed my mom was right about having these people in my life, and they are great. They promised not to tell Alexia about our meeting and Julie knows that Alexia is missing me. Julie is going to take Alexia out the next day to the spa. I will have extra time to get back and prepare for the upcoming plans.

I asked the guys and Kristen to come back a day early to help me. They all are as excited about this as I am. We worked hard all day to be prepared for Alexia's arrival. When we are done, I can't believe what we made. It is perfect. I look at everyone and they seem to be amazed. Kristen even has tears in her eyes. That evening I treat them to dinner and we just hang out for a while. I am glad Alexia has found a friend like Kristen who loves her.

I know the exact time Alexia leaves the airport and gets to her room. I know she will head to the beach, because I know my princess. Kristen helps out by watching her from afar on campus. The first day back, I want to be patient and observe Alexia's reaction to what we all built. As soon as she sees it, she has tears in her eyes. I know she loves it, and now I know that tomorrow will be the day to finally tell her how I feel.

I wake up early the next morning to set up the plans. I still remember last night's dream when I go to school and I sure hope that it comes true today. I park my car and see Alexia walking toward the classroom. I follow behind her and she doesn't even know I'm here. I am really close to her when she suddenly stops in front of the door, making me run into her. She turns around and looks straight into my eyes. It is all I can do to not grab her right now and kiss her.

I tell her that I am sorry for running into her and ask her to please forgive me. She says that she does and asks how am I doing? I tell her that I am better now that I ran into her. I let her know how good she looks and she even blushes. I smile and wave for her to go in ahead of me. I really want to watch her walk and move that body.

I decide right then that I am taking my seat beside her. I noticed that the professor has been letting people sit wherever lately and hope he doesn't notice me changing again. When he comes in, he doesn't seem to care. This will be the longest class since I have plans after.

I love being beside Alexia even if in the seat next to her. Every now and then, I look her way and she would blush. Is she enjoying my being beside her too? This is a good sign that what I am about to do will work. At the end of class, I tell her to have a great day and enjoy the sun. She doesn't say anything back, but looks confused. Why, I don't know.

I know Alexia goes to lunch before another class. That is perfect for the rest of my plans. Kristen and the guys meet up with me to finish the grand gesture. I sit down and write a note while they finish. Do you really want to know what my sappy note says? *Okay*, I will tell you.

"Alexia,

From the first time I laid eyes on you, I wanted to get to know you and even felt love on the first day we met. Each and every day after, I grew more in love with you because you are the person who lights up my life; I was in the dark until my sunshine brought me light.

You are the air I breathe, and when you were in the hospital, I was afraid I could never breathe again if I lost you. Ironic, how I did lose you then. I was hurt because of my past demons, not because you have Gabe's heart. I now believe he gave me another gift beside his liver. He gave me you. If he hadn't died that day, I wouldn't be here today with you. It was his last gift to me and that gift was you. I will always miss him and I know we only have a little while here on earth. Why not make the best of it while we can?

Enjoy today because there may be no future. Today, I beg for your forgiveness. Please, Alexia, forgive me for being stupid and letting you go. I shouldn't have wasted a day without you being by my side. I have been planning today for a few weeks now and I hope you have liked your hearts and castles, because only the best will do for my princess.

While we were on holiday break, I spoke to both our families. Your parents kept it from you. I asked them to and please don't be mad at them. My mom even helped pick out the ring in your hand. I told her you were my princess and she said only a princess cut ring would do. I agreed with her, because it looked like you. When I asked your parents for their blessing, they said yes and they knew that I love you, and would take care of you.

Alexia, my princess, let us not waste another day apart. Today let us start with forever. Would you do me the honor of being my wife? I promise to love you today and forever. I don't want forever unless you're in it. I know this is sudden, but why waste another day? Being with the one you love the most should be the only thing we should do. Never waste a second. By saying yes, I mean for us to be married soon. Yes our parents know what I planned, and even our friends know. They all gave us their blessing.

I need you to look up now and look into my eyes so you can see the man who loves you. Please, princess, say yes to marrying me, now and forever.

I Love You,

Phillip"

Hopefully this note will let her know how much I love her and that she will forgive me enough to say yes and start with forever by my side. I look up and see that everyone is admiring the castle creation, and I believe it is perfect. I can see my princess in a beautiful castle like this, and hopefully, with her by my side, I can give her this and more.

We all hurry up and leave. I know I have to be back soon, and before she comes, I have to leave the ring and note for her to find. I want to make a picnic for her, even if she says no to my question.

Kristen is back at the campus and texts me the minute she leaves. I get back to the beach and place the note and ring in a perfect place. I know soon the sun would hit it in a way that it would shine the brightest. I dusted everyone's footprints away and hid from her in my usual place.

Alexia arrives at the time I knew she would. As soon as her eyes see the masterpiece that our friends and I created, she is shocked by it. She finally moves closer and then sits down facing it. I watch her study everything about the castle- the shape of the heart around it and the shells on the castle. Finally, when the sun hits the ring, she notices it. I believe she is afraid to go check it out. When she gets up and moves to the ring, my heart stops and I can no longer breathe.

She takes a look around to see if anyone is there. Then she slowly opens the note. Reading it, Alexia finally knows who the ring belongs to. I start walking toward her then stop when I see tears going down her face. Does this mean she will say no? I can't live with a no for an answer. I will change her mind no matter what. She looks up and sees me coming toward her.

I stop because now I am afraid of her answer. Tears streaming down her eyes, she clenches the note and ring in her hand. Before I can take a step, she comes running toward me and I open up my arms to catch her. It only takes a moment and now I have her back in my arms. I look into her eyes to see if I can read the answer in them.

I ended up on my knees to I tell her that everything in the note is true and that I want her to be my wife. Now is the time for us to start with forever and I want her to be my wife soon. She surprises me by saying yes. I was prepared to beg if I had to while down on my knees. I'm glad I don't have to. I end up pulling her down on my lap so I can kiss her the way I wanted to earlier today- like a man who was starved. I had missed her so much and now I was never letting her go ever again. Time for forever to begin, beginning now. Plus there's a surprise picnic on the beach yet to come.

Epilogue

5 YEARS LATER

*C*an you believe another five years has passed? I can hardly believe it either. So much has happened in the last ten years that I can hardly comprehend it all. I am sitting here waiting patiently but barely hanging on to my sanity. As I wait, I look around at everyone and know that I am truly blessed right now and have been for a while. At the time, I was on my last heartbeat I received a miracle that day, which came with another miracle. Who knew that a tragic day for one family came with a blessing? That family lost a member but saved others. I now am part of that family and have been since I fell hopelessly in love with Phillip.

Let me catch you up to speed while we are all waiting on another miracle to happen. Since the day on the beach that-my now husband-Phillip, proposed in the most perfect way, I learned that everyone had known it was going to happen, before

I even knew we were getting back together. Yeah, they all kept me out of the loop, but it turned out perfectly. They all knew we both fell in love at first sight on our first flight together.

Both of our parents knew we wanted to get married by Christmas and planned it all while we studied for finals. They planned the perfect beach Christmas wedding. Yes, we got married on the beach at Christmas. What a perfect present to the one you love- yourself, forever. Yes, it was getting cold, but it was perfect for us. All of the most important family members and friends we had, came. We had a reception in the condo building we still live in. Phillip's parents gave it to us as a wedding present. My parents paid for the wedding and are truly happy to have Phillip in their lives. They love him almost as much as I do.

The biggest surprise that Phillip and I had was that while Jacob and Kristen helped Phillip, they fell in love. I know, right? How did Kristen manage to capture the heart of Jacob the womanizer? Phillip told me that Jacob said he'd never be tied down, but when he met Kristen, he fell hard. It took her a while to admit that she loved him too because of his past. They worked it out and now they are married. Tyler is now dating a nice girl, but he's yet to let us all meet her. He says it is because he wants to make sure she is 'the one' before bringing her in our group of friends.

Back to Kristen. She remembered when I was in the hospital that I couldn't have kids. One day Kristen and Jacob came over and surprised us with an offer. Kristen wanted to be a surrogate for us so we could have a child that was ours. We told her no for a while and they even had a kid of their own. When she asked again, we took her up on it. Now that is what best friends do for you!

She and Jacob are going to be our son's Godparents. Our kids will be a year and half apart in age. She had a girl and now we are waiting on our little baby boy, Gabe, to arrive. See? I told you we were waiting on another miracle. Phillip and I decided on naming our son Gabe because Gabe deserved a namesake. Gabe, our little miracle, will learn everything that his uncle did for us and the importance of what an organ donor is. Although Phillip's brother is gone, he forever will be alive with us.

Well the nurse just told me that Kristen is yelling for me. Now I will get to be a part of the gift of life and hold my little bundle of joy. This little bundle of joy will make our lives complete, now and forever.

The End

Acknowledgements

I want to thank the ladies who encouraged me along this journey of writing this book. Without your support, I wouldn't have finished writing **Last Heartbeat.**

Thank you, Reba Bowling, for always being there for me in everything that I do. Your love gets me through everything.

Thank you, Sandy Adams, for telling me what I have written is worth writing and that I should keep going.

Thank you, Tenver Owens, for waiting to read each chapter as it was written and encouraging me to keep up the hard work that went into this book. You always tell me to listen to my heart with every word and I did.

Thank you, Crissy Davis, for all your kind words, making my day when I needed it the most, and always being there when I need you.

Thank you, Keelie Chatfield, for kicking my butt into writing this book, helping me to learn new things in the book world, and helping me with my website. Without your knowledge, I would still be lost. The kind words that you always give me will always be in my heart.

Thank you, Karen Mills-Tribble, for making my day when you told me you loved my book. That day, I was having a hard time going forth, but with your kind words, I made it through.

Thank you, Nikki Montgomery, for always standing by me and being a great friend who encourages me to keep writing.

Thank you, Jami Cole, for crying with me through the end of my book and lifting me up with kind words.

Thank you, Lynoda Howell, for your love and support during this journey.

Thank you, Michelle Kampmeier, for helping me keep my focus in the right direction while writing my book and all your kind words that have helped me through this process.

Thank you, Juliana Cabrera, for being my rock when I needed you the most. Sometimes you had to set me straight with kindness.

Special thanks, to my book club girls for showing me kindness, and for being my friends, always: Diva's Lit'Couture Book Club

You can find the Divas on here:

http://authortrlykins.com/divas-litcouture-book-club/

Thanks to all my fellow author friends who encouraged me every step of the way and inspired me to keep going. You will find these authors on my website at:

http://authortrlykins.com/authors-who-inspire-me/

Thanks to my brother, Bill for all of your support.

Thanks to my mom and dad for telling me I can do anything if I set my heart to do it. The support you gave me while I wrote this book was more than I needed to make it through. Thank you for loving me.

Special thanks to my personal assistant Sarah Long who encourages me every day to continue writing my story and helps me promote my book. Without your help Sarah, I would not get the extra time to finish my stories.

About the author

T R LYKINS

http://authortrlykins.com

https://www.facebook.com/pages/T-R-
Lykins/707698679282037